"Do you always bully people?" Sappha wanted to know.

"I?" Rolf asked. "Bully you? My dear girl, don't you know that the Barons—the bold, bad ones, that is—only bully those who are unable to look after themselves? And from what I have seen of you, you are perfectly able to do that." His face split into a sudden grin.

Sappha was really angry with him, but at the same time she was enjoying every minute of his company. She said slowly, "I'm sorry. I know you wouldn't bully anyone or anything."

Rolf stood looking down into her face, then said quietly, "A remark like that needs celebrating."

Betty Neels spent her childhood and youth in Devonshire before training as a nurse and midwife. She was an army nursing sister during the war, married a Dutchman and subsequently lived in Holland for fourteen years. She now lives with her husband in Dorset, and has a daughter and grandson. Her interests are reading, animals, old buildings and writing. On retirement from nursing, Betty started to write, incited by a lady in a library bemoaning the lack of romance novels.

THE BEST *of*

BETTY NEELS

TANGLED AUTUMN

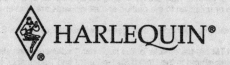

HARLEQUIN®

TORONTO • NEW YORK • LONDON
AMSTERDAM • PARIS • SYDNEY • HAMBURG
STOCKHOLM • ATHENS • TOKYO • MILAN • MADRID
PRAGUE • WARSAW • BUDAPEST • AUCKLAND

ISBN 0-373-51147-7

TANGLED AUTUMN

First North American Publication 2001.

Copyright © 1971 by Betty Neels.

CHAPTER ONE

THE rain fell, soundless and gentle, veiling the dimming heather and all the rusts and reds and brown of the autumn countryside, and almost blotting out the distant mountains while it in no way detracted from their beauty. This view was not, however, shared by Miss Sappha Devenish, sitting behind the wheel of her red Mini. She had been halfway up a moderately steep hill when the little car had coughed, spluttered, hesitated and then continued its climb, only to come to a halt again. The road was a narrow one, the Mini had stopped squarely on its crown, and its driver, calculating her chances of steering it into the side, decided against it. The country was fairly open ahead of her—anyone coming down the hill would see her in ample time to pull up, and anything climbing behind her would be, of necessity, travelling slowly. Besides, she had no mind to ruin her expensive suit and still more expensive shoes—someone would be bound to pass one way or the other, sooner or later. It seemed as though it would be later, she had been watching the rain for more than an hour, and now turned to study the map on the seat beside her.

She had left the main road at Torridon and had passed through Inver Alligin, which according to her reckoning meant that she was a bare five miles from her destination. She glanced at her watch—it was already four o'clock, and her thoughts dwelt longingly on tea, though it was her own fault that she wasn't going to get it. She should have filled up at that last petrol station, but she had been in a hurry to arrive at her journey's end and she had thought that she could just do it. Foolish, and all the more so after her well-

5

planned, effortless two-day trip from London—almost six hundred miles. Well, she had wanted to get as far away from Andrew as possible—the hospital too; it looked as though she had achieved her purpose, for the countryside she was now in was indeed far away.

She had jumped at the chance her uncle had offered her to go as nurse to a patient of his staying in this remote district of the Western Highlands, but now, suddenly, she wondered if she had been wise. Viewed from faraway London, and with the bitter aftertaste of her break-up with Andrew still to be borne, it had seemed a splendid idea, but now, surrounded by distant mountains and an unfamiliar countryside made sombre by the rain, she wasn't so sure. She stared glumly out of the car's windows, beset by the feeling that she shouldn't have come; a feeling that was heightened by the nagging suspicion that she would probably be homesick for the ward she had left behind her at Greggs'.

She had been Sister of Women's Surgical for only a year—she had been a fool to give it up; any other girl, less soft and silly than herself, would have put a bold face on things and stuck it out. She sighed, aware that however reasonable this argument sounded, she would remain soft and silly, although in the last few weeks she had succeeded in acquiring a cool impersonal shell to cover it. She interrupted her thoughts to consider the sound of a car coming up the hill, travelling rather faster than she thought either possible or wise. She turned in her seat and craned her neck to peer out of the rain-washed rear window. It was a Land Rover, coming towards her with a fine burst of speed which took no account of the possibility of there being other traffic. It came to a halt only a foot or so from her rear wheels and its driver did not immediately get out; when he did, his movements were irritatingly unhurried. He was a very tall man with broad shoulders, wearing, she observed, a shabby duffle coat and corduroy trousers stuffed into rubber boots—a farmer, she decided, then felt uncertain of this as

he approached and she was able to take stock of him, for
he didn't look like a farmer at all, not with that dark fierce
face, haughty and hawk-nosed above a straight mouth; dark
hair brushed back from a wide forehead and a pair of
winged eyebrows, so arched and thick that they gave him
the look of a satyr.

She wound down the window, feeling nervous and just
a little silly—justifiably so, as it turned out, for he said
without preamble:

'Of all the fool places to stop—I might have known it
was a woman.' He had a deep voice with the hint of an
accent and he spoke without haste and apparently without
temper, which for some reason caused her own to rise.

'I'm out of petrol!' she snapped, and could have bitten
out her tongue the next instant, for he said at once:

'Naturally.' His dark eyes studied her person in leisurely
fashion. 'A stranger, of course—no one in these parts travels without a spare can, let alone allows the tank to run
dry. You could have got to the side of the road, though.'

Sappha lifted her chin. Even though she was aware that
she had been careless, she didn't much care for the way he
was pointing the fact out to her.

'It's raining,' her glance went involuntarily to her
shoes—hardly made for a muddy road in the more remote
parts of the Scottish Highlands. His gaze followed hers and
his rather stern mouth curved for an instant. He said with
perfunctory kindness:

'I don't suppose that you realised that tweeds'—his gaze
flickered over her beautifully cut suit, obviously he didn't
mean that kind of tweed—'and thick boots are—er—more
suitable at this time of year.' He gave her an enquiring look.
'But perhaps you're only passing through? If you are, I
should warn you that the road ends at Dialach.'

She stared at him, her brown eyes smouldering. 'I
know—I have a map. I'm going to Dialach.'

He received this sparse information with an expressionless face, although she was aware of the glint in his eye as

he straightened up, saying: 'In that case, I'll put some petrol in your tank—unless you would like a tow?'

Sappha felt the stirrings of temper again and quelled them. After all, he was being helpful even though he appeared to find it tiresome.

'No thanks,' she said politely. 'I'll be OK., if I could just have the petrol,' and watched while he fetched a can and filled her tank. When he had finished he came back to stare at her through the window once more, and she asked: 'How much did you put in?' and reached for her handbag. 'I'd like to pay…' to be interrupted brusquely by his 'My dear good girl!' uttered in such a tone of mocking arrogance that she coloured faintly and snatched her hand away from her handbag as though it was red hot, and when he made no further attempt at conversation, she said awkwardly: 'Well, thank you very much,' and switched on her engine, praying that she would make a smooth start. Anything else under those dark mocking eyes would be the last straw, but to her relief the Mini pulled away without a hitch, gathering a little speed as it breasted the hill, and at the corner, between the dripping birch trees Sappha looked in the car mirror—the man was still standing in the middle of the road watching her.

She forgot about him in the next instant, allowing the little car to run steadily while she took her fill of the scene before her. Below and a little to her left she could see Dialach tucked cosily into the trees which lined the loch. It was a small place, with its houses crowded together around the tiny harbour and a scattering of larger houses on the hill behind it. There was a causeway on the left of the town, running out across the rain-smoothed water of the loch to a little island that supported a huddle of dwellings. Sappha, straining to see them clearly through the rain, concluded that they and the causeway were in ruins, and turned her attention to the church, its square grey tower standing in Dialach's centre. Her patient was a guest at the Manse, her uncle had said, so presumably if she made for the church it would be the quickest way of getting there.

She allowed the car to dawdle to a halt and sat, no longer looking at her destination below her, but straight ahead at nothing at all, a little pucker of unhappiness between her beautiful brown eyes. Despite the despondency of her expression, she was an extremely pretty girl, with an oval face framed by naturally dark curling hair, which although confined in a french pleat, had escaped in soft tendrils on either side of her cheeks. Her nose was straight and a little on the short side, and her mouth, released from its present downward droop, was soft and mobile. Her good looks were offset by the clothes she wore—well cut and fashionable, although not excessively so, and her hands, free of her driving gloves, were nicely shaped and beautifully kept. She leaned her rather determined chin on them now, thinking about her new job. When her Uncle John had offered it to her she had accepted without thought. To stay in London in the same hospital as Andrew was unthinkable—it offered a means of escape from an untenable position. She had given a sympathetic Matron her notice, and after a month in which she had learned to hide her real feelings under a cool, impersonal manner she hadn't realised she possessed; she was free. She thought wearily back over the last few months, wondering where she had gone wrong—if, indeed, she had been at fault.

She and Andrew had been engaged for several months, and although the actual date of the wedding had never been discussed, everyone had taken it for granted that it would be soon. She ignored the first spiteful whispers about him; she was sensible enough to know that in a hospital the size of Greggs', there would always be someone ready to start rumours of that sort, and when they had persisted, she had even joked about them with Andrew, because Staff Nurse Beatty, although possessed of a lush blonde beauty, was hardly his type. He had laughed with her and agreed with an apparent sincerity which had made it all the harder to bear when she had come across them in a deserted Outpatients Department. Their embrace had been so close and so long that she had gone away without them even noticing…she had waited two terrible days for him to tell her about it, during which time it had become common knowledge throughout the hospital, and when he did, making out that it had been no more than a momentary impulse on his part and certainly the same on the part of Beatty, she had swallowed her pride and forgiven him, turning a stubbornly deaf ear to her friends' guarded hints, and a still more stubborn ear to her mother's thinly veiled warnings. She had known Andrew for more than a year; they loved each other and she trusted him… She shifted a little behind the wheel and laughed ruefully; at least she was wiser now—it would be a long time before she trusted any man again.

She hadn't believed the Sister from Men's Medical when that young lady had told her, with tact and kindness, that Andrew and Beatty had been seen time and again together in various places by various people—it seemed that London, for all its size, wasn't big enough… She had hotly denied it, because Andrew had told her that he was attending a series of post-graduate lectures, but in the end she had been forced to believe it, for she had seen them together coming out of Wheeler's one evening as she was on her way back to Greggs' after visiting her mother, who was staying with friends in Cumberland Terrace. She had got off the bus to cut through the complexity of small streets to reach the hospital and came face to face with them. This time she didn't wait for Andrew to come to her; she waylaid him on the way to Outpatients the next morning and with almost no words at all had handed him back his ring and then gone straight to Matron's office and resigned.

It was her mother who had enlisted the help of Uncle John without telling Sappha that she had done so, and in any case, Sappha couldn't have cared less what she did. She took the job he offered her so providentially and here she was. She sighed, switched on the engine, and drove down the winding road to Dialach.

The Manse was easy to find, for it stood foursquare beside the church; a solid roomy house surrounded by a pleasant garden in which the autumn flowers and trees made a splash of colour even on such a grey day as this. Sappha drove up its neat short drive and had barely turned off the engine before the front door was opened and the minister appeared on his doorstep. He was a friend of her uncle's, but she hadn't expected quite such a warm welcome—it acted like a tonic upon her downcast spirits, she resolutely tucked her own troubles away in the back of her mind and greeted him with a quiet friendliness of her own which lighted up her face to a quite breathtaking loveliness.

'You're tired and chilly, I daresay, my dear Miss Devenish,' said Mr MacFee. 'My wife has tea waiting for you, and presently, when you are rested, you may like to go and see our district nurse, Miss Perch, so that she may tell you everything there is to know about Baroness van Duyren.'

He had drawn her across the hall as he spoke and now opened a door into a pleasant room with comfortable shabby furniture and a blazing log fire. Sappha, feeling that she was being treated more as a patient than a nurse, allowed herself to be led across the room to where Mrs MacFee was standing, to be greeted by a kindness at least the equal of the minister's, and then bustled into a chair and told to undo her coat and stretch her feet to the fire. She barely had the time to do this before she was being plied with tea and hot buttered toast, while her kind host and hostess talked with gentle inconsequence of the weather, her Uncle John, the excessive rainfall and the delicate flavour of the quince preserve she had been pressed to try on a scone. It wasn't until she had followed the scone with a teacake and that with a slice of rich fruit cake that she was allowed to enquire about her patient, 'for', as she pointed out, 'Uncle John has told me a great deal about the case, and I know he will be down to see her next week, but of course he hasn't much idea of the nursing routine.'

Mrs MacFee smiled comfortably. 'Indeed one would scarcely expect him to, but you'll find Miss Perch most helpful and your patient very co-operative. She and I are old friends, of course—your uncle will have told you that already. We went to school together—Switzerland, you know and we still see a good deal of each other. She and her husband used to come every year to visit us, usually with their children. She has a family of six...' Mrs MacFee, who was childless, paused to sigh. 'After his death she continued to come, but now of course all the children are married, save for the eldest and the youngest.' She paused for breath, beaming kindly at Sappha, who had conjured up a picture of a desicated spinster wearing glasses following Mother wherever she chose to go...she hoped that she was going to like the Baroness.

It had stopped raining by the time she had convinced the minister and his wife that she was sufficiently rested and refreshed to visit Miss Perch. Mr MacFee went with her to the Manse door and pointed out the way she should go— a not very arduous walk as it turned out, for the district nurse lived in the end cottage in the little street behind the harbour, a bare three minutes' walk away. Sappha knocked on the stout door, looking around her as she did so. The harbour was indeed small, and the causeway, now that she was near enough to see it properly, was nothing but a crumbling mass of rocks and stone and wood with here and there rough steps connecting its uneven surface—she wondered if it was still used, and as if in answer to her question she glimpsed smoke rising from the muddle of buildings on the island to which it led.

She turned from their contemplation as the door opened and she saw with pleased surprise that Nurse Perch was a girl of her own age, small, blonde and blue-eyed, who grinned engagingly and said 'Hullo, do come in,' as she put out a friendly hand which Sappha took with quite obvious signs of relief. 'I expected you'd be a tough old battleaxe,' she burst out, 'but don't ask me why.'

Miss Perch giggled. 'And I thought you'd be some high and mighty Ward Sister for ever reminding me of the size and importance of your ward.' They laughed in unison and as they went inside, Sappha said:

'My name's Sappha.'

'Mine's Gloria.'

The sitting room was charmingly odd, for it had been furnished largely by the better-off members of the community, but as most of the inhabitants had contributed something, there was a delightful hotch-potch of Victoriana; handsome rugs, two armchairs with rather startling covers, a modern and very efficient-looking desk crammed into one corner, and a variety of cushions of every conceivable size and shape. The walls supported a remarkable collection of pictures, dominated by 'The Stag at Bay' over the fireplace, on either side of which were two dim sepia-tinted photographs of elderly ladies in the heavily laden hats of a past era, and they in turn were flanked by 'When did you last see your Father?' on the one side and a cross-stitch text framed repulsively in plush and bearing the words 'Flee from the Wrath to come' on the other.

Sappha allowed her fascinated gaze to take in these samples of art before turning her attention to the third wall, which held, surprisingly, a delicate watercolour of the harbour and a pair of coloured prints each depicting a gauze-swathed young woman in the act of encouraging—or possibly repelling—the advances of a young man in a tricorne hat. Sappha was still trying to decide which it could be when her hostess spoke. 'Shattering, isn't it? The first day I was here I swore I'd have the whole lot down, but this place was furnished by practically everyone who lives here and if I moved a single picture I'd hurt someone's feelings.' She made a face and Sappha laughed.

'I've never seen anything like it,' she admitted, 'though I love the watercolour.'

Gloria coloured faintly and looked pleased. 'Oh, do you? Actually I did it myself.' She grinned cheerfully and went on, 'Come and sit down and I'll tell you all about Baroness van Duyren. I'm so glad you've come to take over—I mean I've got my hands full and after all she is a private patient. Mr Devenish is your uncle, isn't he? He comes out most weeks, but anything trifling he leaves to me or Doctor MacInroy.'

She said this name in such a way that Sappha was constrained to ask:

'Is he nice—Dr MacInroy, I mean?'

'Well, he's—we're engaged—that's why I came here, to be a bit nearer him until we marry, but of course we don't see a great deal of each other; when I'm free he's usually up to his neck in measles or something and when he's got a day off I'm delivering babies.' She sighed. 'All the same, it's nice here, the people are dears and the countryside is heavenly.' She eyed Sappha's rather townish clothes with a little doubt not unmixed with envy. 'Do you like the country?'

Sappha, to whom any part of the world would have been preferable to London at that time, replied that yes, she thought she would love it.

'It'll be a bit different from the bright lights of London,' Gloria warned.

'Yes,' Sappha agreed, 'but I—I wanted a change.' She frowned. 'Just for a few months, you know.'

Gloria's eyes slid discreetly to Sappha's ringless hands resting on her lap. She said airily: 'Well, that's all right, and it's good fun here too. There's always something going on here—whist drives and play-readings and dances, and when you can't think of anything else to do you can always come here, you know. I don't lock the door, only on my days off, and I'll show you where I keep the key so's you can just walk in.'

Sappha thanked her warmly. 'I've got a little car,' she said. 'I thought I'd get out and about when I can get off.'

'Walking's better,' said Gloria. 'Now, shall we go over the notes and charts and so on? I've got them ready and a rough routine, though I expect you'll change that to suit yourself. I don't know when you'll get your day off, but I'll pop up and do the necessary when you do...'

'Is she nice—the Baroness? She sounded a bit...' Sappha left the sentence in mid air, but all Gloria said was, 'Well, I'll leave you to form your own opinion—she's Dutch, you knew that, I expect? But her English is as good as yours or mine. She comes to stay with the MacFees at least once a year. She's fifty-four and has six children—the youngest is sixteen and the eldest thirtyish. Lashings of money, though they've had so much for so long that you hardly notice it, if you see what I mean.'

Sappha nodded. 'It's a month since she had parathyroid osteodystrophy done, isn't it? Uncle John was rather pleased with the op—he said it was a nasty tumour. Funny no one found it sooner...'

'Well, it's a rare condition, isn't it? and the signs and symptoms are a bit like rheumatoid arthritis, aren't they? It was her son—the one who's a doctor—who suspected a tumour on a gland. He'd been away for several months, though, and she was already over here on holiday when he joined her, and he got your uncle to see her. He caught her just in time I fancy, and as it is, the poor dear has mild renal failure and to crown everything she fell down the first day she was got out of bed after the op and fractured an arm and a leg—the bones were already a bit softened because of the lack of calcium and the tumble did the rest. Still, she's not the sort to give in and she's on the mend, we hope, but dreadfully depressed at times, poor dear. You can see why she needs a private nurse.' She paused and looked at Sappha. 'Are you sorry you came?'

Sappha said slowly, 'No, it's quite a challenge, isn't it? I think I shall like it.' She got to her feet. 'I should go back. Mrs MacFee said something about me seeing the Baroness before suppertime and I ought to run over these notes first. Is there anything else I should know? Drugs and so forth?'

They bent their heads over the charts and prescriptions and TPR sheets, and presently, promising to ring up her new friend if she found herself in difficulties, Sappha made her way back to the Manse.

Her patient had a large room on the first floor, and the small room leading out of it had been turned into a very comfortable bedroom for herself. She took off her outdoor things, tidied her hair and was led by Mrs MacFee into the Baroness's room. Her first reaction was one of surprise; her patient wasn't at all what she had imagined her to be. Sappha, who had a lively imagination, had conjured up a middle-aged heavily built woman with iron grey hair and a commanding manner. What she saw was a small, extremely pretty woman, whose hair was so fair that the silver in it was hard to see, and whose face, though woefully thin and colourless, was lighted by the sweetest of smiles. She was sitting very erect against her bed pillows and despite the plastered right arm and the bed cradle, managed to look as though she were dressed for a party. Mrs MacFee made the introductions, remarking: 'Now I shall leave you two to get to know each other. Supper won't be until half past seven, and perhaps if…' she paused and looked at Sappha. 'My dear,' she said, 'I'm not sure what I should call you. Sister—or Nurse or Miss Devenish. I know you're a hospital Sister, so perhaps…'

Sappha said at once: 'I'd like it if you would call me Sappha. Sister is a bit stiff, isn't it?' She looked at her patient. 'Baroness van Duyren may wish to call me something else—'

'Indeed no,' said the little lady vigorously. 'We're going to be seeing a great deal of each other for the next few weeks, aren't we? I'd like to call you Sappha if I may.'

This important point having been settled to everyone's satisfaction, Mrs MacFee went away and Sappha pulled a chair up to the bed. 'I've some marvellously clear instructions from Miss Perch,' she said, 'but as she has never been here all day I thought we might fill in some of the gaps between us and then I'll bring you your supper and perhaps you would tell me what you would like to do until bedtime.'

The day's routine was discussed at some length and minor points such as time off and free days for Sappha were settled too. It was at the end of this discussion that the Baroness said: 'You wear very pretty clothes, my dear, if you don't mind my saying so. I'm afraid you'll not have many opportunities to go out here, though Ida did tell me that you have a car of your own. How clever of you to drive—I must confess that I have no idea as to what is under the bonnet. Did you not find the journey from London very tiring?'

'No,' said Sappha. 'I stopped overnight on the way up and the roads are good except for the last twenty miles or so. I was stupid enough to run out of petrol coming up the hill from Inver Alligin, but some man came along in a Land Rover and filled the tank for me.' She looked annoyed as she spoke, remembering the dark stranger who had been so coolly critical of her and her clothes.

'Dear me,' observed the Baroness, 'he seems to have vexed you in some way. Do tell.'

'He looked like the Demon King—you never saw such eyebrows,' said Sappha with ill-humour. 'He—he said that he might have known it was a woman…and he didn't like my clothes. I think he was laughing at me.'

She was interrupted by a tap on the door and the man she was talking about came in, this time impeccably dressed in tweeds and exquisitely polished shoes. He seemed a great deal larger at close quarters and his eyes looked quite black. Sappha sat staring at him, the picture of consternation, her lower lip caught between her teeth, her eyes round with surprise. A surprise not shared by her patient, who looked from Sappha's face to that of her son's and said, so softly that neither of them caught her words: 'Enter the Demon King—how very interesting life has suddenly become!'

CHAPTER TWO

THE Baroness shook out a lace ruffle, raised her voice and said pleasantly: 'There you are, Rolf—how nice,' and turned to smile at Sappha. 'This is my son Rolf, my dear—he's on a short visit from Holland—just to see how I am, you know.' She gave Sappha just enough time to murmur politely before she went on: 'Rolf, this is Miss Sappha Devenish who has come to nurse me back on to my feet again—all the way from London too. I daresay you remember, dear—I did mention...' Her voice took on a vague note. 'I believe you have already met...'

Sappha had gone a delectable pink. She said baldly: 'Yes, we have, I was just telling you.' She glanced across at the man standing so quietly in the doorway, her brown eyes snapping because she suspected that behind the politeness of his expression he was laughing at her. He walked across the room without saying anything at all, kissed his mother, said in a voice deeper than Sappha had remembered: 'Yes, Mother, I remember very well,' and turned to shake Sappha's hand. At close quarters he seemed very large indeed and handsome in a dark sort of way. He enquired gravely how she did and when she looked at him she could see that his eyes were alive with laughter. He said: 'I hope you will enjoy staying here, it is—er—a little quiet.'

He allowed his gaze to sweep over her well-turned-out person so that she made haste to say with a touch of haughtiness: 'I shall be wearing uniform,' and was instantly furious with herself for saying anything so stupid, for his mouth curved in a faint smile and the peculiar eyebrows

19

lifted. 'Of course,' he said mildly, 'what could have made you suppose I should expect anything else?' He sat down carefully on the end of his mother's bed. 'Tell me, did you have a good journey? Which way did you come?'

'The M1—from London, you know.' Her voice had an edge to it. 'And at Inverness I got on to the A832, through Garve and Achnasheen and Torridon—it was a good road all the way, excepting for the last few miles.'

'Ah, yes.' She was sure he was laughing at her again. 'There are very few roads around here—just the one to Torridon. You will enjoy the walking, I have no doubt.' His voice was silky and she had her mouth open to answer him back, but he went on smoothly: 'Am I interrupting something? Would you prefer me to come back later?' Which was so obviously a polite way of asking her to leave that she got to her feet at once with a remark that she would unpack.

She found her way down to the kitchen presently to fetch her patient's supper, having disposed of her clothes and changed into a crisp white uniform and perched her Greggs' cap upon her nicely arranged hair. It was a spotted muslin trifle, goffered, edged with lace and rather fetching. Mrs MacFee, helping in the preparation of the invalid's supper, complimented Sappha upon it. 'Such a refreshing change, my dear, after some of these odd styles—not,' she added hastily, 'but what you looked charming when you arrived.' She set a steaming pipkin of soup carefully upon the tray and added its lid.

'Now, dear, if you wouldn't mind taking this up. I don't feel that I should be telling you what to do, really I don't, but I'm sure you will find your way around in no time at all, and then you must do as you think best for your patient. I expect Dr van Duyren is with her now?'

Sappha said, 'Yes,' and cast around for something else to say about him. She could, of course, have mentioned that they had already met, she could even have passed a remark about his satyr's eyebrows, but Mrs MacFee might find that a little odd. Instead she asked: 'Does he stay here? I mean when comes to see his mother?'

'Oh, yes. Of course he's been coming here ever since he was a very small boy—Mr MacFee thinks of him as a son—he comes and goes as he likes and he knows everyone for miles around. He keeps a Land Rover here and many's the time he's gone to some outlying croft when there has been an accident or a baby arriving too soon and we couldn't get Hamish MacInroy.' She paused for breath. 'They're good friends, anyway.'

Sappha, cutting toast into neat squares, agreed that it sounded most convenient, while the unbidden thought that Andrew—a great stickler for etiquette—would never have countenanced casual help from a colleague crossed her mind. Presumably it was a different kettle of fish in these remote parts. She picked up her tray and went upstairs to find that her patient was alone and looking rather downcast, so when she had arranged everything so that the Baroness could manage with her one hand, she said: 'I want to write up your charts—do you mind if I sit here and do them while you have your soup?'

Her patient lifted her spoon. 'Would you?' she asked eagerly, 'a new face is so refreshing.' She spooned another mouthful. 'You were quite right, Sappha—Rolf does look like a demon king—it's extraordinary that I have never noticed it before.'

Sappha put down her charts. 'I must apologise, Baroness. I should never have said that—I had no intention…'

Her companion nibbled toast. 'Why should you be sorry?' she asked. 'I expect he was wearing some dreadful clothes and muddy boots and probably he hadn't shaved. I believe he went out very early this morning—a broken leg near Ben Eighe and he would have to walk part of the way you know—it was off the road. Hamish was out on a baby case and one really can't leave a person lying with a broken leg, can one?'

Sappha said dryly: 'No, that would be rather unkind,'

and her patient nodded before continuing: 'Really, I hardly recognise him sometimes. At home, of course, he looks exactly like a doctor.' She waved a hand in an expressive gesture, 'and naturally, being the eldest, he tends to throw his weight around—is that the right expression?'

Sappha smiled. 'Yes, though perhaps it's a little severe.'

'Not nearly as severe as Rolf when he's annoyed,' retorted his mother with spirit.

'All the same,' commented Sappha, 'you must be very glad of his support.'

'Oh, I am, child, I am. My husband died when Rolf was twenty-five, and Antonia—the youngest—was only nine. The others are married now, which means that Rolf has more leisure, though he always has time for Tonia—they're so fond of each other.' She smiled a little wistfully. 'She is such a dear child and I do miss her. She's at school and I had hoped that she would be able to come over for a day or so—it's so long to Christmas, but anyway, I shall be home before then.'

Sappha took the empty soup bowl. 'Good gracious, yes,' she said bracingly, 'but surely she could fly over for a weekend? There's an airfield at Inverness...' She stood deep in thought. 'We could at least make a few enquiries.'

'That would be lovely, but I believe Rolf thinks that it would be unsettling for Tonia—she has her studies...'

'Oh, pooh,' said Sappha inelegantly, 'she can do some extra homework to make up for it—shall I talk to Doctor van Duyren and see if he will change his mind?' She was on her way to the door and didn't see the Baroness's face which held an expression of mischief mixed with anticipation.

When Sappha returned after a few minutes with a fricassée of chicken and an egg custard, and having placed these delicacies before her, poured a glass of wine and put it within her reach, her patient said: 'What a great deal of work I am going to give you, Sappha.'

'Indeed you won't—in hospital I ran around all day except when I had to sit at a desk and fill in forms and answer the telephone.'

The Baroness speared a morsel of chicken and asked: 'Will you not be bored just with me to look after?'

'Not in the least.' Sappha spoke with a conviction which wasn't quite genuine, for she had her private doubts on the subject; not only would her working day be far less exacting, her private life was going to be very different too. No more going out on her evenings off duty to the theatre or dinner and dancing or to the cinema. She tried to remember where she had seen the last cinema on the way to Dialach. Probably one had to go back to Inverness, or at least Achnasheen or Garve. Her speculations were brought to an abrupt end by the realisation that even if she were in London there would have been no theatres or cinema or dinners—not with Andrew, at any rate. She said rather abruptly: 'I'll fetch your coffee,' and when she got back her patient had finished her supper and was lying back against her pillows, deep in thought, she roused herself, however, to say pensively: 'Of course, you'll have our Gloria—she's about your age. Such a pretty girl—I expect you know that she's engaged to Hamish—a dear boy, your uncle thinks very highly of him.' She watched Sappha pour the coffee and then obediently swallowed the pills she was offered. 'Loathsome things,' she muttered crossly, and Sappha laughed and said encouragingly:

'Yes, but think how much worse everything would be if you didn't have them.'

'Since no one has told me what they are or why I am taking them, how can I possibly agree with you?' her patient wanted to know, and then on the same breath and with a suddenness which took Sappha by surprise: 'Why are you not married or at least engaged? You're a pretty girl, young—twenty-three or four?—intelligent and well dressed.' And when Sappha didn't reply: 'Perhaps I shouldn't have asked. Forgive me, I didn't mean to be rude, I'm just a curious old woman.'

Sappha managed a smile, 'You're not old, nor are you rude. I'll tell you one day, but just for now I'd rather not talk about it.'

She went downstairs, outwardly calm, but inwardly a little ruffled. She had, after all, come several hundred miles in order to be free from just such questions as the Baroness had asked.

Mrs MacFee was in the sitting room, sitting before the fire, and Mr MacFee was standing in the window, engaged in conversation with Dr van Duyren. They paused as she went in, however, and came over to the fire.

'You two have met, I understand,' remarked Mr MacFee cheerfully. 'Well, now you can sit down for a few minutes and get better acquainted.'

'Just as though,' thought Sappha crossly, 'we can't wait to tell each other how pleased we are to meet again.' She sat down, accepted a glass of sherry and was instantly affronted by the manner in which Dr van Duyren walked as far away from her as possible, saying: 'Oh, we shall have time enough for that, I imagine. I'm sure Nurse would prefer to rest a little.'

She gave him an open-mouthed, indignant look while Mrs MacFee observed: 'Why, of course—such a long journey—how thoughtless we are. You must be worn out, my dear, although I must say that in that uniform you look so fresh and efficient.'

Sappha, murmuring politely, looked up and caught Dr van Duyren's dark gaze bent upon her and it was obvious that he was laughing. She lifted her rather determined chin, nettled at his lack of interest coupled with his implication that she was a useless creature who needed a rest, or worse, that she looked as though she needed one. And calling her 'Nurse' too, she had't been called that for eighteen months or more.

Reading her thoughts with an uncanny accuracy, he said smoothly:

'Forgive me—I have been guilty of demoting you. You

were a Ward Sister, weren't you?' He looked apologetic, although she was sure he wasn't, and when he continued: 'I shouldn't have any idea what to call Gloria,' the remark somehow made things seem worse because it reminded Sappha that she was a stranger in a small community where apparently everyone knew everyone else. She wondered rather wistfully if they would accept her, and then, catching his eyes on her again, unsmiling now, decided that it didn't matter in the least.

She treated him with a cool politeness throughout supper and when that meal was over, asked him if he would spare her a few minutes as she had something to discuss with him, to which he replied that he would be delighted although she saw that he was a little surprised too, if his eyebrows were anything to go by.

Mr MacFee had urged them to make use of his study; a small dark room, cluttered with old copies of the *Statesman* and some dusty volumes which looked like encyclopaedias and probably were. It was furnished with a large desk upon which were laid paper, pens and a great deal of blotting paper—her host's sermon, waiting to be written, thought Sappha as she preceded her companion into the room and took a remarkably uncomfortable chair pushed up against the wall. The doctor had the good sense to rest his bulk against the desk, from which he regarded her without speaking.

She folded her hands tidily in her lap and said austerely: 'I should be glad of your co-operation, Doctor,' and watched the eyebrows arch once more.

'So soon? I am amazed—I thought that that would be the last thing you would wish.' He sounded mildly amused.

Sappha suppressed a desire to answer him back, knowing that it would get her nowhere. She closed her pretty mouth on the words which bubbled to her lips and was silent for so long that he enquired, still very mild: 'You wanted me to co-operate, I believe. How?'

'Your mother is anxious to see your sister—Antonia—

she feels that you wouldn't approve because of her studies. Surely it could be arranged for her to come over by air, even for a day or so?'

He said coldly: 'Antonia's schooling is important. She is doing very well—probably she will go on to a university.'

'Oh, fiddle,' said Sappha rudely and quite out of patience. 'Surely she can do some extra homework or something—your mother's peace of mind is much more important.' She shot him a sharp glance. 'Your sister will probably marry before she even gets to university.'

His cold voice became icy. 'Probably, but as you yourself are aware there is many a slip between the cup and the lip when it comes to marriage.'

Sappha sat very still, staring at him. She had gone rather white even though she appeared quite composed. She hadn't realised that the man standing in front of her would know about her and Andrew, but of course Uncle John would have told him. She felt humiliation, so bitter that she could taste it, well up within her. She took her lovely eyes from his face and focused them on the wall above his head, and said quietly: 'We are discussing your mother, I believe,' and heard his voice, wonderfully kind and gentle saying: 'I beg your pardon, that was unforgivable of me. I am afraid I have no excuse, only the unsatisfactory one of always having my own way with my family and taking it for granted that no one will gainsay me.'

He crossed the space between them and caught her by the shoulders so that she came to her feet, willy-nilly. 'Forgive me—if you will, I'll arrange for Tonia to come over whenever you say.'

Sappha studied his face; his eyes, now that she saw them so close, weren't black at all but brown, and at that moment they looked warm and friendly. She said uncertainly: 'I say pretty breastly things myself sometimes—and I forgive you without the bribery—or is it blackmail?'

'Whichever you like, I'll take the blame for both.' He smiled at her so that his face changed completely and just for a second she caught a glimpse of someone quite different, but only a glimpse, not enough to stop her saying: 'It's rather difficult to put into words, but I think we should understand that...' she paused so as to get it quite right, 'some people don't get on very well—I think perhaps we are all like that.'

'Ah,' he said blandly, 'mutual dislike and so forth—is that what you mean? It has been known. Well, in that case, we must conceal our true feelings for each other under the guise of good fellowship, mustn't we?' He walked a little away from her. 'That shouldn't be too difficult, for I go back to Holland tomorrow and you will have plenty of time to practise a friendly approach before I return. Now, shall we go back to the drawing room? I usually spend half an hour with Mother at this time if you have no objection. I'll be gone early tomorrow morning, so you won't need to strain your friendly approach.'

It wasn't until they had parted with outward goodwill and she was sitting with the MacFees that she came to the conclusion that he had been laughing silently when he had made that last remark.

Sappha had expected to spend a wretched night; leaving London had been a wrench, and the peace and quiet she had anticipated in the Highlands had been strangely ruffled by her meeting with Dr van Duyren. She went to bed prepared to lie awake, and promptly slept, to awaken only when Meg, the little daily maid, came in with her morning tea.

'It's a fine bright day, Miss,' she observed as she drew the curtains, revealing a glimpse of the sea and the rugged coastline beyond the rooftops. 'The Baron left with the sun on him.'

Sappha sat up, tossed her hair over her shoulders and yawned. 'Baron who?' she enquired, not quite awake.

Meg turned a surprised face towards her. 'Why, miss, the Baron, ye ken, though maybe ye call him the doctor, but here in the village he gets his rightful title.'

Sappha sipped her tea. 'Oh, Dr van Duyren, the Baroness's son.'

Meg nodded. 'The Baron,' she stated simply. 'Breakfast
is at half past eight, I was to tell you.' She went away,
leaving Sappha to ponder this titbit of information. She had
never met a baron before; she supposed, after due thought,
that he was very like a baron should be—the very name
conjured up a swashbuckling, high-handed gentleman, for
ever shouting down his inferiors and being charming when
it suited him. She got up and dressed rapidly, reminding
herself the while of everything about him that annoyed her.

Her patient was awake after a good night and very ready
to talk while Sappha performed the few necessary tasks
prior to bringing up her breakfast. Her son, she told Sappha,
had left at first light to board a plane at Inverness and she
wasn't at all sure how long it would be before he would
be coming again, for as well as running a practice with his
two partners, he lectured in Groningen.

'Ah, yes—somewhere in the north of Holland, then,' said
Sappha, shaking down the thermometer, and was taken
back when the Baroness said touchily: 'Not North Holland—our home is in Dokkum, which is in Friesland. Groningen, of course, is not.'

Sappha begged her pardon, made a mental note to have
a look at an atlas when she got downstairs, and besought
her patient to open her mouth.

Uncle John came later that morning and spent a long
time examining his patient, and a still longer time talking
to Sappha about her. He was pleased with the results of the
operation he had performed; the tumour had been removed
before it could do lasting damage and the bones were hard-
ening once more with the increased calcium, moreover the
renal failure was improving at a heartening rate, but he
warned Sappha of the depression which was bound to attack the Baroness from time to time—the aftermath of her
rare disease. 'But we'll pull her through, I have no doubt',

he said cheerfully, then asked without pause: 'I suppose Rolf has gone?'

Sappha gave her uncle a level look. 'You mean Dr van Duyren—or should I say Baron van Duyren?'

He returned her look with an innocent one of his own. 'My dear, how should I know? Everyone around here calls him Rolf—the people in the town address him as Baron, I believe, but I hardly think he would expect you to address him as such. Don't you like him?'

Sappha pinkened faintly. She said crossly: 'How ever should I know, Uncle John? I've hardly spoken to him.' She picked up a batch of forms and went on in a businesslike way: 'Shall I fill these in for you to sign? I expect you're taking them with you.'

Dr McInroy arrived just as her uncle was preparing to leave. He was a sturdy man in his early thirties, of middle height, and with good features and bright blue eyes. After he had greeted the specialist, he turned to Sappha with a warm smile, saying: 'Miss Devenish—I've heard all about you from Gloria and I'm delighted to welcome you to Dialach.' He sounded so genuinely pleased to meet her that Sappha found herself smiling widely as she shook hands, but even as she did so, she had a fleeting recollection of her meeting with Dr van Duyren, who hadn't greeted her at all…but there was no time to indulge her own thoughts; the two doctors began to discuss their patient, and as they seemed to take it for granted that she should stay with them, she concentrated upon the subject in hand, so when she was drawn into their conversation from time to time she was able to join in in a manner which caused Dr MacInroy to look at her with something like respect and remark:

'You know a great deal about osteitis fibrosa cystica— have you seen one before? It's a rare condition.'

Sappha shook her head. 'No, never, that's why I read up all I could about it before I came—I picked a few brains too.' They all laughed and presently she left them to return to her patient.

The Baroness was lying back in bed looking bored. As well she might, thought Sappha, with only one leg and one arm available. She bustled around with an exaggerated cheerfulness getting ready to bedbath her patient, and presently, while she was doing this, asked: 'What else do you do—other than reading?'

'Oh, crosswords—there's nothing else with one hand…' The Baroness spoke listlessly and Sappha made haste to say: 'Uncle John is delighted with your progress—he wants you to do a few exercises each day, so that when your arm comes out of plaster it will be fairly strong. I'm going to get you out of bed and into a chair by the window—there's a lovely view. I suppose you don't paint?'

Her patient looked surprised and faintly interested. 'Yes, I used to—how did you know?'

'I didn't—but I was thinking if we could get hold of some paints and a canvas or some paper, you could amuse yourself.'

The Baroness lifted eyebrows which reminded Sappha of her son. 'With one hand?' she enquired.

'Why not? If I arrange everything within reach—we can find some way of keeping the paper steady, and I shall be on hand for a good deal of the day—would you like to try?'

She had been wrapping her patient in a dressing gown as she spoke; now she pulled the chair alongside the bed and lifted the Baroness in her strong young arms into it and trundled her over to the window.

'I'll get you some coffee and while you're drinking it I'll see if Mrs MacFee can help about the paints.'

Mrs MacFee, when appealed to, not only produced an elderly paintbox of her own but a sketching pad as well and spent half an hour with her friend discussing the best view to start on; while Sappha busied herself making the bed and tidying the room; with such success that Sappha was able to leave the two ladies together after lunch and take an hour or two off duty. She went first to the post office to send a hastily written letter to her mother and then explored the little town and its harbour. The day, which had started off in sunshine, had become overcast and windy, so that the waves beat against the lonely shore; only in the harbour was the water smooth although it looked cold enough.

She was on her way back when she met Gloria, who fell into step beside her saying: 'There you are—how nice. No good me asking you to come in for tea, I'm afraid—I'm just off to see a patient.' She waved vaguely in the direction of the causeway and Sappha asked: 'Where? You're pointing out to sea.'

'Well, she is in a way,' said Gloria cheerfully. 'At least, I have to be rowed over because the causeway's in ruins—there's a baby due any time now and a good thing it's not later in the year, for there's a terrific current and if it's stormy the boat can't make it—the locals think nothing of scrambling over the causeway when the weather's bad, but I'm no mountain goat—even they hesitate a bit unless it's daylight.'

'Who lives there?' asked Sappha, interested.

'The family MacTadd—father's a fisherman and there are Mum, Gran and a clutch of children. There's a plan to rehouse them, but there's nothing suitable for them at the moment, and besides, they don't want to go. They've patched up the croft very nicely, though there's no H and C and no electricity either. Hamish has tried to persuade Mrs MacTadd to go to hospital, but she absolutely refuses, so all we can do is to keep a sharp eye open and pray for fine weather.' She grinned cheerfully. 'I'm going down here—Mr MacTadd will be waiting for me—let me know when you've fixed your days off and I'll pop up and see to the Baroness for you. 'Bye.' She turned away and then paused to say over her shoulder: 'I've fixed Saturday for mine, so don't have that.'

Sappha took her day off on Friday; during the four days she had been at the Manse she had got the routine nicely settled, and in any case, she didn't go until she had got her patient up for the day, arranged with Gloria for that young lady to call in after lunch and arranged with Mrs MacFee that the Baroness shouldn't be left too long alone in case she moped. She then set out with the Mini. The weather was good; she suspected that before many weeks as the autumn settled into winter, she would have to spend her free day in Dialach—it seemed a good idea to explore as far afield as possible while she could. She took the road to Ullapool, where, Gloria had informed her, there was a rather delightful shop selling local handicrafts and tweeds. Besides, she intended to visit the garden at Inverewe—it wasn't the best time of year to do so, but various of her friends in London had urged her on no account to miss it.

She thought briefly of Dr van Duyren as she drove to Torridon—his mother, beyond mentioning that he had got home safely and was very busy, had offered no further information, although she had been voluble enough about Antonia, who, from all accounts, was not only very pretty but a little spoiled and wilful as well. Sappha stopped for a late cup of coffee at the Loch Maree Hotel, feeling breathless from the magnificent scenery she had just passed through, and eager for more. The day was going to be too short. She decided to press on to Ullapool, have lunch there, take a quick look around the town and then visit Inverewe on her way back. Even so, by the time she had reached Ullapool she knew that she would have to return, not once, but several times if she were to take her fill of the scenery.

She lunched at the Caledonian Hotel, and for the first time since she had arrived in Scotland, felt almost happy. She supposed it was the magnificent country through which she had been driving which somehow had the power to make London and its pleasures seem a little unreal. She spent a pleasant half hour looking round the little town, quiet now after its summer season, but she was anxious not to miss the gardens and sped back through the forest land, resisting the urge to stop and gaze at the mountains around her. Next time, she promised herself, going downhill fast towards Gruinard, and then up the other side to Inverewe gardens.

They were lovely even though there was only an aftermath of summer's glory in the flower beds. She left reluctantly, promising herself that she would pay another visit in some distant summer, and stopped for tea in Aultbea, and then, pleasantly tired, took the road back to Dialach. It had been a successful day, made more successful by the friendly people she had met wherever she had stopped and the openly admiring glances of the young man in the deer-stalker cap who had entered the hotel while she was having lunch, and had at once engaged her in conversation while he ate his own meal at a nearby table. It was only after they had parted in mutual friendliness that she felt a twinge of regret that they weren't likely to meet again, for as far as she could see, there weren't many men of her own age in Dialach—Dr MacInroy couldn't be counted, of course, for he was Gloria's anyway, and the Baron, with his peculiar eyebrows and bossy ways, certainly had no place in her thoughts. She spent several minutes convincing herself of this as she changed back into uniform and went to seek out her patient. And felt instantly contrite when she saw her; the Baroness was in bed—Gloria had seen to that before she had left at teatime—and turned a listless tear-stained face to Sappha as she went in; it took a few minutes of patient comforting on her part before she could induce her patient to speak. 'I-I h-hope you h-had a lovely d-day,' she sobbed, 'and this is s-so s-silly, because I d-don't know why I'm c-crying,' and then contradicted herself by adding: 'Rolf s-said he would t-telephone and he hasn't.'

'Perhaps he's been too busy,' said Sappha, who felt strongly that the telephone was a modern blessing which had its drawbacks. How many times had she sat by the wretched instrument in London waiting for Andrew to ring, and all the while... She jerked her thoughts back to her patient; it was really too bad of the tiresome man, he should have squeezed in a call whatever he was doing. 'He'll telephone later,' she said with a conviction she didn't feel, 'and don't worry about being a bit tearful, Baroness—remember what Uncle John said; that you were bound to feel depressed for no reason at all. I'm going to wash your face and tidy your hair, and after supper we'll play that game of draughts we never had.'

The evening was cheerful after all—with the fire alight in the old-fashioned grate and the chintz curtains drawn, the room looked cosy and inviting. Sappha ate a hasty supper and went back upstairs and true to her promise got out the draughts board and allowed the Baroness to beat her soundly before giving her her sleeping pill and tucking her up for the night. She had only just got downstairs to say goodnight to the MacFees when the telephone rang and Mr MacFee, who answered it, said:

'It's for you, Sappha,' he smiled a little, 'a man.'

She could feel her heart pounding in her chest as she crossed the room. It could be Andrew, miraculously in love with her again, telephoning to say so because he couldn't wait to write it. She picked up the receiver and said Hullo in a voice which shook with excitement.

But it wasn't Andrew, although it was a man—a man with strange eyebrows who had laughed at her and thought her clothes were silly, and who had forgotten to telephone his mother. His deep voice came lazily over the wire: 'Oh, dear, I'm not the right one, am I?' he asked outrageously. 'How's Mother?'

She choked back disappointment, furious with him and with herself.

'She's been waiting for you to ring up,' she said sharply. 'She was upset...'

'I'm sorry. I imagine you've given her her sleeping pill by now, that's why I thought I'd better speak to you first.'

'Well, it's no good, she's asleep.' Sappha spoke with some thing of a snap.

'You sound like a love-starved spinster with no looks

and no prospects.' He was laughing, and forgetful of the MacFees, sitting across the room politely not listening, she burst out: 'How dare you!'

'I'll dare anything if I have a mind to,' he said coolly, 'and just for the record, you'll never starve for lack of love, my good girl, and your prospects are about as good as they can be.'

Sappha drew a deep breath, let it out noisily and said helplessly:

'Well!' She was prevented from saying anything else because he went on at once: 'I'm sorry I couldn't telephone earlier—circumstances prevented it. I'll ring in the morning—you can tell her that if she wakes. I hadn't forgotten, it was quite impossible.'

She said: 'Very well' in a stiff little voice and he went on as though she hadn't spoken. 'I've arranged for Tonia to come over with me. It's most inconvenient, but I don't dare face you without her. That will be a week on Thursday. Goodbye.'

He rang off before she had time to open her mouth. She put down the receiver slowly and went back to the MacFees and repeated what he had said, but with a good deal of it expurgated, so that her mild version didn't tally in the least with the heated retorts she had given. This quite escaped her, and the MacFees, beyond a mild comment on the pleasure of seeing Rolf and Antonia again, didn't mention it.

Later on, in bed, Sappha went over all that he had said. She hadn't understood his remarks about her not starving for love and having good prospects and she thought about it for a long time, getting more and more frustrated because it didn't make sense, finally she said out loud: 'Oh, he's crazy,' then turned over and went determinedly to sleep. The following days passed quietly enough and the boredom which she had half expected to settle upon her after a week or so, didn't materialise. Instead, she began to find the days not quite long enough. The Baroness had taken heart again; Rolf had telephoned her several times and she was full of

excitement at seeing Antonia so soon. She had never asked
Sappha if she had spoken to Rolf about her daughter's visit,
nor did she do so now beyond making a comment upon his
kindness and understanding. Sappha, asked to agree with
her patient upon her son's excellent qualities, agreed woodenly, remembering what he had said—she wondered if she
would ever forget his words even though she had forgiven
them. She pummelled the pillow she was shaking up with
unnecessary vigour—he was one of the most unpleasant
men she had ever met.

She had her day off on Wednesday and took the Mini in
the other direction down to Balmarca, so that she might see
the hills of Skye across the Kyle of Lochalsh. She had
lunch at the hotel there and then went on to look at Eilean
Donan Castle on the edge of Loch Duich. She followed on
down the steep road to get a good view of the Kintail
Mountains, but they were fast disappearing in heavy clouds,
so she found a place to turn the car and started back home.
She had promised to have tea with Gloria anyway, and it
was already getting on for four o'clock.

Gloria wasn't home, but Sappha let herself in, poked up
the fire, put on the kettle and then went to fetch the cake
she had brought from the baker's. The cottage had a small
rather cluttered kitchen, gay with gingham curtains and a
collection of copper pans which Sappha coveted. She pottered around, rather enjoying herself so that she found herself reflecting, while cutting bread for the toast, that life in
Dialach was so pleasant that the idea of going back to London seemed quite laughable. A fortunate thing, in the circumstances, because that was the last place she wanted to
be in—probably by now Andrew had married that beastly
little blonde...

She frowned and sighed at the thought, so that Gloria,
coming in at that moment, exclaimed: 'Good lord, Sappha,
what's eating you? You look ferocious—sadly ferocious—
or do I mean ferociously sad? What's the matter?'

Sappha speared bread on to a toasting fork. 'Hullo—nothing, really.'

Gloria cast her hat on one chair, her coat on another and her case on the table. 'Not bored, are you?'

'No, on the contrary—I was just thinking how bored I should be in London.'

'Well, even if you were,' said Gloria, making the tea, 'you won't be after tomorrow. Rolf and Antonia will be here, you can't be bored when they're around. What do you think of Rolf?'

Sappha buttered toast. 'Well, I don't really know him—I mean we only talked a little.'

Gloria laughed. 'But he's not the kind of man you need to talk to—don't tell me he didn't make an impression on you, or you'll be the first woman under ninety who hasn't been bowled over.'

The two of them sat down by the fire in the little sitting room and bit into their toast. 'If you want to know,' said Sappha, her mouth full, 'I found him rude, bossy—and he laughs behind his face.'

Gloria stared at her over her tea cup. 'I haven't asked you yet, but it's obvious to anyone with eyes in their heads that you came up here to get away from something or someone—a man, I suspect. It's hardly fair to colour your impression of Rolf by your own experience.' She put down her cup and held out a friendly hand. 'That was a beastly thing to say—I'm sorry. I know how I'd feel if Hamish...'

'I daresay you're right,' conceded Sappha, privately thinking her all wrong. 'Now tell me, what are you going to do with your day off?'

'Inverness—with Hamish. He's coming for me about nine and we won't be back until the late evening. There's nothing to worry about in the village; old Mrs MacGower is off her penicillin injections and Mrs MacTadd is OK. She should go another three weeks—the babe's a transverse lie, but there's time enough for it to right itself—Hamish has turned it twice already. Are you a midwife? You are?—

good, just in case I'm not about when Mrs MacTadd starts,
I shall warn them to come for you.' She had spoken jok-
ingly and Sappha replied in kind, and Rolf's name wasn't
mentioned again for the rest of Sappha's visit. Before she
went home though, Gloria said with a laugh: 'I'm going to
show you where everything is kept in the surgery, Sappha,
so that if ever there is an emergency you could cope.'

So Sappha was invited to see where the key was hidden
and where the midwifery bag was housed, and the gas and
air apparatus, even the blood taking and giving sets—'For,'
said Gloria, 'we just have to be prepared for everything—
and by the way, there's a litre of O blood, Rhesus positive,
in the fridge—Hamish brought it with him today in case
Mrs MacTadd does the dirty on us.' She went with her
guest to the door. 'Do you want anything from Inverness?'

Sappha considered. 'No, I don't think so, thanks. I
thought I'd drive over on my next day off and do some
shopping, but there's nothing urgent.'

She said goodbye and drove the short distance to the
Manse, where she put the car in the little lean-to at the back
of the house which the minister had put at her disposal,
and ran indoors. The house was warm and quiet; the faint
murmur of voices from the drawing room told her that Mr
and Mrs MacFee were enjoying their usual evening chat
together; she forbore from joining them, for she suspected
that it was probably the only hour in the day when they
could be reasonably sure of being uninterrupted, but went
on upstairs, to pause at the Baroness's door undecided
whether to go and see her first or wait until she had taken
off her outdoor things. She decided to go in; probably the
Baroness was feeling lonely. She opened the door and
poked her pretty head round it.

The Baroness was not lonely at all; she had company—
a very pretty blonde girl curled up beside her on the bed,
and the Baron, crouching on the floor, tinkering with a por-
table TV set. He came to his feet in a surprisingly agile

manner for so large a man and said: 'Hullo—had a nice day?'

Sappha said yes, thank you, a trifle breathless with surprise and some other sensation which, if she hadn't disliked him so much, she would have admitted was pleasure. The Baroness beamed at her. 'Sappha, isn't this a lovely surprise? Rolf brought Tonia a day sooner and he's brought a TV for me too...come and meet my daughter.'

Antonia had left the bed and had pranced over to Sappha. She really was extraordinarily pretty with great blue eyes and dimples, her hair was straight and thick and corn-coloured, cut in a fringe across her forehead. She put out a hand, remarking disarmingly: 'You're far too pretty to be a nurse. I don't believe you're much older than I am—I'm sixteen.'

Rolf said lazily from the floor: 'Antonia, you mustn't ask Nurse how old she is—she might not want me to know.'

'Stuff,' said his sister inelegantly. 'You make her sound like some old bag in her thirties—just because you're thirty-two yourself...' She turned her lively little face to Sappha. 'Tell me later,' she invited, and bounced back to make herself comfortable by her mother once more as that lady said indulgently: 'Tonia, you're not to talk to Sappha like that—you hardly know her.'

'Oh, yes, Mama, I do, you know. Sometimes you meet someone and it's as if you've known them all your life.' She appealed to her brother. 'Rolf, people do feel like that, don't they?'

He looked up briefly, but not at her. His dark eyes dwelt for a few seconds on Sappha, who felt herself turning slowly red under them. But all he said was: 'Oh, yes, of course, only it's more satisfactory if they both feel the same way at the same time.'

'There, you see?' Antonia addressed the room at large and smiled widely at Sappha. 'I know we're going to be friends.' She studied Sappha's heightened colour and went on with devastating candour: 'You've gone very red—it makes you prettier than ever. Rolf...'

He didn't look up and his voice was bland. 'I'm sure Nurse wants to take off her coat.' And Sappha cast him a look of relief mingled with the vexed thought that he had called her nurse again. She said primly:

'I'll be back with your supper presently, Baroness,' and went away.

Hours later, sitting up in bed thinking about the evening, Sappha had to admit that she had enjoyed herself. Antonia had lent a sparkle to the conversation, and so too, surprisingly had Rolf. He was certainly very fond of his sister and she, for her part, was equally devoted to him, and although it was apparent that she could twist him round her little finger, it was also quite clear that she had a wholesome respect for him too. Sappha smiled to herself, thinking about her; she was spoilt and a little wilful but so good-natured and sunny-tempered that she doubted if anyone, even her eldest brother, could be annoyed with her for more than a couple of seconds at a time. And, reflected Sappha, she had been instantly obedient to the suggestion that it was her mother's bedtime, and afterwards, sitting on the end of Sappha's bed while the latter rearranged her hair, she had asked some remarkably sensible questions about her mother's illness and when Sappha had hesitated to answer them, said: 'I know a great deal about it already—Rolf said it would be better for me and for Mother if I did. And of course he's right. He always is,' she added simply.

Sappha thought it wise to say nothing to this; quite obviously, the Baron ruled his family with a rod of iron, albeit a well camouflaged one. She found herself speculating upon the poor girl he would coerce into marrying him and felt fiercely sorry for her. She could imagine what it would be like—'Half a dozen children,' she muttered to herself, thumping her pillows. 'The woman's place is in the home, and all that, however luxurious that home might be.' She had a sudden vivid mental picture of the Baron sitting at the head of a table lined with little barons and baronesses, all with miniature satyr's eyebrows and herself at the end. She pulled herself up short, hastily substituting this ridiculous idea with the interesting question as to what a baron's children were called, but before she could go deeply into the matter she was disturbed by her patient's voice from the bedroom next door, asking if she might have another sleeping tablet because one hadn't seemed to be enough. Sappha got out of bed, her unruly thoughts forgotten. She said soothingly: 'It's only because you've had such an exciting evening—you have been to sleep and you'll soon drop off again. I'll read to you, shall I? Are you quite comfy?'

She made a few deft movements amongst the pillows and bedclothes.

'There, not a wrinkle in sight. Close your eyes—I'll go on with *Jane Eyre*.'

She read for several minutes until the Baroness interrupted her to say:

'What an arrogant man he was—but of course he loved Jane, and she loved him. Was the man you loved—still do perhaps, Sappha—arrogant?'

Sappha looked up from her reading. Her dressing gown was a soft pink, a perfect contrast to the dark hair hanging around her shoulders. She smelled faintly of Roger and Gallet's Violet soap and she looked as pretty as the proverbial picture. Her patient, studying her closely, thought it a great shame that there was no one other than herself to see her.

Sappha said in a wooden voice: 'No, not arrogant. It was just that he found someone else—blonde and sexy and willing to give him what I wouldn't—I'm old-fashioned about marriage…'

'Me too,' said the Baroness briskly, 'and you would be surprised at the number of men who want an old-fashioned girl for a wife—a girl who will love them and run their home with pride. And children—men want children.' She

waved her plastered arm in the air. 'It's no good me telling
you that you will get over it and meet another man—there
aren't any other men at the moment are there? And you're
sure that you will never get over him, aren't you?'

She took another look at Sappha, and it was a pity that
Sappha, instead of looking at her companion, was looking
backwards over the last few disastrous months, for the Baroness's pretty face wore the look of someone who had just
had a brilliant idea. She did, in fact, look very like her
young daughter when that young daughter was plotting
mischief. There was a little pause until Sappha said quietly:
'Shall I go on reading?'

The Baroness yawned daintily. 'I do believe I begin to
feel sleepy again, dear. Would it be too much trouble if I
asked you to fetch me just a little warm milk?'

Sappha padded downstairs and presently, with the milk
in her hand, went back again through the quiet old house,
to stop in the bedroom doorway at the sight of Rolf, still
dressed, lounging over the end of his mother's bed. He said
nothing at all, but his gaze swept Sappha from head to foot.
It was the Baroness who said in her soft voice:

'Sappha, Rolf heard us talking and came to see if anything was the matter.' She smiled at them in turn, giving
her son a bright glance which dared him to imagine otherwise. He stared back at her, his eyes snapping with laughter. 'And now that I see you are in such excellent hands,
I'll leave you to settle, dear Mother.'

He bent and kissed her, said a brief goodnight to Sappha
without apparently seeing her, and went back to his room.

The Baroness accepted her milk with the blameless air
of a good child.

'You poor girl,' she said contritely, 'I've kept you from
your bed, but I'm sure that I shall sleep very well now.'
She finished the milk, allowed Sappha to settle her once
more, said goodnight in a grateful voice and closed her
eyes, leaving Sappha to go back to bed, but not at once to
sleep. It was a pity that her patient had asked her those

questions—answering them had made Andrew very clear in her mind once more, and she wanted so much to forget him.

CHAPTER THREE

THERE was no sign of the Baron the next morning. Sappha busied herself with her patient, helped and sometimes hindered by the well-meaning efforts of Antonia, who, after lunch, declared her intention of sitting with her parent while Sappha went for a walk.

Sappha, who was feeling moody and restless, felt more inclined to sit and brood in her room, but she had some letters to post; she would go down to the post office and take a look at the sea at the same time, so she put on her raincoat and tied a scarf over her hair and went out into the rather wild afternoon. It was raining; not very hard, but the wind was boisterous and the mountains behind the little town stood head and shoulders in dark cloud. She walked around the harbour, shivering a little because the wind was keen as well as strong, eyeing the angry waves beyond the harbour's mouth, they were battering the causeway too. A solitary fishing boat was battling its way in and she stopped to watch it, thankful that she wasn't called upon to leave dry land.

It was after she had been to the post office and was on her way back to the Manse that she came face to face with Andrew. She stopped short, her eyes like saucers, her mouth, bulging with a wedge of the toffee she had purchased along with the stamps, slightly open. Andrew however didn't look in the least surprised, nor for that matter did he look awkward or ashamed of himself, but then, some small detached part of her mind reminded her, Andrew never did. But this thought was swamped by the rush of excitement inside her, emotion caught her by the throat so

44

that, what with her heart in her mouth as well as the lump of toffee, she was quite unable to speak.

Andrew, unhindered by either the one or the other of these encumbrances, stopped in front of her and said with all his well-remembered charm, 'Sappha—darling, how marvellous to see you again! I had a couple of free days— it seemed a good chance to come and look you up.'

Sappha, once more in control of both her breath and the toffee, gave him what she hoped was a cool, unflustered look. She said:

'Oh, indeed. How did you know that I was here?'

'I wormed it out of old Mother Martin.' Mother Martin was Home Sister at Greggs' and a notorious passer-on of gossip. Andrew's good-looking face broke into a smile as he caught one of Sappha's hands in his. 'I thought you would be glad to see me—you are, aren't you, Sappha?'

She caught her breath. Of course she was glad, she was on the point of saying so when she felt the weight of a great arm on her shoulders and heard the Baron's voice, mildly, amused, say: 'Hullo, Sappha, taking an hour or two off?' She felt the arm tighten. 'Andrew Glover, isn't it? Thought you'd show up—the landlord of the pub at Torridon mentioned on the telephone that you were heading this way. My name's van Duyren, by the way.'

Sappha watched Andrew's face as he tried to make up his mind how to treat the Baron, who, she noted, was looking ruffianly enough in a thick sweater and terrible old trousers stuffed into rubber boots—he was swinging a string of fish in one hand too. She choked down a sudden desire to laugh because Andrew had no idea who the Baron was and the Baron had equally no intention of telling him. She looked sideways up into his dark face, changing the toffee lump from one cheek to the other as she did so, a childish action which caused him to blink rapidly while the nostrils of his commanding nose quivered ever so slightly. He said carelessly: 'Why not take the afternoon off, Sappha—or for

that matter, the rest of the day? Antonia and Mrs MacFee
will cope.'

Sappha frowned. For one thing Andrew had said nothing
about taking her out—he'd had no time—and for another,
it made her sound too eager. She was eager, she told herself, but Andrew mustn't know that. She said icily: 'How
kind of you, Doctor, but I've had my off-duty for today
and I see no reason for giving myself any more.' And went
pink under his mocking gaze. It was maddening that he
should spoil this unexpected meeting with Andrew—it
could have been something exciting and even more than
that, though Andrew, at the moment, didn't appear to be
exactly carried away... He said now: 'Are you a doctor—
I had no idea...'

The Baron waved the fish and said mildly: 'Oh, I've a
practice—a small country town in Friesland.'

Andrew smiled with a hint of patronage. 'Oh, a GP.' He
was contemptuous and faintly pitying. 'I've rooms in Wim-
pole Street—consultant you know—a nice little private
practice.'

'You are to be congratulated upon your success.' The
Baron's voice was silky, and Sapphia stirred uneasily under
his confining arm, remembering dimly that the Baroness or
someone had mentioned that he lectured in Groningen and
hadn't she said something about examining? With feminine
unfairness she was instantly up in arms against him—he
was taking the mickey out of Andrew. She said positively:
'I really must go—there are things to do.'

If she had hoped to get rid of the Baron she was sadly
mistaken, for he remarked immediately: 'We'll all go.
Come up to the Manse for tea, my dear fellow—Mrs
MacFee will love to see a new face and you and Sappha
can sort out her time off.'

He turned up the lane leading to the Manse, and Sappha
perforce turned with him. Andrew fell into step beside her.
'A pity you can't manage today,' he remarked smoothly.

'What about tomorrow— afternoon or evening perhaps, old girl?'

Sappha quivered with temper; not only had she been called old girl, her free time was being discussed and arranged for her without so much as a by your leave. She opened her mouth to say so, but the Baron spoke first.

'Of course, tomorrow, why not? And I must insist that you take both the afternoon and evening, Sappha. It's not quite the weather for a drive, but there are some splendid walks—I can lend you a pair of boots—' he flung a friendly aside to Andrew. 'I suppose you're at the pub here. They make you very comfortable and Mrs MacGregor is a good cook—she'll turn out an excellent dinner for the pair of you.'

'I'm not sure—' began Sappha loking at the Baron with frustrated rage, to be met with a look of such limpid friendliness that she was struck dumb; if she hadn't been prepared to think the worst of him, she could have supposed that he was trying to make things as easy as possible for her and Andrew.

They turned in at the Manse gate and walked slowly up the short drive to the front door, and any idea Sappha may have had about keeping Andrew's visit from her patient's ears was scotched by the Baron, who paused and waved at the Baroness's window. Sappha felt sure that even if she didn't happen to be looking out at that moment, Antonia would have seen them. She excused herself in the hall and flew upstairs to change back into uniform. It was foolish, but she felt better able to cope with the situation once she had clasped the silver buckled belt round her slim waist and tucked her hair tidily under her cap.

The Baroness and Antonia were sitting by the window when she went in and although Antonia said nothing, Sappha gained the strong impression that this was because she had been told not to. The Baroness turned her still beautiful eyes upon Sappha and asked merely: 'A pleasant walk, I hope, dear?' Sappha, repeating her impressions of the sea

and relaying the little bits of gossip she had gleaned from
the post office, wondered why her patient didn't ask about
Andrew, for it was obvious from their faces that they had
seen him. She hadn't long to wait to find out, however, for
very soon the Baroness told Antonia to go down to tea and
tell Mrs MacFee that Sappha would be down directly, and
that young lady had barely closed the door when her mother
said:

'So he came after you, Sappha. I hope he doesn't intend
to take you back with him—not,' she added earnestly, 'that
I should dream of stopping you.'

Sappha paused in the clearing up of the bed table in
preparation for the tea tray. She said a little wildly: 'But
he hasn't asked me. I don't even know why he's here—
I've had no chance…we'd only just met when Dr van Duyren joined us.' She added bitterly: 'He insisted on bringing
Andrew back for tea and he's kindly arranged for me to be
free tomorrow afternoon and evening.'

Her patient seemed to miss the sarcasm in her attendant's
voice, for she said kindly: 'Now, isn't that nice? How
thoughtful of Rolf. I expect they took to each other at once.'

Sappha, who had her own opinion about this, muttered:
'Oh, well—they're both doctors,' and remembered the
Baron's modest admission to being a GP.

'Exactly what does Dr van Duyren do?' she asked.

The Baroness closed her eyes the better to think. 'Let
me see now—he has a large practice in Dokkum, but of
course he has two partners, then he has consultant's cham-
bers in Groningen as well as being a professor at the Medical School—he has a teaching round and so on and he's
an examiner—he specialises in stomachs and I never have
understood why, my dear.'

Sappha said weakly: 'He's busy.'

'Too busy,' agreed his mother, 'I sometimes think. But
he seems to like it, though I have warned him that if he's
not careful he'll have neither the time nor the inclination
to marry. When he does, of course, his wife will come

before everything else,' she sighed, 'just as I did with his father.' Two tears rolled down her cheeks and Sappha hurried across to her to put her arms around her and say: 'There there—and how proud you must be to remember that, and I've no doubt that you were worth every second of his time.'

This remark induced the Baroness to give a watery smile. 'Oh, yes indeed I was—and the children too,' she added, 'Rolf's very like him.'

Sappha straightened up. There was no accounting for tastes, she told herself crossly, and after all the Baroness was his mother. She was on her way to the door when the Baroness observed: 'Well, I daresay your young man will tell you why he came when you see him tomorrow. I must say he has a great deal of patience after coming all this way.'

Sappha had thought so too, but it wasn't very nice to be reminded of it by someone else. But it was a long way, surely Andrew hadn't driven hundreds of miles just to say hullo. Besides, there was still the question of Staff Nurse Beatty. Sappha said tonelessly: 'I'll get your tea, Baroness.'

She put off going down to her own tea for as long as possible, so that by the time she went into the sitting room everyone was having second cups and Andrew was explaining at some length just how important it was to have the right sort of practice. He was forced to break off while Sappha was told to sit down and asked if there was enough milk in her tea and was the toast really hot still; she sensed his annoyance at being interrupted even across the room. He had nodded briefly at her when she went in, but it was the Baron who had got up and pushed her gently into his own chair and then, taking no further notice of her, gone over to sit by Andrew, to listen, apparently tonguetied with admiration, to that gentleman's dissertation upon his brilliant future. Sappha munched morosely at a scone and drank her tea, watching Andrew. He was enjoying himself—he had an audience who appeared to be interested in him, even though he wasn't in the least interested in them. She glanced round the room; Mrs MacFee was listening with a charmingly attentive air, so was the minister, Antonia was gazing at him with rapt attention—and so to was the Baron, too rapt, thought Sappha. He looked up and caught her staring at him and returned it with one of his own, a long searching look which ended in a faint smile.

She dressed with care for her meeting with Andrew—a fine wool dress in a warm shade of pink with a high neckline and full sleeves gathered into bands and then ruffled over her hands. She covered it with her raincoat and tied a matching scarf over her hair. Andrew said that they would go for a run before tea and then sit in Mrs MacGregor's parlour until dinner was ready for them. There were things, he had said, which had to be discussed. She pondered this remark while she was putting on her good shoes—a reckless act, she knew, seeing that the weather was worsening every minute, but she wanted to look nice for him.

When she was dressed, however, she sat down on the bed, reluctant to go, even though he had said he would call for her at two o'clock, and it was already past that hour. It worried her that she didn't feel happier or more excited than she was. Perhaps it was the shock of seeing Andrew again which made her so curiously apathetic about the afternoon's outing. She got up and went to the Baroness's room to say goodbye and found that lady straining to see out of the window from her chair. She looked round as Sappha went in and said:

'He's just come, dear—he seems a very smart man, I hope you'll have a lovely time. Antonia is very taken with him, you know, not that that signifies anything—I daresay you will come back with a ring on your finger once more.'

Sappha said slowly: 'I don't know. I think I'd want to wait this time. I—I have to be sure.' She picked up a pillow and put it where it belonged. 'You're sure you can manage? I feel it's all wrong leaving you alone—Gloria isn't here either…'

'Nonsense,' said the Baroness comfortably, 'Antonia is dying to play nurse; you've put out my pills, my exercises are done, and Rolf will be in, I daresay, to make sure everything is all right.'

Sappha said goodbye and went downstairs to where Andrew was waiting, talking amusingly to Mrs MacFee. He smiled at Sappha as she joined them and said casually: 'Hullo there,' looking so completely at ease that she felt a small prick of annoyance because he was so sure of her. After all, it had been he who had let her down even though he had come back to her.

The afternoon wasn't an unqualified success. Andrew was a good driver and he handled his car—a Jaguar—well, but as Sappha pointed out, the wind was now almost gale force and the rain was developing from a thick drizzle to a steady downpour. It seemed foolish to take the road through Shieldaig and Kishorn just so that they might see the heights of Skye from Auchtertyre; in any case, Sappha pointed out reasonably, in such weather there would be nothing to see. To all of which Andrew replied with a laugh. 'Nonsense,' he said, 'we can talk as we go and worry about the scenery when we get there.'

But talking was impossible. At first it hadn't been too bad going down into Torridon, for there was shelter from the forests which lined most of the narrow road and later on the newly constructed road towards Shieldaig, but then the road reverted to its former width, winding up and down the hills so that Andrew had to pay attention to his driving. At Loch Kishorn Sappha suggested that they could probably see Skye from there, but Andrew said sharply: 'What's come over you, Sappha? Don't you want a chance to see the country? We'll go on to Auchtertyre—it's not much further. We'll go there for tea and talk.'

Naturally there was no Skye to be seen, but Andrew at least seemed to have derived some satisfaction from reaching his goal, if only for the reason that he would be able to tell the Baron about it later. They stopped for tea in

Lochcarron, and although the hotel was empty the tea was delicious. Despite herself, Sappha relaxed and began to enjoy herself, Andrew could be an amusing companion and he was making great efforts to please her. They had almost finished tea when he said: 'Sappha, you must know why I came to this outlandish spot...darling, I'm lost without you.'

'What about Beatty?' Sappha asked in a cool little voice which disguised the warm glow of excitement at being wanted again. She gave him a level look. 'Did she find someone else?'

She watched Andrew grow red. 'It was mutual—we weren't suited. I suppose I was a fool.' He caught her hand on the table and held it tightly. 'Listen, darling, come back with me. Leave this awful godforsaken place, you don't belong here. We could have such fun together.'

She stared at him across the table. It was lovely to be wanted; to be missed—London might be fun and perhaps he loved her very much to have come so far to say so. The uneasy thought that he hadn't said so crossed her mind. She withdrew her hand gently and said:

'Look, Andrew, don't expect me to answer you now. I must have time to think about it.' She saw the faint annoyance on his face. 'My dear girl, what on earth do you have to think about? I'm doing you a favour—giving you a chance to escape.'

Sappha said quietly: 'But I like it in Dialach. I didn't think I should, but I do—and I can't leave my patient just like that, where are they going to get another nurse at a moment's notice? My patient has been very ill and she will need care for weeks yet.'

He shrugged his shoulders. 'Good lord, Sappha, stop being such a do-gooder. They'll rub along, and she's got that brigand who calls himself a doctor, hasn't she?'

Sappha put down her cup with a hand which shook a little. 'That's a beastly thing to say. He doesn't look in the least like a brigand.' She felt guilty saying it, for had she not likened him to a brigand herself? She hurried on: 'He's good to her—he comes over from Holland every week or so and he helps the local doctor when he's needed…'

Andrew was laughing at her. 'More fool he. Are you a fan of his? Or perhaps you've fallen a victim to his charm?'

'Neither,' she snapped. 'I—I don't like him, but that's no reason to be spiteful, and I won't leave until another nurse is found to replace me.'

He smiled. 'We'll not argue about that now. We'll go back and make ourselves comfortable round Mrs Mac-Gregor's fire and I'll guarantee to make you change your mind.'

He gave her a look which sent the colour into her face but left her bewilderingly unexcited. She followed him out to the car in silence, puzzled at her lack of response. Three months ago she would have flown into his arms and now she felt herself moving away from the touch of his shoulder in the car. But he didn't notice this nor her silence; he was talking about his future and how much money he intended to make, and not once did he mention her…

The journey back was tricky. The wind, now a gale, buffeted the car, while the rain, coming down in good earnest, made the windscreen-wipers useless. Even on a fine dry day the road needed care, and although Andrew was a good driver, he wasn't a patient one. Sappha was glad when they skidded to a halt before the small brightly lighted inn. Inside it was warm and cheerful and a table had been laid for them in the little parlour behind the bar, and two comfortable chairs drawn up before the fire. Sappha took off her raincoat and scarf and hung them tidily behind the door, then followed Mrs MacGregor up the narrow staircase to one of the bedrooms so that she might tidy herself. The room was spotlessly clean and rather cold; its little window overlooked the houses lining the harbour, and she stood for a moment watching the boiling sea. There was a light twinkling at the end of the causeway and she wondered if Mrs MacTadd was all right. She wondered about Gloria and

Hamish too; they surely wouldn't be driving back in such
weather, probably they would wait until the storm had qui-
etened down or the morning light made the journey easier;
listening to the wind howling outside, she didn't blame
them.

They had finished their sherry and Mrs MacGregor was
in the act of placing two plates of steaming soup on the
table when she was almost knocked over by a boy who
darted in from the bar. He was so wet that the water ran in
little rivulets down his arms and legs and formed pools on
the matting, but even while Mrs MacGregor was scolding
him he had pushed past her and handed Sappha a sheet of
paper wrapped carefully in a scrap of plastic. She put down
her glass and said in surprise:

'For me? Are you sure?'

The boy nodded, 'Aye, miss,' and when she said: 'Well,
take off your wet coat while I read it,' surprised her by
saying: 'Nay, I'll not,' and looked so beseechingly at her
that she took the paper out of its sopping wrappings and
began to read.

'Sappha, Mrs MacTadd has jumped the gun. A shoulder
presenting and well jammed. I'll have to do a Caesar. Go
to Gloria's and fetch her midwifery bag, the gas and air,
blood giving and taking sets and the vacoliter of blood in
the fridge. Keep the boy with you, he'll bring you back.
Ask Glover if he'll give a hand.' It was signed R.v.D.

She looked up from it to find Andrew's eyes on her. He
said irritably:

'Give the boy something and let's get on with our meal.'

Sappha folded the paper carefully. 'No, we can't do that.
Listen, Andrew.' Almost before she had finished explaining
he exclaimed: 'But you're not going, Sappha. The man
must be mad. Why can't he send the woman to hospital?
He's only a GP anyway.'

She answered him patiently. 'How? There's no ambulance in the village—how could she be brought over the
causeway or put in a boat on a night like this, and then be

driven miles?' She added stubbornly: 'He's perfectly able to deal with it himself if he must.' As she spoke she was astonished to find that she believed what she was saying.

She went to the door and took down her raincoat and started to put it on; Andrew strode across the little room and caught hold of her.

'Sappha, you're not to go. Let him manage as best he can.' His voice held a faint sneer.

'He wants your help,' she reminded him as she evaded his hand and tied on her head-scarf. Andrew flung away and went to sit in one of the chairs. 'I have no intention of going. I don't even know that the fellow's a doctor—after all, he's a foreigner, supposing the woman were to die— my reputation—I have myself to consider.'

Sappha turned away without a word. It was funny to think that if this hadn't happened she might have decided to go back to London, if not immediately, then in a short time, not because Andrew had wanted her to, but for some vague reason of her own which lurked somewhere at the back of her mind, and there was too much on that at the moment for her to give it a second thought. She had to help Rolf, of that she was certain. Not looking at Andrew she said. 'Come along,' to the boy and pausing only long enough to ask Mrs MacGregor to send a message to the Manse, she followed the boy out into the storm.

Gloria's house was close by but it was dark and she had no torch; it took precious minutes while she blundered round searching for the key. Inside, she went straight to the surgery key's hiding place and opened its door. As she collected what she needed she sent up a little prayer of thankfulness that Gloria had shown her where everything was kept. Before she locked the door again she possessed herself of Gloria's torch, a solid rubber affair with a vast beam, scribbled a brief note to leave on the sitting room table and went over to the boy, standing patiently by the door. She gave him the torch and said worriedly: 'You poor lad, you're soaked!' She touched his wringing sleeve. 'What's your name?'

'Ian. Are ye ready?'

She nodded. 'Will you take this bag, Ian—I can manage the rest.'

She had got wet coming from Mrs MacGregor's, but when they were out in the lane again, she realised that that had been only a preliminary. Ian crossed over the narrow street, turned down behind the post office and so to the harbour, where the full force of the gale met them with a wall of wind and blinding rain. It was only then that Sappha saw that Ian was heading for the causeway beyond the harbour. She clutched him by the arm and shouted against the wind: 'We're not going over the causeway?'

She heard his answering 'Aye' before he started off again, quickening his pace as she struggled to keep up with him, her bags and bundles banging against her legs as she went. It was like a nightmare; but if this was a nightmare, she had no words for the causeway when they reached it.

For the first few yards it wasn't too bad, for although its stones were broken and uneven, there was some foothold, but then she was confronted by half a dozen crumbling steps, covered in seaweed and lashed by spray. She looked at them and said simply: 'I can't, Ian. I'm afraid.' He made a small grunting sound which sounded sympathetic, then:

'Ma'll die,' was all he said. There was only one answer to that; Sappha put a sodden and completely ruined shoe on the bottom step.

'Will you go first,' she asked, 'and I'll pass you the bags—I must have one hand free.'

She scrambled up somehow, helped by Ian, who put the bags carefully down and came back to help her. It was a mercy that it was so dark, she decided as she landed on her hands and knees, for if she were to see where she was she would probably scream the place down. In obedience to Ian's shouted advice she ducked to avoid the full force of the wind and the rain, trying to keep her balance while she clutched the two bags and the precious vacoliter in wet hands. But now, by straining her eyes, she could see a light ahead and she said involuntarily, her voice snatched by the wind: 'Oh, it's too good to be true!' as indeed it was, for half a dozen staggered steps further Ian stopped and shone the torch on more steps, leading down this time, but not only did they lead down, they sagged sideways as well and in one place her horrified eyes saw that there was almost no step at all.

Ian said something in Gaelic and disappeared to negotiate the impossible with comparative ease, for he was back very shortly to take the bags from her and scramble down again. It was when he came back for the second time and said: 'Come, miss,' that Sappha whispered: 'But I can't—really I can't.' No one heard her, of course, and she went on standing there, unable to move for fright and cold. It was only seconds later that another, more powerful torch spotlighted her feet and she heard the Baron bellow: 'Stay where you are and hang on to that blood!'

Even in her terror Sappha's mind registered the fact that he seemed far more worried about the blood than about her, but she was beyond caring and almost beyond movement, although her hand tightened obediently around the vacoliter. The next moment he was balanced on the step below her, prising the precious bottle from her stiff fingers, to go again before she could make a sound, but he was back in a moment, his voice close in her ear to shatter her eardrums above the roar of the wind.

'Turn round—go on, I've got you safe enough—and do as you're told.'

She did as she was told, muttering uselessly into the gale: 'That's right, bully me, you fiend!' She felt the tears streaming down her face and didn't care; she was already so wet, no one would notice. She felt the Baron's large firm hands clamped on either side of her waist, but it was only after he said: 'Let go—let go, damn it!' that she took her hands from the stone at the top of the steps to clutch frantically at thin air.

'Stop flapping like a wet hen,' besought the Baron—above the gale's scream she heard him laugh. 'Lean back against me.' Which she did; it was like leaning against a tree-trunk, solid and safe and strong and when his calm voice ordered, 'Stretch your left leg down and put your weight on it,' she did so without hesitation. 'Now the right,' came his voice once more. She could feel that she was balanced on a narrow slipery ledge tilting sharply to one side, spray from the sea soaked her legs, the wind tore at her hair—it had whipped her scarf away long since. When the Baron said 'Jump,' she closed her eyes against the awful, noisy dark and jumped, his hands still firm on her waist, and when he shouted 'Good girl!' she felt a warm glow despite her shivering body.

'Two more steps,' he said, 'easy ones.' She could feel their sliminess under her feet and screamed as one foot slipped, unaware that she had screamed his name, but his hands still held her fast; she felt rough grass and boulders under her feet as he caught her by the arm and hurried her the few yards to the croft. Ian was already there, the equipment stacked tidily against one wall. Inside, it was very warm, with a driftwood fire sending sparks up the chimney and a good deal of smoke into the room as well. There were oil lamps on the table and the mantelpiece, and as they entered an old lady came through an inner door carrying another lamp in her hand. The Baron spoke urgently to her in a language Sappha couldn't understand, then turned to her.

'We'll have to be quick before she starts haemorrhaging again.'

Sappha started to unbutton her raincoat with cold shaking fingers, but she made clumsy work of it, so that he came across the little room and did it for her, stripping the soaking garment off her and throwing it into a corner of the room, revealing her dress—her lovely pink woollen dress, plastered to her body, its collar shapeless, the pretty ruffles torn and filthy with bits of seaweed sticking to them. The Baron caught her by the arm, remarking cheerfully: 'A write-off, isn't it? so it won't matter if I do this.' He caught the tattered ruffles and ripped one sleeve up to the elbow and rolled it up tidily, then did exactly the same with the other while she watched with speechless fascination.

'Your hair,' he said briskly, and took the slender suede belt she wore and went behind her, gathered her hair into it and tied it securely.

'Next room,' he said, still brisk, and swept her before him, pausing only to hand her the midwifery bag and pick up the remainder of the clutter himself. The room Sappha entered was small but well lighted by reason of the lamps ranged on the little shelf over the fireplace and the chest in one corner. The patient lay in the big iron bedstead pushed up against one wall; there was a large wooden table in the middle of the room covered with a sheet, and a stand with a basin and several jugs of steaming water upon it. The Baron went past her to the bed and bent over his patient, saying over his shoulder: 'We'll get that blood into her as soon as possible, but first we will get ready to operate.'

Sappha found herself saying meekly: 'Yes, Doctor,' as though she were quite in the habit of preparing for a Caesarean section in a stuffy little room without so much as a cold water tap. She went to open the first of the bags and caught sight of herself in the mirror on the wall. At any other time she would have stared incredulously and then burst out laughing at her ludicrous reflection, but now she scarcely paused, but began setting out the sterile packs with the same careful precision she would have used in the operating theatre in Greggs'.

She was a practical girl as well as a good nurse—the small table under the mirror would do excellently for the instruments—she cleaned its top lavishly with Savlon, draped it in a dressing towel, and laid the packs upon it. The baby's cot was already in the room, she took the tiny

blanket from the midwifery bag and wrapped it around the
old-fashioned hot water bottle already in the cot, then
opened the blood giving set, put it neatly, still in its sterile
wrappers, beside the instruments, and said, with commendable coolness:

'We shall want at least two buckets or bowls and something in which to put the swabs—they'll have to be
checked,' and the Baron bending over his patient, took his
stethoscope out of one ear and shouted through the half
open door into the other room. Presently the old woman
came in with two buckets, a baby's bath and a small wash-
tub. Rolf looked up briefly. 'There you are—take your
choice,' he remarked. 'Are you ready your end?'

Sappha said yes, she was, and wondered why she could
feel so calm about it all—perhaps it was because he was
so matter-of-fact about everything and so quietly certain;
indeed, he was no longer a brigand, nor, for that matter, a
bossy baron, but a man in complete command of an awkward situation. She trusted him completely and was quite
prepared to do anything he might ask of her.

She tied herself into the gown she had taken from one
of the packs, put on a mask and watched him while he
lifted Mrs MacTadd on to the table and covered her with
a blanket. Mrs MacTadd, Sappha saw with concern, was
unconscious, she wondered what the Baron intended to do
about an anaesthetic. As though in answer to her thought,
he observed:

'I've got my case here—I'll give her a spinal—but the
blood first.'

He went to scrub his hands and then over to the little
table Sappha had prepared and she went to the chest and
picked up the vacoliter. As she turned round to give it to
him, it slipped through her fingers. She stood for a frozen
eternity staring at him, the bottle in splinters at her feet
while its precious contents oozed gently in all directions,
waiting for him to utter the blistering words she undoubtedly deserved. But all he said was: 'I hope you're O group,

Rhesus positive.' He didn't sound in the least angry; she had never heard his voice so mild, and when she nodded wordlessly, he said, still mildly: 'Then it's our lucky day, isn't it? Jump on the bed, there's a good girl, and I'll take a pint or so off you.'

She did as she was told, hardly noticing the old woman, who, in answer to another of the Baron's unintelligible shouts, came in to clean up the mess. 'Clever of you to bring the blood donor set,' he remarked cheerfully. 'Can you bear the needle straight in without a local? It'll save time.'

Sappha stared down at his head bowed over her arm. 'Yes, of course I can bear it,' she said in a shamed little voice, 'and don't call me clever.' She choked a little on the word and added: 'I'm sorry.' It sounded inadequate, and perhaps it was, for he merely looked up briefly, said: 'Now,' and slipped the needle into the inner side of her elbow where the vein showed blue. But then he said very kindly: 'If you hadn't come our patient and the baby might very well have been dead by morning—that cancels out any dropped bottles.'

Sappha continued to stare while the elusive thoughts she had buried so firmly under the emergencies of the evening suddenly became very clear indeed. She knew now why she ought to go back to London—and soon. She had fallen in love with Rolf and since she had been fool enough to pick on someone who didn't care for her at all, the quicker she went away the better. The sensible half of her brain approved of this while the other half, which was ruled by her heart, deplored it. She curbed a desire to stretch out her free hand and touch his dark hair and reminded herself sternly where she was.

'Clench your fist, Sappha,' Rolf bade her, and shouted to the old woman again, who poked her head round the door and withdrew it again, while Sappha, for the sake of saying something because she could no longer stay silent with her thoughts, asked: 'Why don't you speak English?'

'She wouldn't understand—some of the older people here speak only the Gaelic.'

'Oh—and you speak it too.'

'After a fashion. I've been coming here for years, you know—it's like a second home.' He tightened the blood pressure armband above her elbow and presently loosened it. 'Mrs MacTadd will bring you some tea and some bread and butter, you'll stay here and have it while I'm getting this into our patient.'

Sappha looked lovingly at the back of his downbent head. 'You won't be able to manage,' she said positively. 'This isn't like theatre or even a hospital ward.'

'I shall manage. You'll do as I say. I shall need you presently and I don't want you fainting all over everything. Feel all right?'

'Yes, thank you. Have you ever done this thing before?'

'Taken blood? Oh, yes, a few hundred times, I should imagine.'

'I mean operating like this—with no mod cons.'

'Yes—never a Caesarean though. An appendix or so and an amputation, and Hamish and I did a bad hernia together—on an old shepherd who had never been to hospital in his life, in any case it was too late to move him.'

He whipped out the needle and she didn't even notice. 'Did they all recover?' she wanted to know.

He laughed a little. 'Of course. People who live close to nature nearly always do—they have faith and trust.' He looked up at her, his eyes twinkling. 'Alas! my poor ego.'

'I didn't mean—' began Sappha. 'That is, I think you could do anything.'

He nodded without conceit, and they didn't talk any more after that. She ate her bread and butter and drank the dark sweet tea and watched him working. He was quick, but his movements were so economical that he gave the impression that there was no haste. Presently he said without looking up: 'OK. Will you clean yourself up? I shall want some help with the spinal.'

It was amazing how smoothly the operation went. Sappha who had been used to half a dozen persons at least in the theatre for a Caesarean section, discovered that, with a little forethought and ingenuity, it was quite possible to manage with two. It was by no means ideal, of course, but once the sterile packs were opened and the sutures had been put ready and the swabs counted out, she was able to scrub up while she listened to Rolf's instructions. She was to remain sterile until they had the baby; longer if possible, so that she could hold the forceps while he tied off, because time mattered now, more than anything else. It helped that Mrs MacTadd was still unconscious, although it was possible that she would regain consciousness before long now that she had had some blood, but Rolf had explained to her hours before what he might have to do; even if she came round before the end of operation she would know what was happening.

'The baby was a little girl. They'll be glad—they've got three boys,' said the Baron as he laid the small wriggling creature on the sterile sheet and turned back to his patient.

Half an hour later, Sappha was making up the bed while the doctor mounted guard over his now conscious patient and the baby. The room looked terrible; it would take hours to clear up, but that didn't matter in the least, because they had got the baby and the mother was safe too. Sappha made the bedclothes into a neat pack, said: 'Ready when you are,' and went to pick up the baby while Rolf lifted Mrs MacTadd carefully into her bed. She was still far from well, but at least she was alive and likely to remain so. She smiled tiredly at Sappha as she tucked her in and gave her the baby and lay quietly while they put up a saline drip; drank the tea she was offered and stayed awake just long enough for her husband to creep in. He kissed her white cheek and she said contentedly: 'It's a lassie,' and smiled again before she was at once asleep.

Mr MacTadd crept out again and returned soft-footed with more tea and an offer to clear up the mess, but Sappha thanked him warmly and said no, she'd do it in a brace of shakes herself, swallowed the rest of her tea and got to her feet. It was, incredibly, just nine o'clock. She looked across at the doctor, sitting on a small folding stool which didn't look as though it would bear his weight. He appeared lost in thought, but looked up immediately as she moved.

'A half-hour pulse chart, I think, don't you? I'll give her some Pethedine when she rouses; we'll get her to hospital as soon as we can, but it's impossible for the moment. You'll have to stay the night, you know that?'

Sappha shuddered, then said with spirit: 'Nothing would induce me to go back over that awful causeway again.'

'Well, we'll have to see about that,' he remarked placidly. 'In the meantime you can sleep here. I would have suggested that you stripped off those wet clothes, but I imagine that they have dried on you by now.'

Sappha nodded and took off her gown to reveal a dress that was a ruin; probably everything underneath it was as well, she thought gloomily; her shoes looked as though she had been walking in them continuously for months on end, and when she put a hand up to her hair, he said mildly: 'Leave it—it's beyond all hope—luckily there's no one to see.' She was getting over this remark when he asked: 'What happened to Glover?'

She was going round the room, bundling the dressing towels and sheets into a tidy heap. She paused with her back to him and strove to make her voice matter-of-fact. 'He—he didn't want to intrude—I mean, it wasn't his case.'

'It wasn't mine either,' Rolf said blandly, and when she turned round to face him she saw that he was wearing his satyr's face. 'I'm sorry,' she said miserably, 'I did ask him.'

The Baron put down his cup and strolled towards her, his face quite normal again. He said kindly: 'It's not your fault and you have nothing to be sorry for.'

She whispered: 'Oh, yes—the blood,' and he waved a hand airily. 'I daresay yours did her a great deal more good,' he smiled so that her heart turned over. 'Thank you for coming, Sappha.'

She had become completely enchanted by the smile. She stood before him trying out several answers and discarding them. One couldn't say 'Delighted,' or 'Don't mention it,' or even, 'It was nothing.' She finally came out with: 'Oh, well…'

He had come very close; before she realised what he was going to do he had bent and kissed her on one cheek. If she had had any latent doubts as to her feelings for him—which she hadn't—they would have been tossed into oblivion, and if a casual kiss on the cheek had the power to make her heart thud against her ribs as it was thudding now, how would she feel if the kiss were not so casual?

It was best not to think about it. She moved back a little and said matter-of-factly: 'I'll have your gown, shall I? If I put everything to soak in cold water, it shouldn't be too bad…'

He made a small sound which might have been a chuckle, divested himself of the garment and said: 'I'll get the water, shall I?'

Sappha made short work of the clearing up, after all for, contrary to her expectations, the Baron proved a willing helper. As good as a nurse, she thought, watching him scrubbing instruments and wishing the night would go on for ever. All the same when he remarked that he couldn't understand why any girl in her senses wanted to do such work for the pleasure of it she answered coolly enough that they liked it anyway and then, 'Do you suppose Dr MacInroy and Gloria will come over here tonight?'

He threw the last of the cleaned instruments on the table and dragged his thick sweater on over his shirt. 'No—not unless they're out of their wits.'

'How did you know—about Mrs MacTadd, I mean?'

'Ian came for me.' He went over to the bed and took his patient's pulse and looked at the chart Sappha had written up between her bouts of cleaning. He said offhand: 'Have you finished? Go and lie down on that folding contraption in the corner, it looks uncomfortable, but you should be able to get some sleep.'

'And what about you?' demanded Sappha. 'You can't sit up all night.'

His voice was cool. 'Certainly I can.'

'Then I shall too.' And wished she hadn't said it when he replied:

'Oh, come now, isn't that carrying good fellowship a little too far?'

It was unanswerable. If she said: 'But I've discovered I love you since I said that,' he would probably give one of his great gusts of laughter, or would look like a satyr and say nothing at all. She went and lay down and after a minute ventured to ask: 'You will call me if you need me?'

He said irritably: 'Of course. I intend calling you at four o'clock anyway so that you can take over until morning.' His voice held a note of finality so that she thought it prudent to say nothing more, so she pulled the blanket up to her chin and closed her eyes.

She awoke to the feel of his hand on her shoulder and his voice saying quietly: 'Here's some tea—it will clear your wits.'

Thus encouraged, she swallowed the strong, hot brew, got up and went to look at Mrs MacTadd, who was sleeping, as was the baby.

'I gave her Pethedine just before two o'clock,' Rolf explained. 'She will probably sleep until six—the baby too. There's a bottle with some sterile water keeping warm by the fire—if she yells give her some, unless Mum wakes up as well—and keep an eye on that dressing.' He gave her the rest of his instructions, said: 'Call me at seven will you?' then went and stretched himself on the little bed and was at once asleep.

Sappha called him exactly at seven, but before then she had seen to the baby and washed Mrs MacTadd and given her some tea. It was surprising how well the patient looked and how serenely she accepted the situation. Sappha left her lying back on her pillows, still pale but cheerful, while she went to rouse the Baron. He was still asleep and she paused to study his face. It looked remote and austere and very handsome, rather like a crusader knight reclining in perpetuity on some ancient tomb; she wondered how she could ever have found him unattractive. When his eyes flew open she gave a gasp and jumped so violently that he asked coldly: 'Do I scare you as much as all that?' and without waiting for her answer, got up and went straight to his patient, and presently, after drinking the tea she had got for him, he went into the other room, presumably to speak to Mr MacTadd. She heard the door open and shut and after a few minutes he came back to inform her that the weather had settled nicely and he had no doubt that Hamish and Gloria would be with them within the hour.

'But it's only seven o'clock,' Sappha protested.

He said reasonably: 'It's only sixty miles or so and Hamish knows the road—my guess is they left around six. Provided the road is clear they'll be here by eight.'

CHAPTER FOUR

ROLF was right, it was barely eight o'clock and Sappha was recording Mrs MacTadd's pulse when she heard the door open once more and Gloria and Hamish came in. Hamish and the Baron exchanged laconic hullos and began, with the calmness of men who knew what they were about, to discuss the case. Gloria, however, went at once to look at Mrs MacTadd, firing questions at Sappha as she did so. 'And how did you get here?' she wanted to know finally.

Sappha shuddered. 'Over that awful causeway—it was pitch dark, and a good thing too or I should never have made it.' She added apprehensively: 'I've just begun to wonder how I shall get back—it will be so much worse because now I can see...'

The two men were talking by the fire; now Hamish said over his shoulder: 'No need to worry, lass, you'll do fine in the boat.'

'Shall I?' enquired Sappha faintly, wondering if she was expected to take the oars herself—perhaps the wretched thing would have an outboard motor, which as far as she was concerned would be even worse. But she was given no time to brood over this problem; the Baron asked her to give her report to Gloria as the latter would be staying until Hamish could get an ambulance organised. Hospital was undoubtedly the best place for Mrs MacTadd—she needed another blood transfusion and some antibiotics to combat the shortcomings of an operation performed in a room there had been no time even to dust. The two men fell to discussing ways and means while Sappha gave details concerning the patient with unhurried calmness. When she had finished, Gloria said:

'OK, and thanks a lot—I never thought when I showed you the surgery that you would have to make use of it.' She eyed Sappha cautiously. 'I heard about your broken date from Mrs MacGregor—she was on the lookout for us—I'm sorry, Sappha, it was rotten bad luck.' She added with engaging frankness: 'You look awful, though if it's any consolation to you, you're the only girl I've met who could still look eye-catching in that deplorable dress—it must have been pretty.'

Sappha nodded. 'I'll have to throw it away,' she remarked, not really minding. She would go to Inverness on her next day off and buy something to take its place. She checked Mrs MacTadd's pulse once more and the Baron said 'Ready? We're going back with Hamish.' He fetched her raincoat and buttoned her into it with the air of a patient man who hadn't much time to spare. As they went out he said to Gloria: 'I'll be back.' He had already talked to Mrs MacTadd, his voice quiet and reassuring, then waited while Sappha said her own goodbyes and then followed her outside into the early morning. The clouds had melted away leaving a pallid sky which wasn't warmed by the thin sunshine, the sea looked mountainous to her anxious eyes, but as neither of the men seemed in the least perturbed, she said nothing, but walked between them to where Ian and Mr MacTadd were holding a small rowing dinghy, and got in when she was bidden to, averting her gaze from the causeway, which, in daylight and at close quarters, looked too awful for words. The equipment was stowed away and she sat silently while the two men got in, half expecting the little boat to sink like a stone under their combined and not inconsiderable weights. It did no such thing, however, and they disposed themselves with the careless unconcern of men who had lived with boats since childhood. It seemed the Baron was to do the rowing; she sat facing him as he sent the craft through the still rough water, looking more

of a ruffian than ever, for he lacked a shave. She supposed
it was the want of sleep that had made his already formidable nose look even more formidable; his brows were
drawn together, his eyes half closed against the spray; he
looked tired and fierce with it. All the same he plied the
oars with the same vigour that a man who had had a good
night's rest and a hearty breakfast might have displayed.
He looked at her unexpectedly with a gleam of mockery so
that she reddened and put a self-conscious hand up to her
hair which the wind had whipped into a tangle, ad the red
deepened as his mouth widened into a smile and he said in
a voice so soft she could barely hear it: 'What does it matter
what you look like?' He bent to his oars once more, leaving
her to guess, without much success, at what he meant. Dr
MacInroy's voice roused her.

'Ye'll have the vacoliter by ye, lassie?'

Sappha half turned to look at him, moving gingerly because the boat was bucketing about on the choppy water.
She said woodenly:

'No, I—I smashed it. I'm sorry.'

'Ah, weel, it was no night to walk the causeway—not to
mind.'

She kept her head turned away from the Baron, who was
grinning at her.

'It wasn't on the causeway—I can't think why not,' she
amended bitterly. 'If I'd known what it was going to be
like…I smashed it, for no reason at all, just as Dr van
Duyren was ready to give it.'

She turned round again and looked steadily at the tiny
jetty they were fast approaching.

'Did ye now?' commented the Scottish doctor. 'Yet I
obsairved that Mrs MacTadd had received an infusion of
some sort.'

Sappha didn't answer. It was the Baron who answered
for her. 'Indeed she did, Hamish—a pint or so of pure English blood from our Miss Devenish here—it served its purpose very well. Here we are,' he added, and Hamish

jumped out to secure the boat while the Baron shipped his oars in a businesslike manner, then stood up, stretched hugely, and plucked Sappha from her seat and set her tidily on her feet upon the jetty. She found herself between them, arm-in-arm, walking through the little lane to the inn. 'We left the car there,' Hamish explained, 'and I told Mrs MacGregor to be on the look-out for us—she'll no doubt have a pot of tea ready.'

She had indeed, as well as a plate of bread and butter and anything else they might fancy. She fussed around them, clucking like a small motherly hen over Sappha's deplorable state.

'That bonnie dress—and the shoes! Ruined—and there, I almost forgot!' She drew a letter from under her apron. 'Your young man—he left an hour since, he asked me to give ye this wee letter.'

Sappha said thank you, took it from her kind hostess and pushed it into her raincoat pocket. She had forgotten all about Andrew; he seemed like someone from another world. She wasn't in the least interested in what he might have to say. She frowned and looking up, found the Baron's eyes on her, but this time they held no gleam of laughter; he said gently: 'He's got his work like the rest of us—he'll be back.' His voice changed; he said briskly: 'Talking of work, how about getting this stuff back to Gloria's place?'

She cast him a grateful look because his remark had made everything normal again. 'I'll see to that,' she said almost cheerfully, 'if you wouldn't mind telling your mother that I'll be back within the hour.'

Rolf got to his feet and as though she had never spoken, said:

'Hamish, be a good chap and let them know at the Manse, will you?'

'I said me,' said Sappha with a regrettable lack of grammar.

He gave her a smile with a hint of mockery in it. 'So you did,' he observed, his voice all silk. 'Are you ready?'

They said goodbye to Hamish and Mrs MacGregor and walked up the street to Gloria's cottage, where the Baron retrieved the front door key from its hiding place with the air of one who had done so many times before. Inside he said briefly: 'You deal with the midwifery bag, I'll see to the rest.'

They worked silently, passing each other on their way to various drawers and cupboards and being carefully polite about taking turns at the sink. Sappha filled with a longing to hear his voice, began several tentative conversations, which he squashed with polite blandness, and she reminded herself sadly that when they had first met she had made no secret of her dislike of him and now it seemed he had accepted that fact easily enough, she thought ruefully, since he didn't seem to like her overmuch in his turn.

He finished a few minutes before her and strolled into the sitting room and when she followed him in to make a list of what they had done for Gloria's benefit, she found him standing in front of 'The Stag at Bay'.

'A revolting picture,' he observed as she began to write. 'I have begged Gloria to throw it away, or at least hang it in some obscure corner, but she's anxious not to hurt the donor's feelings.'

'You don't like stags?'

He turned to look at her, his eyebrows arched. 'Like them? Of course I like them, but I abhor blood sports. Why do you look so surprised?'

She fidgeted a little under his bright enquiring gaze. 'Oh do I? Well, actually, you look as though you might enjoy hunting—things.'

His eyebrows met in a frown and his eyes narrowed. 'And what brought you to that conclusion?' His voice was bland.

Sappha hesitated. She thought that he might have been amused even though her remark had been a silly one, but he was obviously annoyed and she would have to answer him—she knew him well enough by now to know that he liked answers to his questions.

'You look like a—a baron,' she said, feeling foolish, and picked up her pen again and without looking at him, finished her list. If he had liked her, even just a little, he might have laughed; as it was, she wasn't surprised when he said coldly without a trace of humour: 'A bold, bad baron, I presume, Miss Devenish.'

She stood up. 'Yes—since you ask, Dr van Duyren.' And went to the door—but he hadn't quite finished with her. 'You haven't read your letter, you must be longing to do so.'

His voice held the faint familiar mockery which could annoy her so much, so that her voice was sharp. 'I'll read it in my room, when I'm alone,' she said and went through the door and waited while he put the key back and then walked silently beside him through the streets to the Manse. They parted in the hall without a word.

She didn't see him again until midday, by which time she had bathed, changed into uniform, taken in her patient's breakfast and eaten her own before continuing with the usual morning routine, all against a lively background of comment and questions from everyone in the house, with the exception of the Baron; he, having breakfasted and bathed, had left the house again, presumably to assist in getting Mrs MacTadd safely into the ambulance Sappha had seen roll past the Manse during the course of the morning. An hour later, it passed again, going hospitalwards, but there was no sign of Dr van Duyren—perhaps he had travelled with it. Sappha turned away from the window and went on making the Baroness's bed, unaware of the forlorn look upon her face. When the Baroness, who had been looking at her thoughtfully, remarked:

'I've often wondered what Rolf is like to work with— do tell, Sappha,' she paused in her work, glad of the opportunity of talking about him.

'He's super—he doesn't flap, you see, and he knows

what he's doing without being cocksure; he didn't let me flap either, and I wanted to once or twice,' she added honestly.

Her patient nodded. 'He sounds quite human,' she observed with an air of surprise so that Sappha felt compelled to say: 'Oh, but he is. He was sweet to Mrs MacTadd and her family, just as though he were in the habit of doing Caesars in bedrooms and thought nothing of it. I don't think any of them realised...he's not easily deterred from doing what he intends to do, I think.'

His mother smiled. 'No, my dear. He is also in the habit of getting what he wants, whether it's the successful treatment of his patients or the conquest of some pretty girl.'

She spoke lightly and Sappha made an equally light reply which cost her quite an effort. 'I can quite believe that, and,' she added thoughtfully, 'if all Dutch girls are as pretty as Antonia, he must be kept quite busy with his conquests.'

The Baroness didn't answer this, merely remarking that Antonia was a Friesian, not Dutch, and that Friesian girls on the whole were good-looking but rather big. 'Not like you, Sappha, for you are quite a small woman, are you not, though you are what we used to call very nicely covered.'

'What is very nicely covered, Mother?' enquired the Baron's voice from the open door. 'May I come in? I see you're in your chair.' He nodded to Sappha, kissed his parent and sat down beside her, to spend the next five minutes or so answering her questions about Mrs MacTadd, who was now safely stowed in hospital. 'And now answer my question, my dear,' he said mildly. The Baroness looked vague. 'Something was nicely covered,' he prompted. She smiled. 'Of course, dear, now I remember—Sappha...'

He turned his head and stared across the room and Sappha said hastily,

'I'll go and get your lunch, Baroness,' and whisked down the stairs at a fine speed, forgetting to shut the door as she went. It was too bad of the Baroness, although probably she hadn't quite realised—she was sometimes a little vague.

Sappha messed about in the kitchen, getting in everyone's way, until the minister poked his head round the door and asked her to go to the study because her uncle was on the telephone.

And so he was, with the Baron listening to him, sitting on Mr MacFee's desk, swinging one long leg. As she went in he said:

'Here she is now, sir. Hold on.' He gave her a brief smile. 'Mr Devenish is coming to see Mother—he wants to know if tomorrow suits you.' Sappha nodded and he said: 'Yes, that's fine—you want to speak to her?'

It seemed that Uncle John did. The Baron held out the receiver and moved along the desk to make room for her, and when she hesitated, put out a long arm and scooped her up to sit beside him, and as he kept his arm around her and it was impossible to get down again without an undignified struggle, she had perforce to stay where she was while she answered Uncle John's questions about his patient. These satisfactorily dealt with, he went on: 'Are you happy, Sappha? Not too lonely after London, I hope—I expect you find it very quiet.'

She thought of the previous night. 'I find plenty to do,' she said at length. 'I like the village and the people.' Her uncle gave a non-committal grunt, wished her goodbye and rang off, and the Baron moved his arm so that she was able to get off the desk and walk with dignity to the door. But before she was quite there he said: 'Don't go—I have something to say to you.' His voice, though polite, had a ring of authority so that she stopped, albeit reluctantly, and turned to face him. He had got to his feet and was standing with his hands in the pockets of his well-cut tweed suit. He was shaved and well-groomed and she hardly recognised him for the man who had been with her at Mrs MacTadd's; perhaps circumstances had made him seem more approachable—now he seemed remote and when he spoke his voice was impersonal.

'I talked to your uncle before you came in—I told him about last night.'

She said quickly: 'Oh—not about Andrew?' For how could she explain to Uncle John that she no longer cared twopence for Andrew, when only ten days ago he had been instrumental in sending her hundreds of miles away to this job because her heart was broken...

The Baron's voice was very quiet. 'No, not about Andrew. What do you take me for, Sappha?' He looked at her so haughtily that she hastily begged his pardon, but he went on as though she hadn't spoken.

'He agrees with me that I should reimburse you for the—er—clothes which were ruined last night. I will give you a cheque for a suitable amount and you will be good enough to accept it.'

Sappha had gone a brilliant and highly becoming pink during this high handed speech. She said wrathfully: 'I'll do no such thing! I went of my own free will and I'm not in the habit of accepting money from—from...'

'Barons?' he supplied nastily, and went on to enrage her still more. 'My dear good woman, aren't you being a little melodramatic? We're living in enlightened times now, you know. I am not bribing you, nor am I expecting any return for my money; I am in your debt, and I am not in the habit of being in debt to anyone.'

'I couldn't care less about your habits,' said Sappha very crossly. 'If you give me any money, I shall tear it up—I'm well able to afford to clothe myself without any help from you.'

He took a few steps towards her and she saw that he looked as ill-tempered as she felt, and suddenly wished that they didn't need to quarrel. How strange it was that she could argue with him so fiercely and yet love him so much. Unexpected tears filled her brown eyes and ran down her cheeks and she took her handkerchief from her uniform pocket, blew her pretty nose prosaically and mopped her face, took a steadying breath and said: 'I'm sorry, I didn't know I was going to cry.' She gave him a defiant look and found that he was staring at her with such intensity that she caught her breath and hiccupped.

He said evenly: 'If you hope to get your own way by crying, Sappha, I should warn you that you're in for a disappointment. If necessary I shall buy a dress and shoes and personally put them on you.'

She sniffed: 'You wouldn't dare.' He smiled, not at all nicely, so that he looked like a satyr; she saw that of course he would dare. She blew her nose again to give herself time to think, then:

'I shall ask Uncle John's advice,' she said, and watched his dark face break into another smile; there was a hint of patient mockery in it this time so that she felt like a child who had tried to get the better of a grown-up and hadn't. Uncle John was no use at all. He had arrived early and had undertaken an exhaustive examination of his patient with Sappha in attendance. Afterwards they had gone into the study where he had outlined the Baroness's further treatment. 'Very satisfactory,' he remarked. 'There had been a tendency to depression before you came, but it seems to me that our patient has a new interest in life—you have no idea what it is, I suppose, Sappha?'

She thought. 'No, Uncle, unless it's Antonia's visit. It's made home seem nearer, I fancy, and of course she can speak her own language.'

'H'm—I daresay that may have something to do with it. I think we might discontinue the intramuscular gluconate and give calcium lactate by mouth. And now the elbow— I think that next week the plaster might come off. You've been exercising her fingers and wrist and shoulder, haven't you? Yes, well, I feel we could safely remove the splint. I'll get MacCombie to come over and have a look. As for the leg—she's been sitting out for several weeks, hasn't she? There's nothing much we can do there for several weeks. That disposes of the orthopaedic side of things, doesn't it? MacCombie may want an X-ray, but that's up

to him. I'll have those specimens tested and let you know
the results; they should be greatly improved, I fancy. On
the whole, I think we have made considerable headway,
don't you?' He smiled at Sappha. 'And so you've settled
down here, Sappha?'

'Oh, very well, Uncle John. How long is the Baroness
likely to be here?'

He gave her a questioning look. 'Well, it's hard to say.
If this improvement is maintained I see no reason why she
shouldn't go home in say, a month's time—probably less.
She won't be able to bear any weight on that leg, but that
is of no consequence; there's plenty of domestic help, I
believe. Why do you ask? Nothing to do with last night's
little adventure, I hope?'

'No—Yes, it is in a way. I didn't mind going to help in
the least—why should I? There wasn't anyone else.' She
told him about the ruined dress and shoes and Dr van Duyren's insistence that she should accept new ones at his ex-
pense. When she had finished she waited, a little breathless,
for her uncle to speak.

'Well, my dear, aren't you making a mountain out of a
molehill? Why shouldn't you accept replacements of the
things which were spoilt while helping Rolf? I find nothing
unusual in it at all, it seems to me to be a matter of common
sense.'

He took off his old-fashioned glasses and gave her a keen
look. 'Perhaps you and Rolf don't—er—quite hit it off and
I appreciate that at the present time you tend to despise and
dislike all men, but you mustn't allow that to blind you to
good sense. Rolf is a very sound man and the fact that you
dislike him—probably he dislikes you too, my dear—could
make no difference to his doing whatever he feels is the
right thing. I suggest you defer to his judgment.'

So she went back to her patient, and as the Baroness,
naturally enough, wanted to talk about her brightening future, she was unable to give her own concerns any thought
at all, and at lunch, to which Uncle John stayed, neither he

nor the Baron made any reference to the preceding night's activities. The conversation was a rather lofty one about droving and old military roads in and around the Highlands, and as Sappha knew nothing at all about the subject she had to sit and listen with as much interest as she could muster, and was even forced from time to time to give her attention to the Baron, who, with a kindly patience which made her grit her teeth, brought to her notice the more interesting points of their talk.

She didn't see him again for the rest of that day. She had said goodbye to Uncle John after lunch, made sure that her patient was comfortable, and then, leaving her to be entertained for an hour by Antonia, went to her room. The weather was still bad; there seemed no point in going out, so she curled up in the old-fashioned armchair and switched on the electric fire. They had sat a long time over lunch and there was only an hour or so before she would have to fetch the Baroness's tea. It hardly seemed worthwhile writing letters. She sat up with a jerk, remembering Andrew's letter, still in her pocket. She drew it out and turned it over in her hand, then presently got up, fetched an envelope of her own, addressed it to him, put his unopened letter inside and sealed it. Perhaps he would understand from that that she wanted nothing more to do with him.

She stamped it and then sat on her bed, debating whether to take it to the post office or not; there was, after all, no great hurry. She laid it on her beside table and went back to her chair, kicked off her shoes, took off her cap, and curled up once more. It was an excellent opportunity to think; after all, she would have to make some plans for the future sooner or later, but the future, when she thought about it, seemed vague and unimportant and it didn't seem to matter what she thought about anyway, because it was immediately blotted out by the Baron's face. She wondered where he had gone; she supposed that he had a great number of friends and acquaintances living round and about— probably had gone to visit one of them. Her overtired mind conjured up a variety of charming women, all young, beautiful and ready to fall into the Baron's embrace. The thought was so disquieting that she got up and went over to the window for distraction, but her eyes lighted on the rain-washed isthmus where she had spent the night with him and her action did no good at all. She went back to her chair again, telling herself sternly that probably her feelings for him were merely the result of her unhappy affair with Andrew—'caught on the rebound', it was called. Probably in a few weeks' time when she left the Baroness and was once more working in some hospital or other she would laugh... The tears trickled down her cheeks at the thought of it.

The sun was out the next morning and the Baroness remarked upon it with such gaiety that Sappha said cheerfully:

'You are better, Baroness. I'm so glad Antonia came to see you—it's done you the world of good.' She smiled at her patient, hoping that she might tell her how long Antonia and Rolf were staying, but the little lady merely said: 'Yes, I feel marvellous. Mr Devenish said something about Mr MacCombie coming to see me. It would be so nice to have my arm back...I really think I could eat some breakfast this morning, Sappha, and do you suppose the post has come?'

Sappha glanced at her watch. 'It's a bit early, but I'll go and see.' She remembered her letter to Andrew; the postman would take it with him if she asked. She fetched it and ran downstairs and into the kitchen to find the Baron standing at the open back door, drinking tea. The sight of him took her breath, but apparently he had no such sensation on seeing her, for he said casually: 'Hullo, you're early, aren't you?'

'Well, it's a nice day and your mother is feeling so well she wants a proper breakfast—and her post.' Her eye fell on the little pile on the table and he said at once:

'There's nothing for you—Mother's are underneath.' He

put his cup down. 'I'm going to the post office, do you want anything?'

Sappha had handed him the letter to Andrew before she had thought about it. He read the envelope deliberately and gave her a pensive, considering stare; she thought he was going to speak, but instead he turned on his heel and went through the open door. She watched him walk unhurriedly down the kitchen garden path until he turned the corner of the house and she couldn't see him any more. Now he would suppose her to be still in love with Andrew—not, she told herself bitterly, that that would make a ha'porth of difference; Rolf treated her with tolerant amusement most of the time and didn't scruple to be nasty when he chose; she might just as well have been cross-eyed and spotty for all the attention he paid her.

He was away all that day too, although when she came back from her afternoon walk, it was to hear that he had spent an hour with his mother. He quite obviously wished to avoid her, and Sappha, who had been popular all her life and never lacked for friends of both sexes, felt puzzled and hurt and finally, angry. Well, she thought defiantly, two can play at that game. Only it was a pity that she had no chance to play it, for next day he took Antonia to visit the laird, who was, it transpired, Antonia's godfather, and the following day was Sunday. Sappha, standing at the Baroness's window, watched the members of the minister's household cross the short stretch of garden between the Manse and the church. Everyone went, Mr MacFee leading the way with Antonia, and Rolf, darkly handsome and exceedingly well turned out, escorting Mrs MacFee. Meg and the postman, who was the odd job man around the Manse, brought up the rear.

'What is Antonia wearing?' asked the Baroness from her bed. 'She's just started buying her own clothes, you know, and some of them aren't quite…she has a hat, I hope?' she queried anxiously.

Sappha, with her eyes on the Baron's broad back, said: 'Yes—a very pretty one—green felt, I think.'

'Ah yes, good. And Rolf, is he there?'

Sappha replied slowly: 'Yes' and turned away from the window. 'He's with Mrs MacFee.'

'A pity you couldn't go too, dear. I feel such a nuisance...'

Sappha started to arrange cushions in the armchair. 'Nonsense, Baroness, I'm used to working on Sundays—besides, I shall go to church this evening, I expect. Mrs MacFee said she would love to sit with you for a little while.'

Which was what she did, leaving not only Mrs MacFee with her patient but Antonia and Rolf as well. He had barely spoken to her all day and then only a few polite remarks, and Antonia, who had spent half an hour in Sappha's room that afternoon, trying on her hats and looking at her clothes, gave the opinion that her brother had something on his mind. 'A girl, probably,' she said airily, 'though they don't usually have such an effect on him. He's quite forgotten to be bossy and when I asked him if we could stay another day or so he just said "Why not?" I mean, it just isn't like him; he rules me with a rod of iron, you know.'

Sappha laughed. 'Tonia, what a thing to say! I think you have just about everything you want.'

Antonia turned from the mirror where she was trying on the smart little hat Sappha intended to wear to church. 'Yes, I do,' she agreed with engaging frankness, 'but Rolf is very strict—far worse than a father—he says I'm much too impulsive. He won't even let me go out on a date, only if there are several of us, and then he has to know who they are.' She pouted, looking like a discontented kitten. 'We're rich, you see, and Papa left me a great deal of money as well, and Rolf says there are plenty of young men around who would like to get their hands on it.' She gave an exaggerated sigh. 'I suppose he'll make me marry some stuffy man he approves of.'

'I don't imagine your brother numbers stuffy people among his friends for a start, and I'm sure he's far too fond of you to want you to be unhappy. There are quite a lot of wolves around, Tonia.'

Antonia eyed her thoughtfully. 'You sound just like Rolf. Your boy-friend's pretty super, Sappha. I like the way he laughs, and he liked me, didn't he? I could fall for him in a big way, but of course I wouldn't be so mean.'

'No, I'm sure you wouldn't,' said Sappha hastily, 'but there's plenty of time to meet someone like him. I know you're an old maid of sixteen, but there's still hope.' They laughed together and Antonia said: 'I do like you, Sappha—I wish you were in the family. What a pity you don't like Rolf, and he doesn't exactly swoon over you, does he?'

Sappha managed a laugh. 'I'm only here on a job for a few weeks, you know, so likes and dislikes don't matter very much. I shouldn't arrange my future too carefully if I were you—and now go away do, you scheming creature, and leave me to write my letters in peace!'

But she had written no letters at all, only sat thinking about Rolf. Somehow the news that he was rich made everything seem even more hopeless than it already was. What was it Antonia had said? 'He doesn't exactly swoon over you.'

Monday morning was fine, which was perhaps why the Baroness was in such a hurry to be bathed and got up into her chair. She did her exercises with none of the little pauses for a chat which she usually indulged in; she even knew immediately what she wanted to do with her morning. Sappha was adjusting the bed's counterpane to a nicety when the door opened and Antonia and Rolf came in together. They wished their parent a good morning and Antonia pulled up a chair to sit by her mother while Rolf strolled over to the bed, to lean over its high brass end.

'How long will you be?' he enquired mildly.

Sappha gave the pristine bedcover a final pat. 'How long will I be?' she reiterated foolishly, her voice sounding a little quavery because when he came upon her suddenly like this it did something to her breath.

He said patiently: 'Yes—how long will you be? You've finished here, I imagine. Can you change in half an hour? I want to get away by half past eleven.'

'Away? Where to?'

'Inverness—to get your dress and shoes. As we arranged,' he added wickledly, his dark eyes snapping. He grinned at her cheerfully, just as though they were friends of long standing instead of two people who had barely exchanged half a dozen sentences in the last couple of days. She ignored the grin. 'I don't wish...' she began in what she hoped was a severe voice, only to be interrupted by her patient.

'Such a splendid idea of Rolf's, dear. You see, they're going home tomorrow, and if you go today, I shall have Antonia for company—such a lovely day for a drive too.'

Sappha looked at the Baron, who was, she noted, suitably dressed for an outing and as usual on these occasions, well tailored and well groomed, but today, despite the impeccably cut tweeds and the handmade shoes, he wore the distinct air of a brigand. He said softly: 'It's no good, Sappha, you see I've made up my mind.'

Sappha's fine eyes flashed. She had made up her mind too—not to go. It was therefore all the more astonishing when she heard herself say meekly: 'Very well, I'll come.'

Rolf straightened up. 'Good. You can shop while I collect Mr MacCombie. I'm bringing him back to see Mother—Tonia and I can drop him off in Inverness as we go tomorrow.'

For some reason Sappha found this piece of information depressing. While she changed she was forced to admit to herself that she had actually supposed that the Baron had asked her to accompany him to Inverness because he had wanted to, but this was obviously not so—it was merely convenient that way. She ground her splendid teeth together as she surveyed herself in the old-fashioned mirror in the wardrobe door. She looked nice, even in her own critical eyes. Her tweed suit was oatmeal-coloured and she had teamed it up with a nut brown angora sweater which went very well with the round fur hat set jauntily on top of her dark hair. The hat had been made from an elderly stone-marten fur cape of her mother's; too good to discard completely—it looked expensive, luxurious and very becoming. She picked up her gloves and handbag and went back to the Baroness's room, smelling faintly of Madame Rochas.

The Baroness gave her an appraising look. She said gently:

'Very nice, Sappha—what a pretty girl you are,' and Antonia skipped forward to get a clearer look at the hat and said instantly:

'That hat—it's super! Rolf, I want a fur hat.'

He barely glanced at it. 'For Christmas,' he said shortly, 'if you're ready, we'll go, Sappha.'

She got into the Land Rover with the strong feeling that putting on anything more glamorous than a sack was a waste of time with Rolf. Probably he noticed what other women—women he liked—wore; she doubted if he had even a vague idea as to what she had on. She sat silently beside him, working herself up into a fine temper all the fiercer because she was forced to suppress it. When he asked: 'Where shall we go first?' in a quite friendly voice, she replied woodenly: 'Wherever you wish,' and when after a further silent mile or so he remarked:

'I thought we might lunch at Invermoriston. Did you see Skye on your trip with Glover?'

She said 'No.' He persevered. 'I imagined not. We'll go down as far as Auchtertyre—there's a splendid view from there.' He glanced at his watch. 'We've plenty of time.'

Sappha said nothing to this, her bad temper was beginning to wear off; it had struck her that for the next few hours she was going to be in Rolf's company—and what was that he had said about lunch? His voice, very dry, cut into her thoughts. 'I am—er—very well aware that your feelings towards men are not very friendly at the present time. I am also aware that we agreed to a mutual dislike of each other, though I must point out that this opinion was yours—but we did agree to conceal our true feelings, did we not?' He sighed. 'I have done my best to carry on some sort of conversation with you, but really, my dear good girl, you're making no effort at all, are you?'

Sappha's breast swelled with returned temper. 'Well,' she exclaimed explosively, 'and that after two days of barely speaking to me!'

They were approaching Strome Ferry, running along the banks of Loch Carron, and before answering her he remarked upon the beauty of the scenery they were passing through. 'Do take a look around you,' he advised, 'it may help to cool your temper.'

Speechless with rage, she turned her head to stare at the view; she kept it turned while he continued: 'Of course I didn't talk to you—you terrified me.'

This outrageous statement had the effect of causing her to turn her head to stare at him. 'What complete nonsense,' she managed at last, 'you're not terrified of anything or anyone.'

'Your eyes flashed; you wore a thin coating of ice; you haven't smiled since Saturday.'

Sappha ignored the quite ridiculous way her heart was thumping; she returned to the attack. 'You took me by surprise this morning—you expected me to rush into my clothes and tear off to Inverness just because it's convenient.'

He said blandly: 'It took you exactly forty minutes to change, though I admit the result was well worth the wait—quite eye-catching, in fact. I speak in the guise of good fellowship,' he added hastily.

She said in a small, disappointment-clouded voice: 'Oh, yes, of course. I—I thought you hadn't noticed.' She was staring ahead of her and didn't see his smile.

'And we're hardly rushing to Inverness, are we? We could of course do so should you prefer that.'

She shook her head and was thankful when he began to talk about nothing in particular with a charm which she found herself responding to, so that by the time they had crossed the ferry and begun the climb through the hairpin bends of Auchtertyre Hill, her temper had evaporated once more. When they pulled up, she saw with something of a shock that it was where she and Andrew had come, and when Rolf asked: 'Is this where you stopped with Andrew?' she nodded briefly and said with careful casualness: 'We couldn't see anything, though.'

For answer he got out and helped her out too, and they stood together staring across the sea at the hills of Skye. 'So I don't suppose you did this,' he said slowly, and she shook her head. 'Or this?'

He flung a great arm around her, pulling her close to kiss her with deliberation. Sappha allowed herself a few moments of delight and then pushed against the expanse of tweed she was pressed against. He let her go at once, saying with a little laugh and no single sign of regret, 'And if I had been your Andrew I'm damned if I should have let the wind and the rain stop me from kissing my girl.'

'You've no right—' she began, breathless.

'None at all,' he replied cheerfully. 'Haven't you ever kissed someone just because you were feeling happy?'

She thought she knew what he meant then. His mother was better; likely to recover completely in time. It must have been a load of his mind to know that—probably he would have kissed anyone who had chanced to be around. She said: 'I suppose so,' and smiled a little up into his satyr's face.

'Let's cry truce just for today,' he said. 'I'll be gone tomorrow and you can forget me.'

She agreed soberly: 'Yes, I can, can't I?' and knew that she never would.

They lunched at the Glenmoriston Hotel, talking happily

about a variety of subjects while they ate smoked salmon flan, steak and kidney pie, and followed these with pears stuffed with *marrons glacés* and covered with a brandy flavoured cream. Sappha, who had a healthy appetite, swallowed the last delicious morsel and said simply: 'That was delicious. How delightful Scotland is! Somehow, when one lives in London, one tends to think that there is nowhere else...'

Over their coffee, she asked a little shyly: 'Is your home anything like this—oh, I know it's flat in Holland, but is it quiet and peaceful as it is here?'

'Yes, Dokkum is a small town with a moat which gives one a curiously shut-off feeling. Everyone knows everyone else and life there is very pleasant. Groningen, where I work mostly, is big and bustling, but not to be compared with London, of course. You like London?'

She had always thought she had until now. She said uncertainly: 'Yes, but not as much as I used to,' and coloured faintly when he said:

'Naturally. Do you plan to go back there? Presumably your Andrew is waiting for you.'

She said, not looking up: 'I have no plans.' That was the second time he had referred to 'her Andrew'. She was on the point of telling him that Andrew was no longer hers and that by her own wish, when she remembered that his interest was merely the outcome of their truce. Had he not said that she could forget him tomorrow? Presumably for ever.

'You look as though you're going to cry.' His voice was gentle, quite unlike his usual faint derision; she straightened her face hastily. It would be very nice to have a good howl on his broad shoulder—after all, he must be quite used to it with four sisters. She smiled at the thought and he said: 'That's better. Shall we go? It's only half an hour or so to Inverness, that will give you a couple of hours to do your shopping.'

But when they got there it seemed that he had every

intention of coming with her, for when she asked what time she should meet him he smiled down at her and took her arm. 'I'll come with you,' he said. 'I don't have to pick up Mr MacCombie until five.'

Apparently he knew Inverness rather well. They visited a couple of dress shops and several boutiques where she looked worriedly at the clothes because he hadn't mentioned prices, and in the kind of shops he had led her to, they were high. She stood uncertainly before a small elegant window, eyeing a pink angora dress which she instantly coveted. It had no price ticket, but as there was nothing else in the window but a vase of hothouse flowers and a silk scarf with an astronomical figure attached to it, she judged it to be expensive. She was about to turn away when Rolf said: 'Ah, that's it, isn't it?' and propelled her into the grey velvet interior where he said loudly: 'Go ahead, Sappha, and try it on,' which words commanded instant attention from the saleslady, so that Sappha, willy-nilly, was forced to request the removal of the dress from the window. It was a perfect fit and very becoming; she was standing before the mirror in the little fitting room at the back of the shop, wondering what to do about it, when the Baron said in a carrying voice:

'Come out here and let me have a look,' and when she complied it was to find him standing with the saleswoman, cheque-book in hand. 'Like it?' he queried nonchalantly. 'It suits you. Have it.'

Sappha liked it too, but she didn't like being told to have it. She gave him a sneaking glance and said: 'I think not—it's probably a great deal too much money.'

She turned to ask the cost and was at once frustrated by his cheerful 'I've dealt with that. Don't you like it?'

They stared at each other across the little shop and she could see that, as usual, although his face was serious, he was laughing at her. She said with dignity: 'I like it very much. I'll take it.'

Outside the shop she turned on him. 'Do you always

bully people into doing what you want?' she wanted to
know, to be met with a look of such innocence that she
was rendered speechless.

'I?' he asked. 'Bully you? My dear good girl, don't you
know that barons—the bold bad ones, that is—only bully
those who are unable to look after themselves? And from
what I have seen of you, you are perfectly able to do that.'
His satyr's face split into a sudden grin: 'Now we will have
no more nonsense and go and buy your shoes.' He took
her arm again, but Sappha didn't move. She was really very
angry with him, but at the same time she was enjoying
every minute of his company. No wonder his mother and
Antonia adored him. She remembered the truce and he was
going tomorrow, anyway, and she would most probably
never see him again. She said slowly:

'I'm sorry, I've been rude. I know you wouldn't bully
anyone or anything I—I mean that, I'm not just saying it
un-under the flag of truce.'

He stood looking down into her face; presently he nodded to himself, then said quietly: 'A remark like that needs
celebrating. We'll have tea.'

He walked her briskly down the main street and presently
turned into a narrow street leading from it; it was lined
with old houses, some of them converted into small shops.
The tea-room was halfway down its peaceful length, small,
wood-panelled and cosy, with just enough people inside to
make it pleasant. They found a table by the window and
Sappha said:

'I should never have found this on my own. It's super.'

'It's been here for years. Mother used to bring us here
when we were children. The spiced buns are to be recom-
mended.'

They sat over their tea, for suddenly there seemed to be
a great deal to talk about, and Sappha, convinced that she
wasn't going to see him again, found herself telling him
about her home and family, but she didn't talk about Andrew, and Rolf made no effort to ask about him.

The shoes were bought in an atmosphere of complete amiability, and the short time left was spent in the purchase of some handmade chocolates for the Baroness and a flask of Fifth Avenue toilet water for Antonia, purchased by the Baron with an assurance which could only mean that he was no stranger to shopping of that type, a fact which left Sappha a little thoughtful.

They were to pick up Mr MacCombie at his own home; Rolf drew up outside and got out. 'Stay where you are,' he commanded before he rang the bell and was admitted to the house, and Sappha stayed where she was, although it seemed to her that the two men would want to travel together, they would surely have a great deal to discuss about the Baroness for a start. But apparently she was mistaken, for within a minute or two the men came out and Mr MacCombie, after an exchange of greetings, climbed into the back of the Land Rover without a single murmur of dissent.

They travelled back to Dialach on the same road which she herself had taken when she had come from London. It was already dusk—it would soon be dark, but the Baron, who knew the road well, didn't slacken speed. Their talk was desultory and casual, and rather to her surprise, very little was said about the Baroness.

The Manse's lighted windows looked warm and welcoming as they arrived, and their own welcome was no less warm. The Baroness looked a little flushed and excited and Sappha went quickly to her room, changed into her uniform and went to find Mrs MacFee. That lady was in the kitchen putting the finishing touches to supper. She looked up with a smile as Sappha went in and said: 'Hullo, Sappha dear. Back in uniform already?'

'Yes, Mrs MacFee. The Baroness looks a bit excited—I thought if I took up her supper and did the usual evening chores and exercises it might calm her down a little. I do want her to be as well as possible when Mr MacCombie sees her tomorrow morning. I expect he'll see her tonight as well, but only to talk to her.'

Mrs MacFee nodded. 'Yes, dear, I'm sure you're right. It must be hard not to get excited, though. Did you have a nice day?'

Sappha was squeezing lemons at the table. 'Yes, very.'

'And did you get a pretty dress and the shoes you wanted? Those you spoilt were so very smart.'

'Yes—the dress is prettier than the one I ruined—pink angora—and the shoes are just as nice as the others. I'll let you see them later.'

She went back through the hall to go upstairs again and heard the rumble of the men's voices from the study and then the Baron's laugh. It had been a lovely day, he had been charming and generous, and most agreeable to be with. Probably when they met at supper he would be distantly polite again, and mock her with his dark eyes. She turned round and went back to the kitchen.

'Mrs MacFee, would it be an awful nuisance if I didn't come down to supper? I think I'll stay with the Baroness while she's having hers. I could get a glass of milk or something later, couldn't I?'

Mrs MacFee was tenderly removing a bubbling macaroni cheese from the oven. 'Why, of course, Sappha. We shall miss you at supper, of course, but if you think it you better to stay with the Baroness...'

It was after her patient's supper, while Sappha was arranging the room for the night, that Mr MacCombie arrived. Rolf was with him, but Sappha, busy with charts and questions, didn't look at him. It was only when the specialist had drawn up a chair to the bedside to have what he described as a little chat that the Baron came to stand beside her.

'You didn't come to supper,' he said softly.

Sappha said, equally low-voiced: 'No, your mother was a little excited—I thought it might calm her down if I stayed up here.'

He murmured: 'Ah, of course. I had imagined some other reason. Do you want me to tell you what it was?'

She said hastily: 'No' then went slowly red as he said on a laugh:

'So there was another reason.'

She swallowed her heart back to where it belonged and without answering or even looking at him, moved away to stand by the bed and presently slipped away to her own room where she stayed, doing nothing until she heard Mr MacCombie calling her. Rolf was still there, standing at the window looking out into the black evening. He didn't turn round when she went in and after one swift glance at his broad back she joined the surgeon, still sitting by the bed. Mr MacCombie said:

'Tomorrow morning, nine o'clock—is that too soon for you, Nurse? We'll get that plaster splint off before I go and take a look at the leg at the same time.' He patted his patient's hand. 'Your troubles are almost over, Baroness. A few more weeks...'

The Baroness interrupted him: 'When will it be possible for me to go home? I have plenty of help and all that sort of thing.'

She smiled coaxingly, looking exactly like her daughter, and Mr MacCombie laughed.

'Well, shall we say soon? I think Rolf and I must talk about this first, and of course Mr Devenish must be consulted—but I think I can safely say that it won't be long now.'

He and Rolf went away after that, leaving Sappha to calm down her patient once more and get her ready for the night, a lengthy business, for the Baroness wanted to talk. Sappha was reading to her when Rolf came back; she put the book down and left them together—doubtless they had a lot to say to each other. In a little while she heard him go downstairs again and went back once more to tuck her patient up for the night, then crept downstairs to the kitchen. There was some soup keeping hot on the stove;

she poured a bowlful and sat spooning it up, listening to the laughing and talking going on in the drawing room. She debated with herself about going in to say goodnight, and decided that she should. There was a lull in the conversation as she opened the door and everyone looked at her. She glued her eyes to Mrs MacFee's kind face and bade the general company goodnight, then looked at Rolf.

'Thank you for a lovely day, Doctor van Duyren,' she said in a polite voice which didn't sound like hers at all.

Mr MacCombie was quick the next morning. He had the plaster off and was examining the arm before the Baroness had finished wondering if it was going to hurt. The arm looked a little puny, but thanks to Sappha's efforts and the exercises, it functioned quite well. The Baroness sat looking at it as though it wasn't her own while he examined her leg, which he did at some length, saying finally in a non-commital voice:

'Very good progress, Baroness—Rolf and I will have a little chat presently and I may possibly come back with Mr Devenish in a week or so, when I daresay we shall have some good news for you.'

With these heartening words he wished her goodbye, nodded nicely to Sappha, and went. As soon as his footsteps had died away, she said firmly: 'Breakfast first, and then you shall let yourself go.'

There seemed to be no one about downstairs. She assembled the Baroness's modest wants on to a tray and went back upstairs, to find Antonia with her mother. She turned round as Sappha went in, saying: 'There you are, Sappha. I'm saying goodbye—did you see Rolf?'

Sappha put the tray down carefully and said no while she adjusted the bedtable, and presently Antonia gave her mother a final hug and pranced across the room to plant a kiss in Sappha's cheek and say *'Tot ziens'* and then was gone. By the time Sappha had found a clean handkerchief for her patient to cry into, the sounds of parting at the front door had ceased; she got to the window just in time to see the back wheels of the Land Rover disappearing through the gate.

CHAPTER FIVE

THE days seemed intolerably long and empty without the Baron, a fact made worse by Sappha's patient, who, once she had recovered from the excitement of the surgeon's visit, became increasingly depressed. Sappha, assuming a false cheerfulness she was far from feeling, tried everything she could think of to divert the Baroness's thoughts without a great deal of success. She told Gloria about it one afternoon when she had slipped out for an hour while Mrs MacFee kept her friend company.

The two girls were sitting comfortably by the sitting room fire in Gloria's cottage, a tea tray between them and a stray cat Gloria had adopted stretched at their feet.

'I don't know what to do,' mused Sappha. 'I believe she's homesick. After all, she's been here some weeks now—she was here before the op, wasn't she? and by all accounts she's been a marvellous patient—I think she should go home as soon as possible. There are another lot of tests due next week, the last batch were pretty good. Obviously her renal function is almost a hundred per cent—surely they could get her home?'

Gloria bit into some shortbread. 'You sound as though you want to get away,' she remarked sapiently. 'Are you fed up?'

Sappha bent to tickle the cat's ears so that her face was hidden.

'No, not in the least. It's a worthwhile case, isn't it? I was just wondering—I suppose they'll get some kind of help for the Baroness when she does go.'

'Lord, yes. No difficulty there. From what I've heard

96

from Hamish they've more than enough servants who've been with them for ever—though I must say they don't behave as though they had. I don't know what they're like in their own home, but when Rolf comes here for a meal he washes up after to the manner born. He can cook too, and last year when Mrs MacFee was down with the 'flu and he was staying with them, he coped with quite a bit of housework as well.'

Sappha looked at her friend with round eyes. 'He did?' she asked incredulously, 'but he doesn't look as though...'

Gloria smiled. 'No, he doesn't, does he?' She ate a biscuit. 'Hamish told me that Rolf's house sounds as though it runs on oiled wheels. I must say he'll be a prize for some lucky girl.'

Sappha's heart did a double knock against her ribs. 'Oh, is he thinking of getting married?' she wanted to know in an expressionless voice.

'I haven't a clue—whoever knows what Rolf is thinking, for a start? Hamish says he's a bit of a puritan.' Sappha gave her a startled look and she went on cheerfully. 'Not that kind of puritan, ducky—he's not above chatting up the girls, with great success, I imagine, but he once said that unless he could find the other half of himself somewhere in the world he didn't intend to marry.' She licked a finger delicately. 'What a waste!'

Sappha poured second cups. 'Antonia's a dear,' she observed, longing to continue talking about Rolf but feeling that the subject should be changed.

'Yes—Rolf has a very soft spot for her too. I suppose because she was only a little girl when their father died; he was quite a man, I believe. She twists Rolf round her little finger, you'll have noticed that for yourself, and he lets her get away with it, but he's strict with her too, for she's headstrong and gullible and as pretty as the proverbial picture, and that allied to a tidy little fortune spells trouble ahead as far as Rolf's concerned; he's got some very sound ideas about whom she shall marry.'

Sappha frowned. 'Do you mean to say he's going to tell her whom she can marry and whom she can't—why, it's archaic!'

Gloria gave her a level look. 'No, it isn't. There are plenty of heels around…are you going to make it up with your Andrew?'

Sappha's frown deepened. Here was someone else referring to Andrew as hers. She said snappishly: 'No, but no one knows that—it seems to be the accepted idea that I shall go back to London and live happily ever after. Well, I've given him up if you must know, and don't go telling anyone, will you?'

Gloria stared at her over the rim of her teacup. 'No, I won't. Tell me about the other night,' she invited.

It was a relief to talk about it; she hadn't realised until she said it loud how bitterly disappointed and ashamed she had been feeling about Andrew's refusal to help. She remembered how nice Rolf had been about it; probably he was nice like that about everyone, even someone he didn't like, which reminded her rather painfully that he didn't like her overmuch. Her own fault of course, for he had, after all been quite right at their first meeting; she had been silly to run out of petrol and just as silly not to run the car on to the side of the road—but he had looked like some fierce brigand… She said urgently:

'He shouldn't walk about looking like a fisherman or a—a pirate!'

And it seemed quite natural for Gloria to answer at once. 'I know, so deceiving, isn't it? He looks so different. Last Hogmanay we all went up to the Lodge—the Laird gives a do then—Rolf was in a black tie, of course, and there wasn't a woman in the room who could keep her eyes off him and he was completely indifferent, if you know what I mean, and at the same time he was charming and a little bold and bad as well. It's a good thing I met Hamish first or I might have fallen for Rolf.' She turned her blue eyes upon Sappha. 'I suppose you couldn't…'

'No,' said Sappha fiercely, 'we—we don't like each other.'

Gloria digested this in silence, watching the delicate pink wash over Sappha's face and slowly fade again. She said finally in a bracing voice: 'Well, what are you going to do about the Baroness? I suppose you couldn't write; even if you don't like each other, you are his mother's nurse.'

'No,' said Sappha for the second time, 'I couldn't do that. I'll wait another week. Uncle John said he'd be down soon—I'll ask him.'

The week took a very long time to pass. The Baroness seemed a little better; she used her arm just as she had been told to do, got up into her chair, painted and knitted and played endless games of backgammon and demon patience with Sappha, and when Rolf telephoned, which he did most nights, she chatted animatedly with him and never once brought up the subject of going home. And never once did he ask to speak to Sappha.

The evening previous to Uncle John's visit Sappha remarked cheerfully to her patient: 'Well, I wonder what Uncle John will have to say in the morning? He said he would be here about eleven o'clock; he'll stop overnight in Inverness, I suppose. I'll get you up as usual, then if he wants you back in bed I can whisk you back. Why not wear that lovely nightie Dr van Duyren sent you last week? It's such a heavenly pink.'

The Baroness agreed with a heavenly smile. 'Do you suppose it will really help?' she wanted to know, and then, 'I'm sorry, my dear, I'm an ungrateful wretch—of course you shall pretty me up.' She sighed. 'It's just that I seem to have been here for ever.'

Sappha was busying herself setting the night table to rights. 'I know, it's always the last few days which are the hardest to bear—but they are the last, I feel sure. I'm going to give you something to give you a sound night's sleep so that you look really perky tomorrow.'

Later, in her own room, sitting up in bed, hugging her

knees and recalling the conversation, she had to admit that she wasn't quite as sure about things as she had made out. For one thing, there was a great deal to be thought of if the Baroness was to be allowed home. A nurse would have to be found and the journey arranged. She began to wonder vaguely what she herself would do afterwards; she knew she didn't want to go back to London. Perhaps Uncle John would know of something, or she might apply for a post in one of the Scottish hospitals. The future seemed decidedly uninviting and she allowed her thoughts to stray to Rolf—probably he was living it up with one of the girls Gloria seemed to think sat around waiting for him to crook his finger. Sappha started to cry, which, although a great relief to her feelings, did nothing to solve her problems. After a few minutes she blew her nose with pathetic determination, got up and washed her face and composed herself for sleep. Time enough for her to mope about her own sorrows when those of her patient had been resolved.

She got up very early because she hadn't slept for more than an hour or so. She crept downstairs through the quiet house, made tea and then went to peep at the Baroness, who it turned out, was awake too. Sappha went soft-footed to the bed. 'I've made some tea,' she whispered. 'Shall I bring it up here and give you a cup at the same time?'

The Baroness didn't answer immediately, instead she stared at Sappha with disconcertingly bright eyes and said in positive tones:

'You've been crying, child. Why?'

'Oh, no reason at all,' said Sappha. 'I'm going to fetch the tea.'

She was back within five minutes with a tray which she put on the bedside table before she drew up a chair for herself. The fire had burned low, she poked at it gently, put on another log to make a cheerful blaze, then, wrapping her dressing gown more closely around her, poured the tea. They were gossiping quietly over a second cup when they heard a car draw up outside.

'The milkman,' Sappha surmised, and frowned at her watch. 'No, it can't be, it's only half past six, and it's certainly not the postman. Someone for Mr MacFee, perhaps—there's old Mr MacIndoe very ill; his wife was up here yesterday about him. I'd better go down and see.'

She crept downstairs once more and crossed the hall to the front door. The dim light in the porch was left on all night; she could see someone's shadow standing by the door. She wondered why they hadn't knocked and then remembered that they would have seen the Baroness's light. She opened the door without haste because the bolt was old and rasped a little and she didn't want to disturb the MacFees until she knew who it was. It was the Baron who stepped inside, looking larger than ever and rather sinister by reason of his bulky coat. Its collar was turned up against the early morning chill and she couldn't see his face very clearly because she hadn't bothered to put the hall light on. He said softly: 'Good girl—I didn't knock, I counted on you hearing the car.'

She stood gaping at him in utter surprise, her heart thudding. After a moment she managed to say in a strangled voice: 'Good morning, Dr van Duyren,' and was instantly caught in his arms.

'Isn't that a little formal, especially from a pretty girl in a dressing gown with her hair hanging down her back—how about this?'

He kissed her, quite roughly, on the mouth, and then again, gently this time, on top of her tousled head. When he let her go she said in a choking voice: 'Your mother is awake—she'll be glad to see you,' and turned and led the way upstairs with her heart still hammering in her ears. She had shut the Baroness's door when she had gone down; now she paused before it and turned to look at him.

'Would you like to go in? I expect you'd like something to eat and drink.' Her voice was matter-of-fact now.

He gazed down at her, his eyes snapping with laughter.

'Ah,' he said silkily, 'the mantle of friendship—or do I mean the olive branch?'

'Neither—I'm talking about tea and toast.' Her tone was astringent.

His brows described an arc. 'I expect too much,' he murmured, 'but tea and toast will do nicely for a start.'

He opened the door and went inside and Sappha flew down the stairs with the faint echo of the Baroness's excited voice pursuing her.

Ten minutes later she was back again with a tray loaded with a teapot and a plate of well-buttered toast. The Baron was sitting on his mother's bed, a fact which Sappha's strict nursing training deplored; he had thrown off his heavy coat to reveal an exquisitely tailored suit of clerical grey and a richly sombre tie; presumably he had got straight up from his consultant's desk and boarded the plane, a surprise which he confirmed as he took the tray from her.

'Is all this for me? I missed dinner and I almost missed the plane too—I have never had so many long-winded patients as I had yesterday.' He sat down again and cast his eye over the tray. 'Marmalade, too,' he observed, 'what a delightfully practical woman you are, Sappha, and so hospitable. I do believe you would feel compelled to offer any burglar foolish enough to enter a cup of tea before you laid him out with the poker. Do sit down and have some of this—yours must be cold.'

But Sappha shook her head. 'No,' she said, 'I'd finished,' which wasn't true, but she didn't care; she had to get away so that she could become as calm and quiet as he was and school herself to treat him with the same casual air as he was treating her.

She felt a good deal better by the time she was dressed. The simple act of turning herself into a nurse once more helped to steady her thoughts, so that by the time she went back to the Baroness she was, outwardly at least, cool and composed and quite prepared to answer the Baron's civil enquiries. She piled the trays neatly and started for the door, only to have them removed from her grasp and when she remonstrated all he said was: 'I've got to come downstairs to fetch one or two things from the car.' But in the kitchen he made no move to go but sat on a corner of the table watching her tidy away and stack the china in the sink.

'I'm afraid you've had rather a difficult time with Mother,' he said mildly. 'I'm sorry I could do nothing to help—it's sometimes difficult to get away. I knew you could cope.'

Sappha emptied a teapot with rather too much vigour. Flattery would get him nowhere, she told herself crossly. She said out aloud: 'Mr MacCombie and Uncle John are coming this morning.'

'Yes, I know. I telephoned Mr Devenish a day or so ago—that's why I am here.'

'The Baroness is anxious to go home. She's a marvellous patient, but I think she feels she's getting nowhere any more.'

He nodded, cut a hunk of bread from the loaf beside him on the table and began to eat it. Watching him, Sappha found the sight pathetic, which she told herself sternly, was ridiculous, the baron had enough money, presumably, to eat his breakfast at a five-star hotel should he so wish—there was no need for him to eat dry bread. All the same, she said: 'When I've taken up your mother's breakfast, I'll cook something for you.'

He smiled at her so charmingly that she turned her back quickly. He said warmly: 'Generous creature—eggs and bacon and some mushrooms if there are any and a kidney or so—on second thoughts perhaps I'd better cook them myself, you've already offered more than a fair share of the olive branch.'

Sappha dished up a poached egg with great neatness. 'You can't cook in that suit,' she said positively. 'Go and do whatever it is you want to do, I shall be about ten minutes.'

He got down off the table and came and stood beside her, an act which played havoc with her pulse rate. 'I'm overwhelmed, my dear Miss Devenish. Can it be that you have had a change of heart?'

She picked up her tray and went briskly to the door, because it seemed good sense to escape before she said something foolish. 'Ten minutes,' she reiterated.

She found her patient sitting up in bed eager to talk, something which she proceeded to do without pause for some minutes. 'I shall be going home soon,' she said with certainty, 'I must be quite well by now.'

Sappha poured the tea, for it was obvious that the Baroness had forgotten to do it for herself. 'Do let's wait and see,' she begged. 'If you get too excited your pulse rate will go up, and you know how fussy Uncle John is about that.' She whipped the cover off a plate. 'Poached eggs,' she invited, 'you know you like them. Will you eat them while I go and cook Dr van Duyren some breakfast? He says he's famished, and it's far too early to disturb Mrs MacFee. You'll be finished by then, and we can concentrate on making you glamorous.' She was interrupted by a knock on the door and Mrs MacFee, cosily dressing-gowned, came in.

'I heard voices,' she said with no sign of ill humour at being disturbed, 'and I just had to come and see...'

'Rolf's here, Ida,' said the Baroness, 'isn't it exciting? Do you suppose they'll let me go home?' This remark was made with the passionate eagerness of someone who had been inured in some dreary prison for a number of years, and was hardly one to please any hostess, however kind, but Mrs MacFee had been a lifelong friend, and far from taking umbrage, she replied with ready enthusiasm that there seemed to be a very good chance of it. Sappha saw that the two ladies were intent on discussing this possibility from every angle; she went downstairs again and fetched another cup and saucer, and wordlessly poured tea for Mrs MacFee too, inviting her to sit comfortably by the fire. This done, she felt free to go back to the kitchen where the Baron was still sitting on the table with the negligible remains of the loaf beside him. She gave him a severe look and said: 'Couldn't you wait?' At this rate she would be lucky if she got any breakfast for herself.

The Baron got off the table. 'You cook,' he said mildly, 'I'll lay the table for both of us, if you have breakfast now it will leave you free for Mother later on.'

He didn't wait for her answer but set two places, while she, admitting the good sense of this, added more eggs and bacon to the pan and when he asked 'Is there any porridge?' filled a bowl from the saucepan on the stove and put it before him, whereupon he invited her to have some too and when she refused, remarked in a friendly jeering voice: 'I suppose it makes you fat.'

'It does not...' she began furiously, then stopped because he might have said it in order to make her lose her temper. She went on sweetly: 'I have it most mornings, but I don't want it today.'

In fact, she wasn't hungry at all, although she ate what was on her plate, otherwise he would comment upon her lack of appetite. She took a small piece of toast and made it last a long time, telling herself that it was the unexpected events of the morning which had taken away her interest in her breakfast, while being aware that it was nothing of the sort. If this was being in love—besottedly in love, she amended honestly—the sooner she got herself out of it the better. She glanced up and found his eyes on her. He said in a gently ruminating voice:

'I should dearly love to know what you are thinking about to make you frown so and to make your mouth so prim. Don't you like having breakfast with me?'

His smile, coupled with the eyebrows, gave him a positively satanic look. Sappha knew better than to ignore his question; she looked down her pretty nose. 'I have no special feelings on the matter,' she observed in a cool little voice. 'More tea, Doctor?'

He passed his cup. 'How long,' he asked with interest, 'was it before you could bring yourself to call Glover—er—Andrew?'

She went a little white. 'Was it sweet enough?' she wanted to know, her voice sounded quite natural, if a bit thin. He took the cup from her without answering her question, merely spooning more sugar in with a generous hand. 'I have always thought,' he went on smoothly, 'that it should be possible to dislike someone without making the fact too obvious; there are, after all, the conventional politenesses of everyday life—occasionally forgotten, I grant you, in times of stress—I distinctly heard you call me by name on the causeway the other night.'

He helped himself to more toast, more butter and a large quantity of marmalade. 'Call me Rolf,' he invited, 'even if only on occasion. You can go on disliking me as much as you wish.' He laughed suddenly. 'I'll be bound to put your back up whenever we meet, and if I can't think of anything unpleasant to say I can always kiss you instead; I'm sure that will have the same result.'

Sappha sat staring at him across the table. She felt bewildered, dangerously tearful and full of a splendid rage which was too inarticulate to allow her to deliver the telling reply this piece of impertinence on the Baron's part deserved. She opened and closed her charming mouth for several seconds, struggling to form her feelings into the right words and her efforts were not helped by his saying kindly:

'Don't bother to think of anything to say—I'm sure it'll come to you later. You can always write it down and commit it to memory and shoot it at me when next we meet.'

Sappha fought a sudden desire to laugh; fortunately she was able to turn it into a kind of strangled cough. She said with commendable calm:

'I think I should be attending to your mother—you'll excuse me?'

She rose from the table with tremendous dignity which was immediately shattered by the marmalade pot which she unwittingly caught in her sleeve as she stood up. It crashed to the floor where it disintegrated into a dreadful mess of broken glass and stickiness. The Baron got to his feet and walked, without haste, round the table to join her. He stared at the floor for several moments and said at length: 'Ah, well—it's not blood, is it? And since it's my turn to show—er—friendship, I'll clear it up.' He gave her a little push in the direction of the door. 'Go on, girl, before I change my mind.'

Sappha murmured something, she had no idea what, and ran upstairs where she was kept far too busy to give the ridiculous episode another thought.

Uncle John and Mr MacCombie arrived together, both in excellent spirits and disposed to sit over their coffee, telling each other dishonest fishing stories, to the intense annoyance of Sappha who could see her patient becoming more and more nervous as each minute passed, and the obvious amusement of Rolf, who, she felt, should have made some effort to hurry them up. But when the examination finally took place, it was surprisingly short after all. The Baroness had answered their questions in a calm voice, and Sappha, even more calm, because years in hospital had trained her to a calm which allowed of no other feeling, gave her own brief, sensible replies to the more complicated questions they put to her. Finally, Uncle John said: 'Well now, shall we have Rolf back again?' and had looked at Sappha, who went down to the study where he was sitting with the minister and asked him politely if he would kindly come upstairs. He accompanied her back to his mother's room with scarcely a word and went to stand by the window, shutting out so much of the grey morning light that Sappha had leaned forward and switched the little rose-coloured lamp on. From its place on the bed side table it shed a becoming glow over the Baroness and made the room suddenly a cheerful place. Uncle John beamed at everyone and then spoke to his patient.

'Well, Baroness, we consider you fit to return home at

last. No doubt Rolf will make all the arrangements, his plans are already made, I know—it's merely a question of putting them into action.'

The Baroness had gone a little pale. 'You mean I'm actually going home? I'm better?'

He nodded. 'Yes to both, but not, I must add, quite well. Several more weeks of inactivity while your leg fracture heals completely—and still pills to take, I'm afraid, and one or two small tiresome things, but I fancy the time will pass quickly enough?'

The Baroness looked across the room at her son. 'Rolf, have you really arranged for me to go home—I mean soon—today? No, not today, for I've nothing packed. Tomorrow, then?'

He crossed the room and sat down beside her and took her hands in his.

'Darling, I'm going back home today, within an hour or so, I'm afraid. I'll come back in two days' time for you. You'll have to travel by ambulance and plane to Schipol, but that's all more or less arranged.'

She smiled at him. 'What an impatient old woman I am! That will be lovely, dear.' She hesitated. 'Have you arranged for someone to look after me?'

He didn't reply but looked at Mr Devenish who was standing before the fire warming himself, but now he advanced a few steps towards the bed.

'As to that, Baroness, it seems to me that the best thing is for Sappha to accompany you for a week or so.' He transferred his gaze to his niece and smiled at her gently.

Sappha had been standing quietly a little way from the others. She gave a small startled sound and jumped visibly. She had been taken completely by surprise, for never once during the Baroness's frequent musings concerning her return had it been suggested that Sappha should return with her, nor by the merest hint had either of the doctors disclosed their views, and she couldn't believe that Uncle John had spoken on the spur of the moment. She studied his face now; it looked much as usual, kind and wise, middle-aged and a shade pompous. Mr MacCombie looked much the same. The Baroness was looking at her hopefully and Rolf—Rolf was smiling. She knew all at once that he had arranged it all, and having arranged it, was confident that he was going to get his own way, and a pity of it was that she could see no way of preventing him. It would be like slapping a happy child in the face to tell the Baroness that she didn't want to go to Dokkum, besides, she had to admit to herself, she did. She wanted very much to see Rolf's home and most of all, a lot more of Rolf.

She said in a voice devoid of all expression: 'If the Baroness would like that, I am quite willing to go with her,' and was rewarded by the look of relief and delight on her patient's face. She couldn't resist glancing at the Baron too, but his back was towards the company because he was looking out of the window, for all the world as though he had no interest in what was being said. Now however he turned round again and said in a coolly pleasant voice:

'I shall be going away for ten days immediately after we return to Dokkum.' His look was as cool as his voice had been and Sappha at once took exception to them both; obviously he was under the impression that this was what she wanted. That she had never given him reason to suppose otherwise was something she chose to forget. She said a little tartly: 'I daresay we shall manage very well,' and was about to enlarge upon this when the Baroness interrupted her. 'Sappha, you really do want to come? I wanted to tell you before this—even a hint, so that you wouldn't be unprepared, but Rolf...'

Sappha overcame a desire to look at the Baron; doubtless he was smiling in triumph over his easy victory, instead she smiled nicely at the Baroness. 'I shall like it,' she said cheerfully. 'For one thing I'll be able to see you on your feet again before I leave you, and I've never been to Holland.'

Mr Devenish coughed. 'Well, now, that's all nicely set-

tled, is it not? I felt sure that you would agree to go, my
dear. I think perhaps you should have a little talk with Rolf
presently in order to settle details.' He gave another little
cough. 'If you should worry about your passport, there is
no need. I had occasion to telephone your mother a day or
so ago and I suggested then that she should post it to you—
just in case you may need it—you should receive it by
tomorrow, I imagine.'

Sappha said, 'Yes, thank you, Uncle John,' which wasn't
at all what she would have liked to have said, but it would
be hardly fair to shock the company with the explosive
words which she longed to utter. She cast the Baron a sear-
ing look, for she had no doubt at all that it was he who had
thought of that too. He met it with a blandness which in
no way diminished the look of satisfaction upon his face.

They had their little talk later in the morning. Sappha
followed the Baron downstairs to Mr MacFee's study, feeling light-headed; a sensation possibly due to the champagne
Rolf had produced for the company to drink his mother's
health; any other reason she chose to ignore. She swept
past Rolf into the pleasant, shabby room and sat herself
down on the same uncomfortable chair against the wall
while he closed the door and went to lean against the table.

'Do unburden yourself,' he invited silkily. 'You've been
swallowing back fiery words all the morning; much better
to get them off your chest—besides, bad temper is so bad
for the looks.'

Sappha's delightful bosom swelled with rage; she looked
thunderous. It was a pity that all she could manage to say
was 'Well…!'

He said to infuriate her still more: 'Oh, dear—it's worse
than I had imagined—you're actually bereft of words. A
pity, for you're worth watching when you're in a temper.'
He frowned with sudden fierceness. 'I've no intention of
apologising, you know. Certainly I arranged everything,
why should I not? You are the obvious person to return
with Mother, and as I was at pains to tell you, I go away

the day following our return home, so you'll not need to conceal your dislike of me—and you'll be no further from Glover than you are now, so don't try and use that as an argument.'

He got up and wandered over to the window and presently said in a quite different voice: 'I had hoped that we could have achieved a more friendly footing—it seemed once or twice...'

Sappha's cheeks took on a fine glow; perhaps this was her chance to tell him that she didn't dislike him any more. She began with a hopeless incoherence: 'I—I...but I...it's not...' to be stopped by his terse:

'All right, you've no need to say anything, but at least let us be honest with each other,' so that she subsided, for what was the good of saying anything if he didn't want to know anyway? And the moment was past now, for he turned back from the window and went to sit at the desk, looking so very like his senior colleagues upstairs, that she straightened up in her chair just as she would have for their instructions.

He said now in a quiet voice: 'As regards the journey back to Dokkum, will you have Mother ready to leave in two days' time, directly after lunch. An ambulance will take you both to Inverness—I shall be driving the Land Rover and will meet you at the airport. We shall spend the night in London and fly to Schipol the following day. We shall be driving from there.' He paused, waiting for her comments, and when she said nothing, continued: 'Your mother lives in London at present, I believe—please make any arrangements you like to see her while we are there—you can talk that over with my mother if you will.'

He stood up slowly and came and stood in front of her so that she was forced to stretch her neck in order to look up into his face.

'I hope you will be happy with us,' he said formally. 'I'm sure that Tonia will be delighted to know that you are coming.'

Sappha got to her feet, for she could see that the interview was over. She replied woodenly: 'I shall be quite happy, thank you,' and walked to the door. He was ahead of her though, holding the door shut with one hand. It was a large, strong hand, it would be hopeless and rather silly to try and wrest the doorknob from him, she put her own hands behind her back and stood waiting, her eyes fixed on his tie.

When he said gently 'Sappha,' she dragged her eyes away and looked at his face. His eyes looked very dark and she thought she had caught a gleam in them before he dropped the lids so that she couldn't see clearly any more. His voice came mildly. 'We shan't be seeing a great deal of each other, and that for only a few more weeks. Do you suppose we might—er—conceal our true feelings for that time? I promise I'll not say a word or do anything to ruffle you.'

He smiled, a smile of such charm and warmth that she caught her breath and clenched her hands tightly behind her. It was a pity that she couldn't tell him how she felt and how silly she had been over Andrew, who now seemed like a misty nobody not worth remembering. She sought hastily for the right thing to say. 'Yes—that is a sensible thing to do,' she agreed in a polite voice. 'I'll—I'll try very hard...' and stopped because his eyebrows had arched themselves so violently that he looked like a satyr once more. At any moment he would laugh; he did no such thing, merely opened the door.

She didn't see him again, and he left again at teatime. The house seemed hollow without him and she found herself on the verge of ridiculous tears because he wasn't there. When she settled a jubilant baroness for the night, she retired to her own room on the pretext of writing letters and sat huddled by the fire, thinking about Rolf, which got her nowhere at all. She undressed slowly and had a bath and got into bed, where she forced herself to stop thinking about a nebulous future which wasn't going to happen anyway and concentrate on the weeks immediately ahead of her. She supposed that she would be in Holland for a month at least, although nobody had been prepared to say. All the same, it would take at least that time to get the Baroness walking with a stick. She probably wouldn't see much of Rolf during that time—had he not said that he would be away and even when he was home, his work would occupy a great deal of each day and she didn't suppose that she would be invited to join in the family's social activities. It was at this point that she realised that she could be as friendly as she wished towards Rolf; it wouldn't matter, he would merely suppose that she was fulfilling her part of their bargain. She chuckled at the idea and then burst into tears.

She went to see Gloria the next day while the Baroness, happily exhausted after a morning of planning and packing, took a nap after her lunch. Sappha, in her tweed suit and a thick sweater with a scarf tied over her hair, walked down to the harbour. It was a cold day under the great puffed-up clouds flying before the wind and she shivered as she stood looking at the grey water. She would have to telephone her mother to bring her some thicker clothing when they got to London. She shivered—again for quite a different reason as she gazed at the causeway, wondering for the hundredth time how she ever managed to scramble its treacherous length. She looked away hastily, knowing that she would face worse than its slippery danger if Rolf needed her. She wondered if Mrs MacTadd was home yet—there was a wisp of smoke from the croft, torn away by the wind as it emerged from its chimneypot. She would have to ask Gloria.

She retraced her steps to her friend's cottage and thumped with the knocker on its stout door before going inside. Gloria was just back from her visits and came out of the surgery as she entered. 'Hullo,' she said, 'I guessed you'd come—be a dear and make some tea while I change.'

She went up the narrow stairs leading from the sitting

room, still talking. 'I hear you're going the day after to-morrow—Rolf popped in yesterday on his way over to the MacTadds' place.'

Sappha digested this piece of information. 'Is Mrs MacTadd back?'

'Yes—two days ago—didn't have a chance to tell you, but I guessed Rolf would. I thought you might have gone over with him, but he used the causeway and I expect he remembered how you felt about that.' She came tearing downstairs again, wearing a wool trouser suit. 'Oh, lord, it's cold,' she observed, and pulled the chairs close to the fire. 'I hope you've got fur-lined undies, Sappha—it'll be even colder in Dokkum, I should think. Aren't you excited? Weren't you surprised?'

Sappha put the tea tray down, let in the cat from the tiny back garden and sat down again. 'Yes,' she said dryly, 'I was. Everyone seemed to know about it but me.'

Gloria poured the tea. 'Do you mean to say that no one told you that Rolf had arranged for you to go?'

'Yes,' Sappha bent to stroke the cat so that she didn't have to look at her companion.

'I suppose he was afraid that you might say no—after all, he is interfering with your love life, isn't he? I mean, Andrew might not like it—I know you've given him up, but if he hears about it it might make him interested again, you know what men are. But Rolf doesn't know you've given Andrew up, does he?' She frowned thoughtfully. 'I think you should tell him.'

'Why?' Sappha wanted to know. 'It wouldn't make the faintest difference—he has no interest in my private life.'

Gloria gave her a sharp look and said 'Um?' in a non-committal way and helped herself to a bun. 'I'm coming your way tomorrow to say goodbye to the Baroness—will that be OK? I shall miss her, though I expect she'll be back before long for a visit.'

'When are you going to get married?' asked Sappha. 'You might not be here.'

Gloria went a faint, happy pink. 'Well, yes—we thought we might have the wedding just before Christmas. A terrible time of the year. I shall be blue with cold, but Hamish says he doesn't care if I am. I wonder where you will be, Sappha—you will come if you can, won't you? Where do you plan to go next?'

'I don't know,' Sappha replied thoughtfully, 'I shall have left the Baroness by then, don't you think? I—I suppose I'll get a job in a hospital. I think I'd like to stay in Scotland, I love it here even though it's miles from home. Mother can come up for a holiday and I'd go home for a week or two first.'

Gloria needed. 'Sounds all right. How are you going tomorrow? The village doesn't seem too sure.'

Sappha laughed and told her: 'You know, the more I think about it the more scared I become—I can't speak a word of Dutch and it sounds complete nonsense when I hear it. And I don't know what clothes to take.'

'Everything warm you can lay your hands on,' said Gloria practically, 'and some pretty things too—though I'm sure you've got masses of those. From what I hear the van Duyrens' life is a lot more social than it is here.'

'Maybe, but I'm the nurse, remember?' Sappha frowned in thought. 'I'm going to telephone Mother this evening. Dr van Duyren suggested that I might be able to see her in London. I must get her to bring me a thick coat and perhaps a couple of dresses.'

Gloria said quickly: 'Why do you call Rolf...' then changed her mind and said instead: 'Something long, I should think. What have you got?'

They spent a pleasant few minutes discussing clothes until Sappha saw the time and jumped to her feet. 'I must fly! The Baroness is so thrilled and excited that she's quite capable of doing something silly like trying to walk. See you tomorrow—why not come to tea? You know Mrs MacFee loves you to call in.'

She bundled herself into her jacket and scarf, said a hasty goodbye and hurried back to the house.

She found her patient just awakened from a refreshing nap and full of plans for the future. It amused Sappha a little that the Baroness had given no more than a passing thought to the actual journey; Rolf had told her that he would arrange everything and it seemed she saw no reason to doubt him. Even when he telephoned later in the evening, her talk was all of seeing her various children again and no word was said about the journey. Sappha did her own telephoning later that evening, only to remember at the last minute that she had no idea where they were to spend the night. She had been stupid not to ask Rolf, and the Baroness, of course, had no idea. She arranged with her mother to telephone the next morning before they left—surely Rolf would be with them by then, and she could ask.

She packed the next morning, completed her patient's packing too and then went for a final walk through Dialach, saying goodbye to the friends she had made there. She would have liked to have taken a run in the Mini, but it had gone that morning—perhaps she had been silly to allow Rolf to arrange for it to be sent back to her home—it only meant that when she returned to England she would have to go and fetch it and drive all the way up again—still, she would probably have her mother with her and it didn't really matter. She walked to the edge of the causeway and stood staring along it. She would have liked to have said goodbye to Mrs MacTadd, but she knew that she couldn't possibly cross the causeway on her own and there wasn't a boat in sight. She turned her back on it and fought her way against the wind, suddenly very sad at leaving.

But she wasn't able to indulge her unhappy thoughts for long, for Gloria was at the Manse when she returned and they all had tea in the baroness's bedroom while Gloria examined over the gorgeous nighties the Baroness had given her. It was only when Meg came up to say that the minister was wanted on the telephone that the party broke up, and Gloria, clasping her present, made her final good-byes. Sappha went to the front door with her; she was going to miss Gloria, she was gay and contented and happy—above all happy. She watched her get into her elderly Morris and nodded vigorously when Gloria shouted: 'See you at the wedding!' and, with a terrible grinding of gears, drove away.

There wasn't much to do that evening, for the MacFees spent a great part of it in the Baroness's room, making cheerful plans about future visits and remembering fresh messages every few minutes for the Baroness's family. It was late when they finally left Sappha to settle her patient for the night, and later still when she got to bed herself. She wakened early, and because she was far too restless to lie in bed and wait for Meg to call her, she got up and pottered around her room. The Baroness was still asleep; Sappha hoped she would stay so for an hour or so yet, for the day would be long and tiring. She opened her door and tiptoed downstairs, made tea and sat by the stove and drank it, then presently decided that she might as well go upstairs again and get dressed. She had her foot on the bottom step of the stairs when there was a movement on the landing above and she looked to see the Baron, in a dressing gown of a startling splendour, coming downstairs two at a time. She stepped back hastily, fearful of being run down, but he stopped just short of her and said pleasantly: 'Hullo—you have no idea how startled you look.'

Sappha closed her open mouth. 'I am startled,' she said reasonably. 'I didn't know you were in the house.'

He sat down on the stairs, reached up a long arm and swept her down to sit beside him. 'No, neither did you,' he remarked cheerfully. 'I remember now I asked Mr MacFee not to mention that I was coming, Mother might not have slept.'

Sappha said of course, she wouldn't have slept either, but that was something he didn't need to know. She went on sedately: 'Did you have a good journey?' and tried, without success, to ignore the arm he had flung around her shoulders.

'Yes, thanks. I slept—I mostly do, you know.' She thought with sudden pity that he hadn't had much time for sleep. 'What time did you get here?' she wanted to know, and when he told her: 'Did you have something to eat?'

She felt his hand tighten on her shoulder. 'Practical Sappha—yes, I did. Mrs MacFee, bless her, left some odds and ends out for me. I'm going to make some tea—have some?'

'I made some half an hour ago, but I'll make you some fresh before I go upstairs.'

He got up, pulling her with him. 'That'll be nice, only you must have another cup with me. It's not good to drink alone.'

Sappha laughed. 'You're being ridiculous, that means strong drink.'

He opened the kitchen door. 'But I like my tea strong,' he protested as he went to fill the kettle. It was while they were drinking their tea that she remembered about meeting her mother. She told him and he said easily: 'Telephone her as soon as you like—we'll be staying at the Savoy.' He paused to stare at her. 'What's the matter? Don't you care for the place?'

Sappha shook her head and said rather faintly: 'How should I know? I've never been there, only looked at it from the outside.'

'It's comfortable,' he went on carelessly. 'I've got rooms overlooking the river. There'll be an abulance to take you there from the airport.' He looked at his watch. 'Seven o'clock, will your mother be awake?'

Sappha thought. 'Yes, she always gets up early, and her sister—my aunt, you know—sleeps like a log and never hears anything, so it wouldn't matter.'

He stood up and caught her by the hand. 'Good, we'll telephone now.'

She found herself in the study, obediently telling him the number of her aunt's flat while he dialled it. She thought he would have gone away by then, but he sat himself on the side of the desk, quite obviously intent on hearing every word she uttered. She said cautiously: 'Mother? About tomorrow—shall I come to Aunt Caro's or will you?' but got no further, for the simple reason that Rolf had taken the receiver out of her hand, giving her a smile which made it impossible for her to do anything at all. He said quietly: 'Mrs Devenish, this is Rolf van Duyren. I wonder if you could manage to dine with us tomorrow evening at the Savoy. You could bring whatever it is Sappha wants and have time to talk. You will? Good. I'll send a taxi for you at half past seven.'

He handed Sappha back the receiver, smiled again and went out of the room. She stood gaping stupidly after him while her mother's voice came thinly over the wire: 'Sappha—Sappha! Are you still there?'

She said, a little breathless still: 'Yes, Mother, I—I...'

Her mother's voice sounded soothing. 'There, now you don't have to worry about anything. I'll see you tomorrow evening, and darling, how do you feel?'

Sappha smiled at the receiver, knowing what her mother meant. 'It's done me a lot of good being up here. Goodbye, Mother dear.'

She replaced the receiver and went back to the kitchen. She might as well take a cup of tea up to her patient. There was no sign of Rolf, but when she got to the Baroness's room, he was there, building up the fire. He gave her a half smile, said 'See you later,' and disappeared.

The Baroness was dressed and ready in her chair by ten o'clock, so that when Rolf suggested to Sappha that she should go with him to see Mrs MacTadd, there was absolutely no reason why she shouldn't. It was a little warmer than it had been and although it drizzled the wind was almost gentle. She asked anxiously: 'By boat?' and when he said yes, went to get her raincoat and scarf, knowing that if he had decided to use the causeway she would have gone just the same.

'Do you know anything about boats?' Rolf asked as they left the jetty. She shook her head. 'Almost nothing—I think I'm a bit scared of them.'

'Probably, but only because you haven't had much to do with them. I must teach you how to handle one.'

She let this pass. Where, in heaven's name, was he intending to teach her, and when? She dismissed the remark as a meaningless civility and sat gingerly, watching him row.

She found the visit not altogether successful; from her point of view at any rate, for although it was nice to see Mrs MacTadd up and about again, and to admire the baby and talk to Ian, it brought back too vivid memories of the night they had worked together—there had been no question of dislike between them for those few busy hours and it had given her some idea of how pleasant it would be to be on permanent good terms with the Baron. It was true that for the moment at least, they were on the best of terms with each other, but only because he had suggested it, and she was reminded of how precarious those terms were when, on their way back, they called in to say goodbye to Mrs MacGregor, who wanted to know if Sappha had heard from her young man. She had said no and looked at him, longing to explain and quite unable to do so because, although his expression hadn't changed, she could sense his withdrawal from the lighthearted companionship they had achieved during the morning. They walked on up to the Manse, still talking in the friendliest fashion, but now it was like speaking lines in a play. She could hear her own voice becoming more and more stilted as they went along.

There was no opportunity to speak to him during their early lunch, nor during the subsequent bustle of their departure. Only at the last minute, as she was getting into the ambulance beside the Baroness, did he look as though he was going to speak to her, but he turned away and got into

the Land Rover without a word. She gave a final wave to
the MacFees and then occupied herself making her patient
comfortable for the first leg of their journey to Holland.

CHAPTER SIX

THE Savoy Hotel, viewed from the back window of the
ambulance which had brought them from the airport,
looked impressive. Sappha felt a faint prickle of excitement
as the ambulance driver opened the door and invited her to
get out. She did so, wishing that the Baron was there because she wasn't quite sure what she was supposed to do
next. Did she march through the foyer beside the stretcher,
or should she go to the desk first and discover the numbers
of their rooms, in which case, surely it would be better to
leave the Baroness in the comparative comfort of the ambulance while she did so. It was a pity that by the time she
had reached this conclusion, the stretcher had been lifted
out. She looked around, a little at a loss, and saw the Baron
advancing to meet them. He said in a businesslike voice:
'Hullo, come straight up, the lift's waiting.' He saw them
safely stowed into it and then disappeared again, leaving
them to be carried to the next floor. Sappha didn't see him
again for twenty minutes or so, by which time she had her
patient sitting comfortably in an armchair by the fire while
she unpacked her night things. Her own room was next
door, though she had had no time to inspect it, and she had
had a glimpse of another room leading from the Baroness's,
where presumably Rolf was, for she had heard him talking
to the ambulance men. Presently, when she had got the
Baroness comfortably settled, she would take a look round:
in the meantime, it was time for her patient's pills.

The Baroness, who had enjoyed a nap in the ambulance
was gently talkative. 'A pleasant journey, was it not, Sappha?' she commented happily. 'I don't care for flying, but

I must admit it is far less fatiguing, and we have only a short flight tomorrow.'

'How long does it take from Schipol to Dokkum, Baroness?' asked Sappha, and was very little the wiser when that lady replied vaguely:

'Well, dear, it's all according to how fast Rolf travels and which car he will be driving.'

Sappha, biting back an enquiry as to what sort of cars Rolf usually drove, hoped that it wouldn't be a Land Rover. She knew there was a Mini because Antonia had once mentioned it, but that would be equally impossible—probably he had something more sober in the garage. She would have to wait and see. She opened the Baroness's leather beauty case and began to lay its fragrant contents on the massive dressing table. 'I don't know what time we're having dinner,' she said cheerfully, 'but would you like anything now?'

'A glass of sherry,' said the Baron's voice from the door. 'It will help the pills down. Tio Pepe, I think, chilled. You'll join us of course, Sappha.'

He gave the order and went to sit by his mother, and Sappha, pottering busily to and fro and aware that he was watching her, thought crossly that she had had no time to do anything to her hair, which was probably hanging in wisps. She tried to remember when she had put on the last lot of lipstick—it must have been hours ago, probably her nose was shining too. Her ruminations were interrupted by Rolf saying:

'You look as though you have stepped straight out of a bandbox, whatever that is, Sappha. However do you do it? And Mother looks as fresh as a daisy too.'

His remark caused Sappha to drop a sponge in a fluster and pick it up again with great clumsiness. She mumbled: 'Oh, I don't know—you can't be looking very closely,' and was glad when the sherry arrived at that moment and saved her from uttering any more feeble commonplaces.

The room next door turned out to be a sitting room,

which opened in its turn into Rolf's room and another bathroom. Sappha thought it rather an expensive way of spending the night, and some of her feelings must have shown
on her face, for Rolf said: 'I thought it would be pleasant
for Mother to dine with us,' and she agreed faintly, still
doing sums in her head. If he chose to throw his money
around it was none of her business; besides, he had spoken
with a tinge of arrogance, just sufficient to remind her that
he was a baron and a rich one. He went on:

'I daresay you think me extravagant,' in a voice which
implied that he couldn't have cared less what she thought,
so that she remained prudently silent, merely contriving to
look so meek that he burst out laughing and the Baroness
said in her light voice:

'Don't take any notice of Rolf, my dear, he's a dreadful
tease, as you've no doubt discovered.'

He went away presently, leaving her to change her patient's warm woollen dressing gown for a more glamorous
one of blue quilted silk with ruffles at its neck and wrists.
While they were busy with this task she remarked: 'I think
when you get home you shall start dressing each day. It'll
be a splendid exercise for you and you'll feel much better
for it, too.' This remark led, not unnaturally, to their discussing clothes until the Baroness said: 'Do go and have
half an hour to yourself, Sappha—did you bring anything
to change into? Though you look pretty enough…'

Sappha looked down at her tweed suit—the one she had
when she had met the Baron for the first time—and wondered why it was that nothing that had happened before
their meeting seemed to matter any more. 'I put in the dress
I bought in Inverness,' she said slowly.

'Wear it,' commanded the Baroness instantly. 'I've only
seen it in its box—besides, you can show it to your mother.'

Sappha nodded. It seemed a good reason for wearing it,
and she had been wanting one. She went presently to her
own equally luxurious room where she did things to her
face and hair and put on the pink angora. It looked terrific

even in her own hypercritical eyes. Even in the eyes of such a man as the Baron, whom she suspected of having a connoisseur's judgement in such matters, she might pass muster. She went back to the Baroness to receive a sufficiently flattering comment upon her appearance as to bring a pretty colour to her cheeks, which was still there when the Baron entered the room a few minutes later. It was a pity that he entirely failed to notice that she had the frock on—indeed, it needed prompting on his mother's part to make him aware that Sappha was in the room at all—or so it seemed to her—a slight exaggeration, she admitted later, for he had nodded at her briefly as he came in. Which, when she came to think about it, made it all much worse. However, when his mother pointed out to him that he himself had approved of the dress in Inverness, he said pleasantly enough: 'Ah, yes—very nice.' With which very masculine remark she was forced to be satisfied.

The Baroness had barely been made comfortable in the sitting room when Sappha's mother arrived. Sappha kissed her warmly, performed the introductions with unaffected grace, and went away with her mother's coat. When she returned it was to find her mother sitting by the Baroness while Rolf poured the drinks. Sappha paused in the doorway for a moment, watching her mother with a little smile. Mrs Devenish was still a very pretty woman despite her grey hair and the laughter wrinkles round her eyes. She looked up now, smiled at Sappha and said gaily:

'How well you look, Sappha dear. Scotland agreed with you,' and Sappha said yes that it had, aware that her mother was studying her to see if she had recovered from Andrew. She hadn't told her about his visit, she didn't think she would, not at present. She went and sat down on the other side of the Baroness and asked: 'Did you bring my things, Mother?'

Mrs Devenish took the glass Rolf offered her and smiled at him before she replied. 'Yes, darling—I gave the case to someone downstairs who said he'd bring it up.' She turned to the Baroness, remarking cheerfully:

'You know, Baroness, I think one of the luxuries I enjoy most is giving someone something to carry when I am quite capable of carrying it myself.' And the Baroness, who had probably never carried anything heavier than her handbag in her sheltered life, agreed fervently, which led, inevitably, to a pleasant discussion on the habits and ways of their own generation. The two ladies became entirely engrossed in the fascinating subject and after a few minutes, Rolf got up and went to sit by Sappha. He said quietly: 'Tell me about the journey. Did you have all you wanted—were you comfortable?'

Sappha was glad of his prosaic questions, for in the answering of them in her most matter-of-fact manner, her pulse rate, which had doubled at his approach, settled down to near normal. She asked a few questions of her own concerning the journey the following day and he answered her with lazy good humour, coupled with a twinkling eye which made her feel that she was being unnecessarily fussy. Presently she fell silent, looking into the glass she held between her hands, and when he took it from her she folded her hands together and looked at them instead. He said, half laughing: 'Our mothers, at least, have no need to pretend—they appear to be fast friends already.'

Which was true enough, for the two elder members of the party were so absorbed in conversation that they had apparently forgotten their companions. Sappha lifted her eyes long enough to note this fact and then allowed herself to look at Rolf. She wasn't normally a shy young woman; it was quite ridiculous that she couldn't bring herself to behave naturally when she was with him. He wasn't looking at her now, but eased himself more comfortably into his chair. 'What are you going to do when you come back to England?' he wanted to know.

She gave the question her serious attention, just as

though it hadn't been on her mind for days past. She said at length: 'I haven't quite made up my mind—it depends...'

He said smoothly: 'Upon Andrew? Of course. Did you get a reply to the letter I posted for you?'

Sappha stared round the spacious room, seeking inspiration from the various articles of furniture. If she said no, he might ask why not, and she would have to make up some cock-and-bull story or tell him the truth. She didn't fancy doing either. She said nothing at all and merely tightened her lips when he said mockingly: 'Put in my place, am I?' and then with a sudden change of tone: 'I've ruffled your feelings, and I said I wouldn't—I beg your pardon. Let us enjoy a calming talk about something impersonal to us both. Ah, yes, I have it—I will tell you the history of Dokkum.'

Under her bewildered eyes he discoursed at some length, so that her ears rang with a great many outlandish names and a selection of dates. The doctor knew his history well and seemed intent upon airing it, when he broke off suddenly and said: 'You're not listening—I thought you were an intelligent woman, thirsty for information...' She stifled a giggle. 'I think I'd rather quarrel,' she said weakly, and broke into a laugh when he replied instantly: 'Good—so would I. What a pity we have no time to do so. Our parents, unless I mistake, are wanting their dinner.'

During dinner Sappha said no more than a dozen words to Rolf. Immediately they were seated at table, the Baroness engaged her in conversation, leaving her mother to get better acquainted with her host—something, Sappha was quick to notice, which that lady achieved in a remarkably short space of time. She loved her mother dearly, but with one ear strained to hear their conversation, while giving her attention to the Baroness, she was vexed to hear the illuminative replies the Baron was getting to his friendly but searching questions. She didn't feel that he really wanted to know that she had played in the school hockey team, nor that she had worn a brace on her teeth until she was twelve, still less that she had been Gold Medallist at Greggs'. She ate her way through a delicious meal, but the *Mousse de Sole au Champagne* and the *Fraises Romanoff* might just as well have been fish pie and bread and butter pudding for all the notice she took of them. It was possibly the Médoc followed by a splendid claret and topped off by the green Chartreuse with the coffee which caused the evening to become progressively enjoyable, so that by the time dinner was over, she joined in the general conversation with something like pleasure and presently found the opportunity to have a few words with her mother—casual words, it was true, because it was neither the time nor the place for anything else, and her mother, thank heaven, forbore from asking her any leading questions.

Mrs Devenish got up to go shortly after and Rolf got up too saying that he would be delighted to take her home, so that Sappha had no more opportunity to speak to her mother even if she had wanted to. She was left alone with her patient, who was more than ready for bed. Sappha wheeled the Baroness back to her own room and made short work of the evening chores.

'You won't need a sleeping pill tonight,' she said cheerfully. 'You're sleepy enough—if you wake in the night, ring your bell and I'll come and do something about it.' She smiled at the Baroness, who smiled back, looking very pretty and a little bit guileful. Sappha, while she took her pulse, studied her patient's face, and wondered why. When she removed the thermometer the Baroness said happily:

'What a delightful evening. I should like to meet your mother again—we have a great deal in common. We are both widows for a start, and she tells me that she enjoys painting too.' She cast Sappha a faintly reproachful look. 'You didn't tell me that your home was in the Cotswolds and that your mother was only staying in London.'

Sappha finished counting the pulse. She said good naturedly: 'Mother comes up for a change sometimes, but she would hate to live here. We live near Cheltenham; she can go there to shop and take the car—she wouldn't dare do that in London.'

The Baroness shuddered. 'So she was telling me. I should like to invite her to visit us—you think she might? When I'm recovered from this wretched illness, of course.'

'I should think she would love to.' Sappha tucked the sheet in firmly and switched off all but one small bedside lamp and said goodnight in her kind voice, for she could see that the Baroness was disposed to chat, and there was more travelling to do the following day. She went to the door. 'I'll leave it open,' she said with her hand on the knob, 'and come in again just before I go to bed.'

She had gone through the door when her patient called her back.

'Sappha,' she said urgently, 'you will wait up for Rolf, won't you, just in case he wants to tell you something or give you a message from your mother.'

Sappha stood in the doorway and thought about it. 'Well,' she said at length, 'I hadn't intended to, but if you wish me...'

'Oh, I do—please, Sappha. I'm sure he won't be long.'

Sappha said: 'Very well, Baroness,' and walked back into the sitting room, where she chose a comfortable chair, picked up a magazine thoughtfully provided by the management and began to read. She read for several minutes without being in the least aware of what she was reading about. She wondered how long the Baron would be and if he would be disposed to talk—she rather hoped so; the wine had made her a little reckless.

He came ten minutes later, casting his coat down on a chair as he entered and exclaiming with casual surprise: 'What, still up? Surely you should be in bed by now—tomorrow will be a long day.'

Sappha got to her feet. The effects of the wine, which quite plainly had had no effect upon him, were wearing off. Just for a little while they had given her the illusion that anything might be possible. She said quietly: 'Your mother asked me to stay up in case there was anything you wanted to tell me about tomorrow.' She started for the door and was glad that he couldn't see her face when he said with a trace of impatience: 'But we have already been over that, have we not? You should have told her so and gone to bed.'

She had reached the door and paused long enough to say in a smouldering voice: 'So I should, but I'm afraid I haven't mastered your technique of doing what you wish without regard to other people's feelings.'

Having delivered this parting shot, she went out of the room, closing the door with a snap behind her.

She had been in bed an hour or more, mulling over the evening when she heard a movement in her patient's room and was on the point of investigating it when Rolf, with a perfunctory knock on the half-open door, came in. She tugged instinctively at the bedcovers and heard him chuckle as he sat down on the end of the bed. He said softly: 'Don't worry—it's too dark for me to see anything.'

Sappha let this pass. She said urgently: 'What's the matter?'

'Nothing—Mother's asleep. I've come to apologise for being so arbitrary just now. You see, I didn't expect you to be there.'

She said 'Oh?' in a polite little voice, wondering what difference that could possibly make. She added: 'That's quite all right. Thank you for a pleasant evening. I'm sure my mother enjoyed herself.'

He moved and she felt the mattress sag a little under his weight.

'A delightful person,' he remarked. 'I look forward to seeing her again.'

She couldn't see his face clearly; it was impossible to know if he meant it or whether he was just being polite, probably the latter.

'She's marvellous,' she whispered, 'but then your mother is too.'

He agreed. 'How unpredictable life is,' he went on, showing no signs of going away. 'Our mothers are two splendid women who liked each other on sight, and yet you and I don't get on very well—those were, I believe, your words.'

He got up and the mattress sprang back with a thankful twang. 'By the way, I have been most thoughtless. I daresay you would have liked to see Glover—you could have done so easily and I should have thought of it. At least you can telephone him in the morning.'

He went soft-footed to the door and was gone; his good night reached her so faintly that she wasn't sure if she had heard it or not.

Sappha was up early, re-packing the things her mother had brought her and then, while the Baroness sipped her morning tea, packing her patient's things as well. She was rather dreading the day, partly because she wasn't sure what would be at the end of it. But the first part at least went without a hitch. The Baron had anticipated everything, so that she found herself sitting beside the Baroness in the plane with quite half the things she had been worrying about already dealt with by him with an assurance which she wholeheartedly envied. It was a pity it was such a cloudy morning, for she could see nothing of Holland as they approached its coast, and at Schipol she was occupied enough with her patient not to have time for more than a glimpse of the airport. She waited beside the Baroness's wheelchair while Rolf dealt with the Customs and luggage, feeling a little out of it because everyone was speaking Dutch, until Rolf had returned and caught sight of her face and said quickly: 'It's all a little strange, isn't it? I'm sorry you have to wait, but the car should be outside.'

It was neither a Land Rover nor a Mini, but a sleek, highly polished black Rolls-Royce. Sappha watched him lift his mother into its dove-grey interior, then got in to arrange the Baroness's various shawls and wraps and dispose cushions where they would do most good. This done, she looked at the Baron, leaning on the door watching her. He said without asking: 'No, you're coming in front with me.'

She slipped meekly into the luxurious seat beside his while he shut the door on her and walked round the car to get in his own seat, saying as he did so: 'All right, Mother, it won't be long now.'

The big car slid forward, slowly at first, and then as they joined the motorway into Amsterdam, the Baron put an elegantly shod foot down on the accelerator and overtook everything ahead of him. He drove, Sappha noted, with the same economy of movement as he operated and with the same easy confidence. She gave an unconscious sigh of pleasure and settled back to enjoy herself. It was a grey day, inclined to rain and giving promise of a wet evening ahead, but that didn't matter. She was pleasantly tired after a long morning of attending to the Baroness, who, because she was so excited, was inclined to be more demanding than usual. But now Sappha, turning round to see how her patient was faring, saw that she had closed her eyes. 'Asleep?' queried the Baron without taking his eyes off the road.

Sappha nodded. 'I think so—she must be tired, although she wouldn't want to admit that.'

'We'll keep her in bed for a couple of days, I think—there will be plenty to occupy her, and Antonia will be at home. She's bound to want to catch up on the running of the house and so on.' He slid past a string of cars. 'We're coming into Amsterdam—we shall take the road running around the city, cross the Ij and then go more or less straight up to Den Oever. There's a map in the pocket beside you, perhaps you would like to have a look.'

They travelled in silence for five minutes or so while Sappha picked out the route, mispronouncing the names of the towns most abominably and then struggling to get them right when he corrected her. She laid it aside shortly, however, to gaze at the outskirts of the city which she thought privately were a little dull. As though Rolf had read her thoughts, he said: 'Don't think this is the real Amsterdam—most of our cities are ringed round with modern flats and houses, but their hearts are still old and beautiful—you shall see for yourself one day.'

They were leaving Amsterdam behind. 'Do you always come this way,' she asked, 'you must know the road very well.'

He laughed. 'Indeed yes. This is the quickest way and the dullest, but I want to get Mother home. There is no reason why you shouldn't borrow the Mini and explore for yourself while you're over here.'

Sappha thanked him nicely, though it sounded dull on her own, but possibly Antonia would go with her and she might even make a few friends in Dokkum. It sounded rather as though she would have to rely on her own resources and she reminded herself once more that she was the nurse, primarily there to look after her patient, then forgot all about it in the pleasure of watching the barges chugging along a canal. Presently a succession of windmills came into view and the next half hour or so passed pleasantly enough while Rolf explained their various types and how they worked. Once or twice she had the suspicion that behind his placid face he was laughing at her; probably he found her company tedious. She felt suddenly out of patience with him and herself too and said a little sharply: 'You must find it tiring—explaining everything.'

'Bored?' his voice was silky.

'No,' she sounded snappish, 'of course not, it's all new to me, but you must have travelled this way a dozen times.'

'Hundreds, I imagine,' he amended, still silky. 'But we do misunderstand each other so frequently if we become too personal, don't we? Windmills seem a safe subject; you see, you don't know anything about them, so there is no fear of you disagreeing with me.'

She gave him a quick sidelong glance. Even in profile he was wearing his most satyr-like expression. It seemed a good idea to change the subject. She said hastily: 'I expect you're glad to have finished with your journeys to Dialach.'

'Yes—my partners have had rather more than their fair share of work during the last few months, and I have had to cancel meetings and committees.'

She asked a little dryly: 'What do you do when you're not working?' and was immediately sorry that she had put the question, for he answered suavely: 'I should have thought that you would have guessed. I date the prettiest girls I can find—one at a time, of course. We tear round the country, visiting one night spot after another and—er—living it up.'

Sappha gave a snort. 'What nonsense,' she said roundly. 'I don't believe a word of it.'

'No? I felt sure you would—isn't that the sort of thing you expect me to do?'

She went pink. 'Yes—no.' She shot him a frowning look and found him smiling again. 'It was my fault for asking.'

She waited to hear what he would have to say to that; instead he observed blandly: 'We shall be crossing over the Ijsselmeer by the famous Zeedijk. It is a remarkable engineering feat of which we are very proud.' He sounded like a schoolmaster, detached and controlled, and she gave a sudden splutter of laughter. 'Oh, we can't quarrel,' she begged. 'I simply can't—my mind's still full of windmills.'

He eased the car past a bus without decreasing speed. 'I'm relieved to hear it,' he said on a laugh, 'for now I come to think about it I can't remember much about the Zeedijk—I can't think of anything to quarrel about either, can you?'

Sappha took off her gloves and then put them on again, hardly aware of what she was doing. The conversation was getting them nowhere. Rolf said quietly: 'Let's start again, shall we? I'll try and give you some idea of what I think we should do about Mother.'

He had become remote again and impersonal, but nicely so, like a family doctor. She listened carefully to what he had to say and then asked: 'Who is in charge of the Baroness? One of your partners or someone from the hospital?'

'The hospital in Groningen. She will have to have some more X-rays taken in a couple of weeks. If I'm not around perhaps you'll drive her there. We have a gardener who takes Mother to the shops and so on, but he doesn't care to go to Groningen.'

Sappha wondered what sort of man the chauffeur might be; she didn't think she cared to go to Groningen either. She asked faintly: 'Not this car?'

'Good God, girl, no. A Rover 416—you're up to driving that.'

She said with dignity: 'Of course. What is that ahead of us?'

'The sluices of the Zeedijk. Is Mother still asleep?'

Sappha had looked several times, now she looked again. 'Yes. It would be nice if she slept for the rest of the journey.'

He slowed a little as they passed the sluices. 'Probably she will. We're on the Afsluitdijk now. The Ijsselmeer is on your right, the North Sea on your left, only you can't see it. Take a good look, because I intend to make up some time.'

The car responded to the touch of his foot and Sappha watched the needle of the speedometer swing round. They didn't seem to be travelling any faster, only the land on the further side was advancing towards them at a great rate. As they flashed past the monument Rolf observed: 'There's a splendid view from the top, but it's a poor day for sightseeing anyway. If you look hard, you can see both coasts.'

Sappha obediently turned and twisted and stared. The water looked cold and grey and empty. Only an occasional seagull, sitting on the sticks which marked the fishermen's nets, showed any sign of life. Scotland, she thought, had much more to offer, and was once more taken aback to hear Rolf say: 'You must be comparing this with Dialach, but wait until we are at our journey's end before you pass judgment. The scenery is different, but it has a charm all its own.'

They were on the mainland now, tearing past towns she would dearly have loved to stop and inspect. Franeker offered a tantalising glimpse of old houses and canals before they were once more in the open countryside. Though the afternoon was beginning to close in now, she could see farms, standing each with its complement of trees and fields and cows, lonely from one another. There were churches too—wherever she looked there were churches, and now and then a large square house, standing as lonely as the farms. She wondered who lived in them, and tried for the hundredth time to guess what the Baron's home would be like.

The Baroness woke up as they were going through Leeuwarden. Much refreshed, she embarked upon a description of the country around them, begging Sappha to look first left and then right at familiar landmarks, which in the early dusk were now almost impossible to see. She was glad when Rolf said: 'There's Dokkum ahead,' and turned off the main road into a street of modern houses, neat and orderly and a little dull, which, once they had crossed the railway, led in its turn to a narrow thoroughfare lined with old gabled houses which presently opened on to a cobbled road alongside water, running at right angles. Even in the half light Sappha could see the old houses on the opposite side, lining the water; she craned her neck to see more as they crossed a bridge, where they turned to the right and drove along by the water's edge before turning up one of the streets leading to the centre of the town.

She turned to speak to the Baroness and so missed the turn Rolf took down a narrow little street and over an even narrower bridge. They were on the road which circumvented the town now, with water on one side of them and walled gardens on the other. She was just in time to see a pair of wide-flung gates as they passed between them into the grounds of a house which she could see at the end of the curved drive, which was short, while as far as she could see, the grounds around them were of a moderate size, laid out with trees and shrubs and a smooth lawn. The house looked square and roomy with a gabled roof cut straight across at the top, so that it looked as though the builder had changed his mind before he had quite finished his work. Rolf had stopped the car before shallow steps leading to a heavy front door and as though this had been a signal, light blazed from the downstairs windows. Obedient to the Baron's invitation to alight, Sappha did so, removed the wraps and shawls from her patient and stood silently while Rolf lifted his mother from the car.

She had moved forward to help, but he had waved her back as an elderly man came down the steps, and after an exchange of greetings, lent his assistance, so that there was nothing more for her to do but follow the little procession into the house, across the hall, and up the broad staircase. She would have liked to look around her, but the Baron's speed, even with his mother in his arms, was such that she had only a glimpse of the black and white tiled floor, the ornate plaster ceiling and wall, the panelling, the heavy carved furniture and the vast number of portraits on the walls. The stairs led to a square landing, thickly carpeted and with a variety of doors and passages leading from it, while another, smaller staircase rose steeply from one corner.

One of the doors was open as they crossed the landing and Antonia stood holding it wide, so that they could go through. She said *'Moeder!'* in an excited little voice and then, rather to Sappha's surprise, stood quietly in a corner of the room until the Baroness had been sat in a high-backed chair by the open fire. Only then did she run across the room to fling herself into her mother's arms, breaking into excited speech as she did so. Even then, when Rolf said:

'Sappha's going to put Mother to bed, Tonia. We'll leave her to do so, shall we?' she went obediently to the door

with him. He flung a brotherly arm around her as they went
out. Before he closed the door he said casually to Sappha:
'Ring if you need help.'

How like a man, thought Sappha sourly, to walk off
without even telling her which door led to the bathroom.
She flung off her coat and hat, smiled at her patient and
said briskly: 'Bed, I think, don't you? I can manage your
chair, it's on castors.'

She prepared the bed, a vast one with an elaborate headboard of carved oak and a fringed counterpane of rose-
coloured brocaded velvet. Her patient, sitting against the
big square pillows, looked small and tired and very happy.
'A wash,' suggested Sappha, 'a pretty bedjacket, supper—
which I have no doubt will be something you fancy—and
then an early night.' She was going round the room as she
spoke, opening and shutting its several doors.

The Baroness laughed. 'Oh, you poor child! No one has
told you anything. What could Rolf have been thinking
of—or any of us for that matter? You must think us all
very unkind and thoughtless, but I'm afraid we are excited.
The bathroom's the next door on your right, Sappha, and
the door over there leads to your room. The other doors are
closets.'

Sappha had her hand on the bathroom door. She said
soothingly:

'Of course you haven't been unkind—I can imagine how
you feel and there's plenty of time for me to find my way
around. The thing is to make you comfortable.'

She plunged into the bathroom—a splendid apartment,
tiled in palest pink with a carpet of great depth and thick-
ness which exactly matched the green towels, and an array
of soaps, jars and bottles which merited a leisurely inspec-
tion. But her sharp eye had already discerned the jug and
basin standing ready; someone had been very thoughtful.
She rolled up the sleeves of her sweater and went to fill
the jug.

Half an hour later the Baroness was ready. Sappha, roll-

ing down her sleeves, asked: 'How do I let everyone know
you're ready, Baroness?'

Her patient waved a hand in the direction of the fireplace.
'There's a bellrope.'

It was a handsome affair of silk cord with a great tassel
at its end; a charming if old-fashioned method of summon-
ing anyone. Sappha gave it an experimental tug and waited
for something to happen. Almost immediately the door flew
open and Antonia came in, followed rather more quietly by
Rolf, who was followed in his turn by an elderly woman,
tall and angular, with a sharp nose and pale blue eyes, carrying a champagne bucket. She put this on a table, answered the Baroness's greeting with guarded but obvious
pleasure and went away again, casting a curious look at
Sappha as she did so. The room had come alive—Antonia
was getting glasses from a small walnut cabinet and talking
at the top of her voice while the Baron and his mother
carried on a calmer conversation which they constantly interrupted in order to answer her.

Just for the moment Sappha felt herself to be forgotten.
It seemed an excellent chance to go to her room and do
her hair and her face and perhaps unpack. She edged towards the door which she knew to be hers, her eyes on the
Baron's back. He had the champagne bottle in his hand;
she judged that he would be nicely occupied for a moment
or so. She had actually reached the door when he said without turning round: 'Where are you going? You must have
a drink.'

She opened the door and turned to face him.

'No, thank you,' she said pleasantly. 'I should like to
unpack.'

He took no notice of this. 'Has anyone shown you your
room? No, of course not—you can't have had a moment
to yourself since we arrived.' He smiled at her. 'I'm sorry.'

'It doesn't matter in the least—I don't need anyone to
show me my room—if you would be good enough to let

me know when you would like me back...!' Sappha smiled in her turn, went through the door and shut it quietly.

She walked straight to the window without bothering to look around her and stared out into the evening. She had no idea which way the room faced, but she could make out trees and a high wall and water gleaming fitfully beyond; it looked lonely and the sound of distant traffic seemed to make it more so. Presently she drew the curtains across; heavy silk damask curtains of muted pinks and blues which, when she turned to study the room, exactly matched the bedspread on the bed—it was smaller than the Baroness's but its headboard was just as elaborate. The room was smaller than her patient's too, but furnished with great taste. Sappha, examining everything, thought that the furniture was probably Hepplewhite. Having taken her fill of the furniture, she tried the doors. The first, by the bed, opened into a fitted cupboard which could have taken her entire wardrobe and still looked empty. The second door gave on to the landing, the third was the one she had entered by, the fourth and last opened on to a small bathroom, pastel blue this time, with neatly piled towels in various shades of pink and a bowl of soaps in the same pleasing colour; there were jars of bath salts too. Sappha lifted their lids and sniffed appreciatively, then kicked off her shoes and began to take down her hair.

Later, as she unpacked, she wondered if she had been a little childish to refuse Rolf's offer of the champagne; she hadn't meant to be rude, but she had felt out of it. It would be better when she had met the rest of the staff, then she would feel more at home. Rolf had said that he was going away—she wondered for how long; perhaps she wouldn't see him again before she went back to England, for she still didn't know how long she was to stay in Dokkum. A cold lump of unhappiness in her chest began to spread slowly all over her body so that she actually shivered. It was a relief when there was a knock at the door and Antonia came in. She said in her prettily accented English:

'Rolf has gone to see some patients—he'll be back soon, he said if you would come to Mother now she would like to explain the house to you.'

The Baroness, looking all the better for her champagne, greeted Sappha with a smile. 'Your room is comfortable, I hope, Sappha? You have all you want? When Rolf has time he will show you the house and introduce the staff to you. They have been with us for so long, we think of them as friends and we hope you will too.' She eyed Sappha with eyes which positively sparkled. 'And now we will have a little more champagne, I think, if you will pour it, Tonia, and remember, only half a glass for yourself—and now, I will try and tell you all you need to know.'

The Baron came in half an hour later and although he saw the glass still in Sappha's hand, he said nothing, although his eyebrows rose just enough for her to be aware that he had draw his own conclusions. She expected him to come out at any moment with some chilling remark about not wanting to drink with him, but all he said with businesslike friendliness was: 'If you've finished your drinks and chatter, how about coming downstairs and meeting the rest of us? You must see the house too, but I think that will be better in the morning. I don't leave until after lunch.'

The three of them went downstairs and Sappha tried to forget that he was going away, and answered Tonia's happy chatter in the same light tone, although Rolf remained silent until they reached the hall when he requested her to accompany him to the kitchen, where she met the tall thin woman, who turned out to be the housekeeper, and was called Annie; the elderly chauffeur-gardener, called Jan, she had already seen when they had arrived, a fresh-faced girl, who, Sappha thought, could only have been described as strapping and who had the peculiar name of Joke, and a small round woman with white hair and bright blue eyes, who, when they shook hands, said, 'Weel, noo, here's a bonnie lass,' in a soft Highland voice, and laughed at the surprise on Sappha's face. 'The young maister said not a word about me, I'll be bound, but dinna fash yesel', Miss Devenish, for ye can ask me ainything ye'll need to know.'

Sappha said happily: 'Oh, how marvellous—I was a little worried about the language, Mrs Burns.' She turned to the Baron beside them. 'You did say Mrs Burns?'

He nodded. 'Our cook and friend for a great many years—she will tell you about meals and trays and anything else you may wish to know. I'm afraid none of the others speak English, but I'm sure you will pick up a few words and Mrs Burns or Antonia can always help you.'

He turned towards the door. 'And now come upstairs.' Which Sappha did reluctantly, partly because she disliked being told to do anything in such a forthright fashion, and partly because she would have liked time to examine the kitchen, which appeared to be a most agreeable combination of the old-fashioned and the very modern. Back in the hall, she asked: 'Why didn't you tell me about Mrs Burns?'

'I thought it would be a pleasant surprise and might cheer you up at a time when you might be feeling lonely and uncertain, as I believe you are—am I right?'

Sappha said yes rather shortly because she hadn't realised that her feelings showed like that, but he didn't appear to see her cross look, but went on in the most civil voice imaginable: 'Come and have a drink, then you shall go and see about Mother's dinner.'

He led the way across the hall and into a large room with a high ceiling bearing a great deal of plasterwork. There were three windows, tall and narrow, each curtained and elaboratedly pelmeted with red velvet. The floor was of polished wood upon which was a fine carpet, dim with age but still of great beauty. The furniture was for the most part Regency with a number of high-backed armchairs covered in tapestry place. The walls were white-painted, picked out in gold and almost covered with large paintings. Sappha, walking slowly to the chair the Baron had indicated, thought it looked very like one of the rooms in an English

stately home, only this room was lived in—there were magazines strewn over the sofa table behind the chesterfield,
some knitting pushed into one corner of a chair, and a tabby
cat asleep in another. There were flowers everywhere and
by one of the armchairs there was a waste basket crammed
full with screwed-up paper and envelopes, while a pile of
unopened letters lay on the floor beside it. Without doubt
the Baron's chair, though he made no attempt to sit in it
but walked across to a small wall table saying blandly: 'Am
I to be snubbed if I offer you a glass of sherry? I was
disappointed in you, Sappha—we have managed to be quite
civil to each other for a day or so, I had thought we might
have kept it up until I go.'

She asked without thinking: 'Are you going for a very
long time? Will you not be back before I return to England?'

He gave her the sherry before he answered. 'Why do you
want to know? Can you not wait to start quarrelling again?'
His voice mocked her.

Sappha stared at her shoes. She said loudly: 'I wish I'd
never said that!' A remark which should have been explained, but apparently he needed none, for he said softly:
'Ah, I have been hoping that you would discover that for
yourself.'

She lifted her eyes from her shoes and looked at him
instead. He was staring down at her, the gleam in his eyes
made them seem blacker than ever before and he was smiling, and there was nothing of the satyr about his face at
all. It was unfair, she thought fiercely, that he had only to
smile like that for her heart to turn over and hammer against
her ribs and take her breath. She said uncertainly: 'I don't
know what you mean.'

He put down his glass. 'Oh, Sappha,' he said on a laugh,
'you're saying that because you've just remembered Andrew Glover. Well, I haven't forgotten him either, though
not perhaps for the same reason as you. I'll tell you now
that as far as I'm concerned Andrew doesn't exist.'

Sappha's eyes were riveted on his face for the simple reason that she was unable to take them away. A wave of delight surged through her; now she could at least explain that Andrew didn't exist for her either. Her mouth was open to say so when the door opened and Antonia came in.

She said gaily: 'Hullo there, you two. I've been with Mother. She wants you, please, Sappha, right away.'

Sappha went upstairs and dealt calmly with her patient, trying not to wonder too much what Rolf might have said if Antonia hadn't come in. She busied herself with the Baroness's dinner and presently went down to have her own in a dining room as splendid, in its own way, as the drawing room, where presently they went for coffee. Rolf and Antonia were amusing company, she could have stayed with them the whole evening, but she still had to settle the Baroness. When she got up the Baron rose too and opened the door and wished her goodnight in the formal tones of a polite host which chilled her to the bone. It was still early, she had expected to be asked to return to the drawing room, but apparently this was not to be expected of her, nor, it seemed, did he wish to talk to her. She went upstairs, the lovely glow of happiness inside her turning steadily colder as she remembered what the Baroness had said about her son—that he liked his own way, especially when it came to the conquest of a pretty girl. Presumably having added herself to his collection, he had lost an interest which could never have been very great anyway; he didn't like her enough.

CHAPTER SEVEN

SAPPHA didn't see Rolf until well after eleven o'clock. By then she had finished her morning's duties, dealt firmly but kindly with her patient's slight peevishness, due to the excitement of her homecoming, and persuaded her to stay in bed for the day in order to recover from the journey. She had gone downstairs to breakfast in a small room behind the dining room, cosily warm from the old-fashioned stove as well as the central heating which had been skilfully concealed around the house. The room overlooked the garden and was furnished with solid, comfortable Empire furniture and bright chintz curtains whose colours were echoed in the breakfast china. She had been joined after a few minutes by a rather sleepy Antonia, still in her dressing gown, who revived after her first cup of coffee and went on to make a splendid meal. She had dealt with ham, cheese and a variety of breads and was contemplating the black cherry jam and some rusks when she noticed Sappha's empty plate and exclaimed: 'Sappha, aren't you hungry? I don't believe you've eaten anything. Are you unhappy—is anything the matter?'

'No. nothing.' Sappha answered the last question first. 'I'm just not hungry.'

Antonia eyed her across the table. 'Does your Andrew know that you are here?' she wanted to know, 'and does he mind?'

Sappha ignored the first question. 'Why should he mind?' she asked in a matter-of-fact voice. 'I really must go back upstairs. I expect we'll see each other later,' and made her escape.

She was writing up her brief report when Rolf came in. He kissed his mother, enquired how she did and said to Sappha: 'Throw that out of the window, and come round the house. I haven't much time.'

She gave him a cold glance which he countered with a twinkle.

'I know,' he said equably before she could utter, 'I order you about shamefully and if only you had the time to think of a good excuse you would doubtless offer one. Never mind, I'll be gone in an hour or so and you'll have plenty of time to think up cutting replies to blast me.'

Sappha burst out laughing, suddenly happy again. 'You really are ridiculous—you behave just as if…'

'I'm bold—bad—unscrupulous? But of course, didn't you know? I try my utmost to annoy you.'

Sappha got to her feet, avoiding the Baroness's eye. 'I'm quite ready when you are, Doctor,' she said soberly, whereupon he gave a great bellow of laughter, caught her by the arm and walked her to the door, telling his mother, as they went, that he would return Sappha within the hour.

'We'll start at the top.' He still held her arm as they crossed the landing to the little staircase she had noticed when they had arrived, where he went ahead of her, her hand still held fast in his. The steps were steep and the stair narrow, but its woodwork was old and beautiful and shining with constant care. It opened on to another landing, only a little smaller than the one below, and like it, had two windows overlooking the grounds in the front of the house. There were four doors, two on each wall, and an open arch leading to a short passage facing the windows. The doors opened on to bedrooms, with tiny, beautifully appointed bathrooms between each pair. The bedrooms were furnished with the same care and luxury as those on the floor below and when Sappha exclaimed:

'Oh, how pretty they all are!' the Baron answered: 'We use them for guests—when my nephews and nieces come to stay, we put them up here—they can make as much noise as they like and they love being on their own.' He led her through the arch and opened another door. 'This used to be the schoolroom, we were banished up here to do our homework, and the girls came up here to sew and paint—there's a pleasant view.'

Sappha followed him to the window and stood looking at the well-kept garden below; beyond the wall she could see a glimpse of water.

'The town moat,' explained Rolf, 'and from the other side of the house we can just see the river Zijl—there's a gate at the bottom of the garden leading to the path running beside the moat—if you feel energetic enough you could walk round the entire town—it's very pleasant.'

'Yes,' said Sappha, not having heard a word, for he had put an arm around her shoulders and for the time being at any rate, she was unaware of anything else. But she heard him clearly when he said quietly:

'I think that you have changed your mind, Sappha,' and she knew that he was referring to her remarks about them not getting on well together. She didn't answer at once, because somewhere at the back of her mind an ugly voice was reminding her that probably he just wanted confirmation of his conquest. When she still hesitated he turned her round to face him and said with a kind of desperate patience:

'Oh, we disagree, don't we?—we always shall. I enjoy stirring up your temper to watch the splendour of your rage. But when we've not had the leisure to argue, haven't you noticed how well we fit? Could we not be friends, dear girl? Let's cry quits; bury the hatchet—so long as we are to be together.'

He put a finger under her chin so that she was forced to look up at him. His face was grave although his eyes gleamed. He bent his head and kissed her mouth gently. 'Kiss and be friends,' he said, 'isn't that an English saying? or if you prefer, *absit invidia*.'

Sappha, still shaken by his kiss said weakly: 'Oh, an absence of something or other...'

He laughed, still staring at her. 'Let there be no ill-will.' He took his hand away from her chin and put an arm around her shoulders again. 'Do you agree, Sappha?'

She nodded. He had said: 'So long as we are to be together,' remembering that made her sad, but she had to say something. 'Yes, all right—but you're going away...'

She shouldn't have asked that, for he said at once: 'Yes—will you miss me?'

Sappha saw the chance to rectify her mistake. She said matter-of-factly: 'Yes, of course, just as the rest of the household will miss you.'

He looked away from her, out of the window; presently he said mildly:

'You'll learn quite a lot about me while I'm away, and that will be a good thing.' He drew her away from the window and said, his voice brisk again: 'Come and see the rest of the house.'

The rooms on the landing below were large and furnished with a collection of antiques which nonetheless gave an air of comfort and homeliness. There were silver and china and magnificent paintings too—they were mostly small and delicate landscapes, miniature family portraits and several flower studies by Bosschaert. The last room they inspected was at the back of the house with three large windows all to itself. Its walls were white picked out with gilt, and the carpet was blue, an admirable foil for the damask pink of the curtains and bedspread on the wide bed; there were a pair of bergSres in the windows, also covered in the same brocade, with a small table between them—it was round and gilded and its top was of painted porcelain. Sappha went to examine it and Rolf followed her over to explain: 'It's Louis the Fifteenth—the top is Sèvres, made by Carlin—I don't much care for it, but a very long time ago an ancestor gave it to his bride when he brought her here, and here it has been ever since.'

Sappha put a gentle finger on its intricate gildings. 'That's such a nice story it would be heartless to move it. I expect she loved it and I daresay it's rare.'

'Very.' His voice was dry and she went pink. He would think her abysmally ignorant, the whole house was full of treasures and she had had to ask about nearly all of them. She wandered over to the dressing table—chinese lacquer, at least she knew that, but its date eluded her. She turned her back on it and said too loudly: 'I know almost nothing about antiques, our furniture at home is old, but it's not—not like these.' She waved an expressive arm which the Baron was quick to possess and hold.

'But you like it?' he said pleasantly. 'I wanted to know what you thought of my home.'

She said honestly: 'It's beautiful. It must be wonderful to live here day after day in the middle of it all—only I don't know enough about it.'

She was puzzled when he said: 'That doesn't matter in the least—not if you like it—and you do like it, don't you? Come downstairs.'

She had already seen the drawing room, now she wandered round it, looking her fill at its treasures; the bracket clock by Thomas Tompion on a shelf all to itself, a collection of enamelled watches under a glass-topped table; a cabinet of marquetry in which was displayed a row of engraved goblets; a carved wooden side table with an ormolu mounted Battersea enamel casket upon it. The dining room seemed almost severe after the drawing room's richness, although it had a fine collection of silver upon its carved oak sideboard.

'You've seen the breakfast room already,' Rolf said. 'There are some rather nice pen and ink drawings and a collection of pewter there.' He had his hand on a door which he now opened. 'This is my study—if patients come to the house, I see them here. I share a surgery in the town with my partners, of course.' As he spoke he ushered her into a comfortably sized room with a large cluttered desk and several comfortable chairs. The walls here were of panelled wood and the ceiling was elaborately plastered. The only pictures were some dark portraits of dead and gone van Duyrens; the women looked calmly at her from their heavy frames, the men, she was quick to see, displayed the same handsome dark looks as Rolf.

Rolf went before Sappha could get down to lunch. The Baroness, still a little crotchety, had delayed her so much that by the time she had reached the dining room he was on the point of leaving the table. She sat down and began on her soup, listening to his feet taking the stairs two at a time while she turned an attentive face to Antonia. It was only when her companion ceased speaking and looked at her enquiringly that she realised that she hadn't heard a word. Antonia looked at her kindly.

'I expect you're tired,' she said. 'Mother's a little cross, isn't she? What I said was, it's partly because her dog Leo isn't coming home until this afternoon—he's a peke and he's at the vet's having some teeth out. Rolf's dog is there too—he's an alsatian—he went too because Leo pines if Charlie's not with him.'

Sappha banished her thoughts of Rolf in order to consider this interesting piece of information. 'You mean to say,' she said with some amazement, 'that Charlie has to stay at the vet's...but he's your brother's dog, doesn't he go around with him?'

'Of course. To the surgery each day—he sits under Rolf's desk, and they go for a walk together early in the morning every single day, and when Rolf goes to one of our farms, he goes too. Rolf wondered if you would like to come with me to fetch them this afternoon—it would be a good opportunity for you to try out the Mini. Rolf said you might.'

Sappha bristled; for two pins she would have utterly refused to drive anything while she was in Dokkum. She was about to say something to this effect when Rolf came back, with his coat over one arm and a briefcase in his hand. He stood patiently while Antonia hung round his neck, gave her a brotherly slap on that portion of her anatomy best suited to receive it, and crossed the room to where Sappha was sitting at table. She got up, for the simple reason that his elegant largeness was so close and overwhelming. She said breathlessly: 'I'll remember what you told me about your family coming and the telephone numbers and the specialist coming tomorrow—and Antonia has just told me about the dogs.'

'Did you remember anything else?' he asked quietly.

Sappha went a delicate pink. It was true she had remembered all these things, but far more vividly did she remember their conversation in the school room. She said carefully, her eyes on a level with his chin:

'I haven't forgotten anything you said.'

'Good. Think of me a little, Sappha.' He caught her hand and kissed it swiftly on its palm and went away. She heard the front door bang as she sat down to her cooling soup.

The house seemed a great deal larger and very empty when he had gone. Sappha was glad, once lunch was over and her patient tucked up for a nap, to change into a sweater and skirt and a thick tweed topcoat and go with Antonia to the garage down by the gate, where she found the Mini as well as the Rover 416. She drove the little car out of the gates under Antonia's direction and found that driving on the wrong side of the road wasn't as bad as she had imagined, probably because everyone else was doing the same thing. By the time she had negotiated the town and was heading the car northwards, she felt quite at ease. The vet lived just outside the village of Brantgum, only a few miles from Dokkum, and presently, with the dogs safely stowed in the back, Sappha drove carefully back again, feeling rather pleased with herself; besides, it had helped to pass an otherwise rather dull afternoon.

It was better with the dogs in the house. Charlie, who looked fierce and was in fact excessively good-natured, was a willing companion to any member of the household who would accept his company, but Leo stayed with the Baroness, baring what remained of his teeth to anyone who went near her, although after an hour or two of Sappha's company he seemed to realise that she was an indispensable part of the Baroness's life and contented himself with curling a lip at her.

After dinner that evening, Sappha, mindful of Rolf's instructions to her, went into his study, sat down at his desk and studied the timetable he had written out for her. The specialist would be coming the following day, and this she welcomed, for there was the chance that he might allow the Baroness to stand at least, but she was a little nervous of the following days, for the Baroness's children were coming to visit her, all at once, and although she didn't expect to see much of them she thought they might be a little overpowering—Antonia was great fun and perhaps they would all be like her, though a good deal older—all the same there would be four of them, each with husband or wife. She got up with a shake of her head at her silliness and went back upstairs to play backgammon with her patient.

The specialist from Groningen was a delightful surprise. He was a large man, and as he got out of his Mercedes, Sappha saw that he was portly as well. She and Antonia had gone down to the hall to welcome him and he had greeted them in a voice as large and exuberant as himself. He shook her hand with a strength which almost cracked her bones and boomed cheerfully: 'De Winter—and delighted to meet you, Miss Devenish.'

They all went upstairs, Mijnheer de Winter firing remarks at them in an English as English as her own. But once in the Baroness's room he lapsed into Dutch and only when he needed information from Sappha did he speak English. But even though he spoke a different language, his methods were the same as Mr MacCombie's; she thought she would have understood him in any language. The examination over, he spent another ten minutes passing the time of day with the Baroness before he said:

'Well, everything seems splendid—I must commend the work of Mr Devenish and also the good Mr MacCombie. I see no reason why our patient should not get on to her feet once more.' He was stopped by his patient's little shriek of delight. 'I say on to her feet, but I do not mean to walk, only to stand and do the exercises with the help of our so good Miss Devenish. When Rolf returns, he will bring you to Groningen and you shall have an X-ray—the last, I hope.' He beamed at the Baroness and then at Sappha, who smiled back at him, but not quite so broadly, because as soon as the Baroness was well again, she herself would return to England. All the same, it was a happy morning for everyone. Mijnheer de Winter stayed for coffee and then, declaring that he had a full day's work ahead of him, made his farewells. Sappha, enjoyed to accompany him downstairs, submitted to having her hand crushed for a second time while he warned her what the Baroness might and might not do. 'And I will telephone Rolf myself this evening—he will be already there.'

Sappha asked 'Where?' before she could stop herself, and he looked a little taken aback. 'You do not know where he is?' he asked. 'But supposing there should be an emergency?'

Sappha explained about the telephone numbers on Rolf's desk. 'Just numbers,' she said, 'no names. Has he gone very far?'

'No—no, Brussels for a couple of days, then Paris and Zurich. Ten days in all, I believe.'

Her heart lifted absurdly. Ten days wasn't a long time. It was a pity that her companion spoilt her pleasant thoughts by saying with a chuckle:

'Rolf will be working hard each day—he is very good at his job, you know, but he will doubtless enjoy his evenings.' He allowed a rich chuckle to escape him. 'All work, is it not, and no play?'

He ran nimbly down the steps to his car, got in, waved in a most friendly fashion and drove away as though his very life depended on it.

The first of the visitors came the next day after lunch. It had been an exciting morning, with the Baroness standing proudly beside her chair with Sappha to support her and what was more important, restrain her from the walking she was sure she was quite able to do. The entire household had come upstairs to watch this triumph and Sappha had been bidden to pour sherry so that everyone could drink to the occasion. Lunch had been a little late in consequence so there had been no time for the Baroness to take more than half an hour's nap before the sound of tyres on the drive below heralded the first of her family. It was Victoria, the youngest but one, a young woman of twenty-two or -three, almost as pretty as Antonia and as dark as Rolf. She had her husband with her and a very small baby in a Moses basket. They had only time to embrace the Baroness, offer her an extravagant bouquet of flowers and exhibit the baby to both the Baroness and Sappha when Annie ushered in the Baroness's two elder daughters. They were alike; fair and tall and blue-eyed and in their late twenties or early thirties. They had their husbands with them too, prosperous-looking men older than their wives and laden with more flowers.

Sappha liked them all; they were a good deal quieter than Antonia, who was talking enough for the entire company anyway, but they were nonetheless friendly and almost embarrassingly grateful. It was to Sia, the eldest, that Sappha explained that she was only waiting for the fourth member of the family to arrive before leaving them for the afternoon. 'For you must be longing to talk,' she said, 'your mother has been so looking forward to this day. I would have gone sooner, but the Baroness wanted me to meet everyone first.'

'Of course, we've heard so much about you—I must say Rolf described you very well.' She turned to get corroboration of this from Ariana, which gave Sappha's faint flush time to fade. 'Of course, we all wanted to be here when Mother came home, but Rolf said that no, it would not be good for her, but he suggested this afternoon and made us promise that we would go if Mother found us too much all at once. So you will tell us, please, Sappha, if we make too much—what is the word?—disturbance.'

'I'm sure you won't,' said Sappha warmly. 'I thought it would be nice if Joke brought the tea up here so that you can all be together. I'll come back about five o'clock, or is that too early? I think perhaps the Baroness will be getting a little tired by then. Do you have far to go?'

Sia shook her head. 'Leeuwarden—less than an hour's drive. Arianna and Bas must return to Apeldoorn and that is perhaps two hours' journey. Victoria and Franz live near Zutphen and that is about the same. Theo, he comes from Hilversum and I think perhaps he will stay the night.' She smiled at Sappha, which made her look like Rolf. 'Did Rolf tell you that?'

Sappha said that no, he hadn't, and was prevented from saying more by the arrival of Theo. He was very like his elder brother, even to the eyebrows, but slighter in build and a little shorter. His wife was a small and dainty girl with a large quantity of mousy hair and large dark eyes. They added their quota of flowers to the display arranged around the room and went around the room, greeting every-one in turn and ending with Sappha whose hand Theo shook with a grip which made her wince. 'Old Rolf is right,' he remarked at once, 'he said you were the prettiest girl he had ever met—and he should know.'

Sappha massaged her hand gently and digested this re-mark. 'I expect I should feel flattered,' she said doubtfully, at the same time feeling pleasure at Rolf's opinion of her looks. 'I understand that you and your wife will be staying for the night—that will be delightful for the Baroness.'

Theo nodded. 'I had to promise Rolf to do as you asked,

though—if Mother gets tired or you have things to do for her will you say so?'

Sappha smiled faintly. 'To be sure I shall. Your—your brother seems to have made me out to be a proper battle-axe.'

'If that word means what I think it does, then no, I would say he meant quite the reverse.'

The only way to answer this was with another smile and Sappha slipped over to the Baroness, exchanged a few words with her, smiled again in a general sort of way to the crowded room, and went away.

She had some letters to post; she changed into a thick coat and dress and went out into the town. The post office was easy enough to find and the clerk obligingly spoke English; she had no difficulty in buying stamps. It was a rather different matter with a dictionary, though. She found a bookshop easily enough, pausing on her way to look at the old gabled houses and the Weigh House. The shop was at the bottom of the main street where it joined the street running alongside the river. She plunged inside, full of confidence after her success at the post office, only to find that the one assistant there had only a few words of English, none of which had any bearing on her wants. They were walking rather desperately round the shop looking for what she wanted when the owner walked in and settled the business with a few neatly turned phrases. Within minutes Sappha had her dictionary, besides a map of Dokkum and a useful little guide to the town as well. She paid for them out of the Dutch money Rolf had thoughtfully provided her with before he had gone away and asked where she could get tea.

'Across the street,' her newfound friend beamed at her, 'there is an hotel—De Posthorn—you see it? Enter the door on your right when you go in and they will give you tea. English is also understood and spoken a little.'

The hotel was nice. It faced the water and had a red-carpeted entrance hall and a large number of clocks hanging on every wall. Their gentle ticking welcomed her as she opened the door on the right and found herself in a brown-panelled room, furnished with small tables and chairs grouped around a large centre table, upon which was neatly arranged a number of papers and magazines, presumably for the pleasure of the few people who were sitting around drinking coffee. They all looked up as she went in and murmured what she took to be the equivalent of Good Afternoon, so she answered them politely and went to sit at a table by the window. The view was delightful, with the water just across the street and on the other side of it a row of old brick houses, each with a different type of gable, and not one resembling its neighbour.

She gave her order for tea to a fatherly waiter who presently returned with a little tray which he presented with a little flourish and the hope, sincerely uttered, that she would enjoy it. Which she did, leafing through her books as she did so until the afternoon began to darken and she got up to go. It had been pleasant in the warm room; she promised herself that she would go again, as well as exploring the little town, and one day, when she had the time, she would walk all round it by the path Rolf had told her of. She hadn't meant to think about Rolf, but this set up a train of thought which kept her mind occupied until she reached the house. She was in no doubt as to her own feelings about him, but very doubtful indeed about his for her. He had been, from time to time, very charming; he had also been most unpleasant, she reminded herself, which more than cancelled out the occasions when he had kissed her. On the other hand when she recollected what he had said before he went away she felt a little surge of hope. She dismissed the whole thing firmly from her mind and rang the bell.

Inside, Jan, instead of going away, beckoned her over to the little room where she had breakfast and opened the door, smiling as he did so. There was a bright fire through the stove's window, and a comfortable chair drawn up to a small table, carefully set with delicate china and a silver muffin dish—there were cakes too, and tiny scones. The sight of it all, arranged with such care, brought a lump into her throat so that all she could do was to smile at him as she took off her coat.

It was Mrs Burns who brought in the tea. 'There, lassie,' she said, 'the master said you were to have everything for your comfort and I thought to myself that a good wholesome tea is one of the best comforts in the world. Now, eat it all—they've got their tea upstairs and they'll not be going for at least another half hour.'

She smiled cosily and went away, leaving Sappha to drink yet more tea and make healthy inroads into the muffins and cakes and ponder meanwhile upon the effortless comfort which lapped the entire house. She looked round the room. It certainly spoke of wealth, but not aggressively so. Nothing looked new—it was as though everything had been there a very long time so that nothing could be valued in terms of money any more. When she thought about it, she couldn't remember either Rolf or the Baroness ever talking about money—Antonia had, but she was still very young and she hadn't been boasting—presumably they had so much of it that it wasn't important to them. She sighed without envy and went away to change back into her uniform.

Sia, Ariana and Victoria left first, Sia and her husband in a Volvo estate car. 'Clumsy great thing,' commented Antonia from the step as they watched them go, 'but they've got four children and dogs besides.'

Ariana and Bas had a Mercedes Benz convertible, although as Antonia informed an interested Sappha, they had a Fiat as well, 'Though they'll have to get a bigger car soon—they've only two children so far, but we all like large families. I daresay I shall have a great number when I marry.' She broke off to wave to Victoria and Franz who were getting into a rakish Porsche coupé, a means of transport which Sappha felt would need to be changed if Victoria shared the rest of her family's enthusiasm for children.

The remaining car she supposed to be Theo's—it was a Buick GS400, beautifully kept and very fast. She liked Theo, she liked his wife too, and wondered how long they had been married; not long, she imagined, for they looked very much in love.

The evening passed pleasantly, although the Baroness was tired when at length Sappha got her to bed. She agreed willingly enough to spend the day in bed on the morrow and when Sappha said: 'I'm sure it's a good idea. I think the doctor…'

'You mean Rolf?' enquired his mother dryly. 'Yes, when he telephoned me yesterday evening he did suggest it, but he was sure that you would think of it. I would be a very stupid woman to ruin all the good work which has been put into me.' She smiled up at Sappha from her pillows. 'You like my children, I hope, Sappha?'

Sappha was pouring medicine into a glass. She corked the bottle neatly and gave the Baroness a brief sidelong glance as she did so.

'Yes, I do—very much. How proud you must be of them all.'

Her patient nodded happily. 'Indeed I am. A pity Rolf couldn't be with us—we all depend on him a great deal, you know. I have been meaning to ask you, my dear, do you still regard him as a brigand?'

Sappha was unwrapping the blood pressure apparatus. She didn't look up but said carefully: 'I'm sorry I ever said that. No, he's not a brigand. I—I think…that is, he's very…I was mistaken,' she finished inadequately.

This lame rejoinder seemed to satisfy the Baroness, who relaxed against her pillows, looking faintly smug. 'Now isn't that nice,' she murmured. 'You know, Sappha, I believe I shall sleep very well tonight.'

The days fell into a neat, tranquil pattern again, enlivened by Antonia's happy chatter when she returned from school each day. Undeterred by the amount of study she had to do, and the fact that she had to leave home soon after seven

each morning, she appeared to enjoy life to the full. Sappha
suspected that she did a large part of her homework on her
journeys to school and back, and as her mother had told
Sappha that Antonia was a brilliant scholar, it seemed that
she had brains as well as beauty, she was certainly a delightful companion; Sappha began to understand why it was
that Rolf was so devoted to his young sister.

By the end of the week Sappha had explored the little
town thoroughly. She could have done this easily in half
that time, but she had taken over the task of exercising the
dogs each morning during Rolf's absence, besides which,
although Dokkum was small, there was plenty to see. She
had spent two afternoons in the Herformde Kerk because
her guide book told her that St Boniface had built it—it
was a large lofty building, with whitewashed walls and
plain glass windows, which had a grandeur even when it
was empty. The floor was paved with gravestones, a great
many of them in Latin, a language which she had enjoyed
learning at school. She had peered down, teasing her brain
to remember long forgotten words and was delighted to find
that hard thinking enabled her to read at least part of the
inscriptions.

She discovered with a little thrill that there were van
Duyrens everywhere; lying beneath her feet since the fifteenth century, while the later, more elaborate wall plaques
adorned the walls. It was a pity that most of them were in
Dutch, although she was able to make out the names. Rolf
and Theobald occurred with monotonous frequency, as did
Sia and Antonia; probably the Dutch liked to keep their
names in the family from one generation to the other. She
wondered which name Rolf would choose for his son when
he had one, and found the thought so disturbing to her
peace of mind that she walked briskly to De Posthoorn and
had a cup of coffee.

She had examined the Weigh House too, and the Town
Hall, where she had been left to roam around on her own.
The Baroness had counselled her to view the painted wall

in the Council Chamber, which she did, but found the portraits of the bygone men of Dokkum much more to her taste. They stared at her with their steadfast gaze out of magnificently painted faces, and she stared back, wanting to know more about their lives and what they had done and thought; the guide book just wasn't enough. She wished with all her heart that she could speak Dutch so that she could have asked—perhaps Rolf would have time to tell her when he returned.

She visited the museum too—it was a stone's throw from the hotel and faced the water. It had a long unpronounceable name, and was very old, but so well restored that she was unaware of this until the curator told her. He was a silent man, but when he saw that she was really interested, he did his best to answer her questions, although sometimes his English failed him, and she was forced to fall back on her own guesses, but on the whole they managed very well between them. The second time she went he allowed her to go where she wanted, for she had the place to herself; the season was over, he told her, and in any case, touring foreigners seldom stayed long in the little town, and even more seldom paid him a visit.

She did a little tentative shopping too, armed with her phrase book which she thrust under the nose of anyone disposed to help her, so that she had acquired a handful of useful Dutch words even though she didn't understand a word of what was being said around her.

Rolf's partners had called to see the Baroness a few days after he had gone. They were quiet men, about his age and speaking an English as faultless as his. They were on the best of terms with the Baroness and charming to Sappha, offering help and advice if she should need them. When they had gone the Baroness remarked on their long friendship with Rolf. 'They were boys together,' she explained, 'and even when they were little they all swore that they would be doctors and share a practice, and as you see, they have done just that.'

Sappha was massaging her patient's legs. She said, her hands still busy. 'They're nice—I suppose the practice is a large one?'

'Oh, yes. A great many patients live outside the town, but Dirk and Pieter have the lion's share because Rolf has his work in Groningen as well as his lectures which take him from home from time to time. He'll be back in a few days. It will be nice to see him again, won't it?'

Sappha said yes briefly and urged her patient to put a little more energy into her foot exercises. The Baroness gave her a thoughtful look and when she spoke again it was about something quite different.

The day before Rolf was due back was a Friday and Antonia came home early from school. Sappha, having just settled the Baroness for her afternoon rest, was on her way downstairs to give Annie a message when Antonia burst into the hall. Sappha stopped short on the staircase. 'Tonia, how did you get home? And so early.'

'A friend gave me a lift, Sappha dear. There was no class because my schoolmaster has a cold. Isn't it delightful? Now I'm free until Monday and if I do all my homework now I shall be able to spend the weekend with Rolf, unless,' she added wickedly, 'he's got some girl he wants to take out.'

Sappha said nothing to this but continued down the stairs. In the hall she stopped, eyeing Antonia closely.

'You look as though you're up to something, Antonia,' she said abruptly. 'Have you spent your allowance on something wickedly expensive?'

Antonia skipped across the space between them and put an arm in Sappha's. 'Me?' she asked innocently. 'How can I get up to anything when I have to go to that stupid school every day?' She smiled with charm at Sappha and said coaxingly: 'Don't look so suspicious—if you must know I've got plenty of my allowance left. Are you going to the kitchen? I'll come with you, for I'm famished.'

Sappha laughed, shaking the uneasy feeling away that

Antonia was up to something. She was a lively girl, given to having her own way, and Rolf, who was the only person she listened to, wasn't here.

'I'm sure Mrs Burns or Annie will love to find you something to eat. Are you really going to stay home until tea-time, Tonia? Because if you are I'd like to walk round the town—you know, along the path which follows the moat. It's not bad weather and I've been wanting to do it ever since…'

'Rolf told you?' finished Antonia. 'He takes the dogs every morning.' She went on without pause: 'Do you miss Andrew, Sappha? Wouldn't you like to see him?'

Sappha paused with her hand on the kitchen door handle; she didn't look at her companion. 'But how could I possibly see him? He has his work too, you know.' She went into the kitchen quickly so that Antonia shouldn't have the chance to ask any more questions.

She set off briskly half an hour later, wrapped in her tweed coat, and with her hair tied into a silk scarf, for the wind was keen. Earlier in the day it had been fine, but now the sun was fighting a losing battle with the cold looking clouds edging it from the sky. Sappha went out of the back gate, turned to her left, and started along the path by the water. It was very quiet save for the rustling of the dry branches of the trees and the occasional lonely cry of some water bird. She passed a few small boys pottering, after the manner of their kind, along the water's edge, and once an old gentleman, warmly clad against the wind and smoking a pipe, which he removed in order to bid her a polite *Goeden Dag*, and which she, equally polite, replied to in her awkward Dutch.

The path was interesting, for it wandered around the edge of the town sometimes following the water which encircled it, sometimes passing over little wooden bridges or alongside a row of centuries old houses. From time to time, too, it bisected the watergates, and here Sappha lingered to catch a glimpse of the old-world roofs of the town. She inspected the windmills on their bastions, paused again to watch some barges on the water and came eventually to the Town Hall and the picturesque houses which faced it across the Zijl. The early dusk was falling by now and she slowed her steps to peer into the lighted windows of the houses as she passed them, but the sight of De Posthoorn reminded her of tea and she quickened her pace once more and turned the last corner on to the stretch of path she had started from; the house was barely five minutes walk away although she couldn't see it yet.

She was two-thirds of the distance when she heard a faint sound. She told herself, doubtfully, that it was a bird, but when she heard it for a second time she stopped to listen. It came from her right and now she knew it wasn't a bird. She walked to the bank and looked about her as well as she was able in the steadily deepening gloom. Where she stood there were no bushes or trees, but a few yards further there was a thicket and a few small trees, almost in the water; the sound came from there. She went forward cautiously, aware that the bank sloped steeply and was more mud than grass, and bent down carefully to peer into the tangle of branches. There was a small sack, a brick tied to the rope which fastened its neck, but the rope had caught in the branches of the trees overhanging the water, and now the sack hung an inch or so above water. As Sappha watched something inside gave a convulsive wriggle and she leaned forward, intent on freeing it. The next instant she had slipped and toppled into the water. It was cold, regrettably smelly, and she was appalled to feel mud and weeds sucking at her boots. She had fallen sideways so that her head and shoulders had remained free and dry, but the rest of her was up to her waist in water and a quick look convinced her that she was going to have an awful job to climb out.

The contents of the sack whimpered again and she forgot her own plight in the need to rescue whatever it was inside. She put a hand underneath to support it and tugged at the rope, with no success at all. She needed a knife, a pair of scissors, even a nail file—all of which she had in the hand-bag she had left on the dressing table in her room. But at least she could ease the small creature's misery while she thought what to do. She poked the tough strands of the sack and made a tiny hole. When she put her finger in a small tongue licked it gratefully. She left the finger there and talked soothingly to the owner of the tongue while she decided what to do. If she could scramble out she could go and fetch Antonia or Joke—it would be a simple matter with two. She suited the action to the thought and let the sack go while she gripped the bank with her hands and tried to lever herself up. Frighteningly, it didn't work—the mud around her ankles tightened around them as she strained to lift her feet, and the weeds, which she had quite forgotten, felt like nylon cords. She waited a moment, aware of the numbing cold of the water, and tried again. It was no use, and what was worse, she had slipped a little further down into the mud.

The creature in the sack made a small, enquiring sound and she said, rather more loudly than she needed to because she needed cheering up as well. 'We'll have to have patience, whatever you are...' she broke off and uttered a gasp which was almost a scream as something brushed through the thicket and plopped into the water. Sappha was ready to scream properly when there was another move-ment in the bang above her. She looked up fearfully into the gloom and made out Charlie peering down at her with wise, friendly eyes. He gave a short bark and was joined almost immediately by his master.

Sappha didn't understand a word Rolf said. He spoke in his own language for a start and in a rough voice quite unlike his usual deep quiet tones. 'Something rude, no doubt,' she thought hazily, a trifle lightheaded with relief and fright and cold. He peeled off his top coat as he added in a subdued roar: 'What in the name of the Almighty are you doing there?'

She watched him place a large sure foot on the bank and said through chattering teeth: 'There's something in a bag—I tried to reach it and f-fell in. It's t-tied with a rope and I can't get it f-free.'

He was just above her, taking a knife from his pocket, uncaring of the water lapping his shoes. He leaned across her, cut the rope and swung the sack gently on to the top of the bank where Charlie welcomed it with gentle blowings and gruntings. Rolf had an arm round her now; without much effort he tugged her loose of the mud and weeds and heaved her unceremoniously up the bank. She landed on her hands and knees and Charlie abandoned the sack and came to blow on her instead. Seconds later Rolf was beside her, hauling her to her feet, wrapping her in his coat.

'N-No,' she essayed through chattering teeth, 'you'll ruin it.' It was, she remembered clearly, an extremely handsome and well-cut garment and must have cost a good deal of money. She pushed ineffectively against his hand fastening the buttons and he said, still roughly: 'Be quiet, do!' His voice sounded so fierce that she lapsed into miserable silence and then tears. They poured down her cheeks and she did nothing about them as it was almost dark by now and he couldn't see them. She was quite unprepared when he caught her suddenly close and touched her face with a gentle hand and spoke in his own language again. She didn't understand what he was saying, but she knew that the words were kind and tender, as was his voice. When he bent his head and kissed her wet cheek and then her mouth, the tears, the mud, the wet and cold dark melted away and for a brief moment she was in a star-spangled fairyland.

The next instant Rolf said in a perfectly ordinary voice: 'Let's see what we've got,' and took out his knife once more. It was a puppy, but what kind of puppy they would have to find out later. Rolf tucked it under his arm, caught Sappha round the shoulders, spoke briskly to Charlie who was inclined to go ratting, and walked quickly towards his home.

Minutes later they were in the kitchen, where Sappha was stripped of the Baron's coat, her own coat and boots and wrapped in a blanket which someone had produced, then told to drink the large brandy Rolf was holding out to her. She took a sip and he said equably: 'The lot, my girl, or I'll pour it down your throat for you.'

She did as she was bid, knowing that he would do exactly as he said, and felt the rich glow surge through. It made her feel instantly better so that she sat up straight and looked around her for the puppy. He was already before the fire, a thin, ugly little creature with a wizened anxious face. The anxiety turned to delight as Annie put a bowl of milk under his nose and he gave a whimper of pleasure and lowered his deplorable head, while Charlie brooded kindly beside him.

Sappha, who, what with brandy and cold and fright, was feeling peculiar, said: 'He's very ugly…'

Rolf was leaning against the table in the centre of the kitchen watching her. He said lightly: 'So would you be if you had been tied up in a sack.' He smiled very kindly at her. 'I can think of a lot of people who would have walked past and pretended they hadn't heard him. I'm glad you didn't.'

A little colour tinged her white cheeks. She unwrapped the blanket, speaking slowly because she felt peculiar. 'I'll go and have a hot bath and change.' She got to her feet and the Baron put down his glass and came across the room to her. 'You'll look after him?' she asked hazily.

His eyes looked black, a smile tugged the corners of his mouth. 'Yes, of course—he shall join the family, but I think I'll look after you first.'

He whipped her off her feet and carried her upstairs, calling over his shoulder for Joke to follow them and run the bath.

An hour later Sappha felt perfectly all right again. Antonia had rushed in while she was dressing and begged her, unsuccessfully, to stay in bed. She had the puppy under

one arm, from where it peered with uncertain delight at a
world which had suddenly become good to live in, and
once she had been convinced that Sappha had taken no hurt
from her ducking, engaged her in the interesting task of
finding a name for the animal. 'You must choose it, Sappha,
for you rescued him. It must have been horrid in that water—all slimy and cold and rats, I daresay.'

Sappha shuddered delicately as she pinned on her cap.
'Yes,' she said, 'and then I looked up and there was Charlie
and—and the doctor.'

'Why do you call Rolf "the doctor"?' Antonia wanted
to know.

'Well, he is.' Sappha tried to sound matter-of-fact.
'There, I'm ready. I'm going along to see your mother.'

'You've had no tea.'

'Never mind—I had a huge glass of brandy instead. I
can miss tea.'

But she was mistaken. When they reached the top of the
stairs, Rolf was in the hall. Without raising his voice, he
said: 'Come down, Sappha. Mother's all right for a little
while.'

She had no intention of going down. She had her hand
on the Baroness's door when he said again: 'Sappha.'

She went downstairs, telling herself that she was a weak
fool as she went. He came across the hall to meet her.
'You'll feel better for tea,' he said cheerfully, 'and don't
glare at me in that enchanting manner or I might kiss you
again.'

She went scarlet, and after one quick look at him, preceded him into the breakfast room and he shut the door as
he followed her. The tea tray looked inviting. She sat down
on a bergere and he sat opposite her, saying blandly as he
did so: 'Don't worry, dear girl, Tonia will be here long
before I can press my unwelcome attentions upon you.'

He smiled at her with lazy good humour and her scarlet
cheeks faded to white. She had, for the last hour, been
living in a happy, slightly hazy dream world in which his

kiss had been a very real thing. Now it seemed that it was part of the dream, to be discarded with it.

She said dully: 'In that case, shall I pour out the tea?' and without waiting for him to reply, lifted the silver teapot. It was mortifying that her hand shook so badly that he leaned forward and took it from her, murmuring: 'Perhaps I had better?'

In the night, lying sleepless, she told herself that she was behaving like a fool—a lovesick fool, she amended, determined to be honest with herself. She forced herself to make plans for the future, but it was a fruitless occupation. She was still thinking about Rolf when she at last went to sleep.

CHAPTER EIGHT

ROLF came in through the front door as Sappha went downstairs the following morning. He shut it behind the dogs, said good morning pleasantly enough and stood staring at her, which didn't surprise her in the least, for she was aware that after her miserable night her face looked as plain as a suet pudding. She said grumpily: 'Good morning,' and returned his stare as he removed the puppy from under his arm and set it on the floor, removed his coat, flung it in a chair and said: 'Under the weather?' He sounded as though he was speaking his thoughts out loud. 'Starting a cold, I daresay,' he cocked a crooked eyebrow at her, 'pneumonia perhaps.'

Sappha found herself on the verge of laughter despite her crossness as he said coaxingly: 'Come and say hullo to our puppy!' She crossed the hall to pick the scrap up and stroke its head. The little beast wriggled, licked her hand with a small pink tongue and barked in a shrill treble so that she said urgently: 'Oh, hush, puppy, hush!' and Rolf exclaimed: 'An excellent name—he shall be Hush from now on.'

Sappha did laugh then. 'I wonder what sort of breed—breeds—he is?' she wanted to know, and laughed again when he said:

'That I think is something we should gloss over, but it will be interesting to see what he grows into—have you had your breakfast?'

She shook her head. 'No—I've been with your mother—early morning chores. I'm just going to take her breakfast up, but if you wanted to see her...?'

He took Hush from her. 'No hurry.' He smiled at her and her heart missed a beat. She said uncertainly: 'Well, in that case...' and made her way to the kitchen. When she emerged presently with her patient's tray, he had gone and so had the dogs.

It was some twenty minutes later when she came down to her own breakfast. The Baroness was in a chatty mood, and not only did she want to know all about Sappha's health after her ducking, she wanted to know about the puppy too. She had demanded to see it the previous evening and while deploring its appearance, agreed that it must join the household. Now she wanted to know if anyone had exercised it and whether it had been fed. Sappha gave placid affirmatives to her questions, rearranged her pillows, put her letters and newspapers exactly where she wished to have them, agreed that it had turned cold overnight, explained away her own drab little face as best she might, and left her patient to her breakfast. When she entered the breakfast room a minute or so later, it was to find the Baron sitting at the table, scribbling notes in his diabolical handwriting, which she privately considered would be of no use to him at all, because he was reading the paper at the same time. He went over to the sideboard as she sat down, saying as he went:

'Scrambled eggs? Bacon? A kipper?'

She settled for the eggs, poured them both coffee and asked: 'You haven't been waiting for me, have you?'

He sat down opposite her and when he spoke his voice was silky. 'Yes—did you hope that if you delayed long enough I might be finished and gone?'

She looked at him in bewildered surprise and saw that he had become a brigand with a satyr's grin. She forced herself to answer reasonably.

'No, what a ridiculous thing to say—your mother was feeling like a chat, and I had no idea that you would be here.'

She didn't add that she had hoped that he would be. She

drank some coffee and waited for an answer which she never received, for Antonia came in, dressed and ready for school. She flung herself down in a chair and grumbled: 'How lucky you two are, having time to eat your breakfast.' She looked at them enviously. 'What fun it must be, having another cup of coffee and being able to talk.' She sounded so melodramatic that Sappha hid a smile as she said soothingly:

'Never mind, Tonia—not much longer now, then you'll be able to do the same.'

The Baron looked up from his perusal of the leading article in his newspaper. He said crisply: 'You could do that now if you got yourself out of bed an hour—even half an hour—earlier in the morning.'

Antonia pouted at him and then smiled angelically at him. 'You're an old bear,' she said fondly, 'and the trouble is no one ever tells you so or answers you back.'

She swallowed her coffee, got up, threw her arms round his neck to hug him fiercely and went to the door, where she turned. 'Actually,' she said kindly, 'you're rather nice—though I do hope your wife answers you back sometimes. Sappha does, someone like her would do very well.'

She waved airily at Sappha's startled face, blew her brother a kiss and went out, closing the door with a good deal of noise.

Sappha, aware that the Baron was watching her, fixed her eyes on her plate and because the silence became unbearable asked at last:

'Can I give you some more coffee?' and when he handed her his cup without a word, she plunged into small talk which became more and more involved and vaguer and vaguer until he cut into the jumble of senseless remarks.

'I have arranged for Mother to be X-rayed tomorrow— I shall have to go into hospital in any case, you may as well both come with me. Could you get her ready to leave the house by nine o'clock? I have a teaching round to do but I daresay I can be free shortly after lunch, when I will bring you back.'

She took a quick peep at him. He was no longer a brigand, but detached and coolly friendly, as was his voice. She said quickly:

'Yes, of course we can be ready. I expect you will wish to tell the Baroness yourself.' She broke off as Hush, who had been sitting by the stove with the other dogs, came uncertainly across the room and made a determined effort to climb into her lap. He looked so woebegone when he found that he couldn't quite manage it that she felt constrained to lift him up and give him a cuddle, looking uncertainly at Rolf as she did so. It was a relief to see a decided twinkle in his eyes as he said blandly: 'You're quite right—I don't approve, but like you, I feel that a little spoiling won't hurt him for a day or two.'

Sappha gave him a grateful look and he went on: 'He slept with the cat in the kitchen, it was Mrs Burns' idea and it seems to have worked, for when she came down this morning they were sharing the cushion on her chair.'

Sappha studied Hush, who was pretending to be asleep. She said quietly:

'Thank you for taking him in, it was kind of you. I—I wouldn't have known what to do with him...'

'No, you wouldn't, would you?' he agreed affably, 'though I daresay you would have persevered until you had found someone foolish enough to give him a home. How's Andrew?'

The abrupt change of topic was too much for her. 'Andrew? I—I...that is, I'm sure he's quite all right. Why do you ask?'

He got up from the table. 'Search your memory, my dear girl,' he advised suavely, 'then you can answer that question for yourself.'

She hardly saw him for the rest of that day, for she spent the morning with her patient, ironing out the knottier points of the Baroness's clothes for the trip to Groningen and trying gently to curb that lady's excited certainty that she would be perfectly able to walk the moment the X-ray had been taken. Sappha ate her lunch alone, with Joke serving her, a circumstance of which she was glad, for it permitted her to try out her rudimentary Dutch with only Joke to laugh at her in a friendly way.

Tonia came home about four, looking so pretty and excited that Sappha's uneasy feelings returned to worry her. Had the girl got a boy-friend no one knew of—someone Rolf might not approve? Despite her pertness, Tonia was unsophisticated and so sweet-natured that she would fall an easy victim to the first plausible wolf to catch her eye. And when Rolf came home presently, Sappha was more than ever convinced that Antonia was concealing something from him. She went up to bed, wondering about Tonia, who despite her up-to-date appearance had been reared in a strict Protestant household, and Sappha had already realised that some Dutch Protestants were very strict indeed. She might have the thin veneer of a modern girl, but Sappha suspected that, under her fashionable suede jerkins, high boots, chain belts and trailing scarves, Antonia was still very young.

She was up early the following morning, because the Baroness, although one of the kindest and most sweet-natured women she had ever met, was quite incapable of being hurried. Sappha had reflected on several occasions that it was a good thing that her patient lived in comfortable circumstances and was surrounded by people who made it their business to see that her life was made as pleasant as possible—indeed, Sappha had found herself doing her utmost to smooth her patient's monotonous daily path, for although the Baroness had a great deal more than most women, she was invariably grateful for any small kindness and had shown great courage in the face of an illness which could have cost her her life.

The drive to Groningen was uneventful. Rolf had lifted his mother into the back of the car and when Sappha had got in beside her he had made no demur. It was left to the

Baroness to point out the places of interest along the route, and she did this with obvious pleasure and a great number of asides as to the various castles and museums Sappha should visit.

'Menkemaborg Castle,' she mused, 'you must certainly go there—it isn't large, but it is old and some of the furniture is of great interest. If I remember aright, there are some splendid leather-covered walls in the gun room. The castle belonged at one time to a distant branch of my family.' She added as an agreeable afterthought: 'They make delicious *pannekoeken* in the restaurant there.'

Sappha, whose head was already filled with an indigestible mixture of windmills, churches, old family friends, museums and the like said rather faintly: 'Oh—how nice,' and heard Rolf laugh as he said:

'Poor Sappha—faint but pursuing. Have you had any days off yet?'

She stared at his back until she realised that he was watching her in the mirror above the windscreen. She said levelly: 'No—but I've had ample time to myself—I've explored Dokkum...'

'We'll have to do something about that.' His tone was crisply friendly. 'There's a great deal for you to see. I'll look into your free time this evening.'

She sat back a little so that he couldn't see her any more, and stared at the toes of her high brown boots, wishing she had a new coat to wear. The one she was wearing was warm, it was true, and a very good tweed, but it was last year's and she wanted to look absolutely eye-catching because she was with Rolf. She failed to realise that she looked quite a dish anyway, for the coat was a rich orange and brown and cream mixture, cut on military lines to show off her pretty figure, and her hat was of orange velvet, small and head-hugging. She looked good enough to eat, but unaware of this, she sat hankering after some dreamy spectacular outfit which would turn Rolf's head permanently in her direction, obediently turning her attractive head this way and that while the Baroness enlarged upon the geography of Groningen—and seeing none of it, because she had eyes only for Rolf, who was taking no more notice of her than he might have done of say, one of his mother's friends and according her the same polite attention. By the time they drew up in front of the hospital entrance she had almost persuaded herself that she really didn't care what he thought of her, but he smiled so delightfully at her when she got out of the car that she was forced to admit that nothing was further from the truth.

The hospital was large and put her in mind of all the other hospitals she had ever seen. There were the signposts telling you where to go—always provided you understood the language—there were the usual swing doors, the porters, the trolleys, the housemen, either in a great hurry or no hurry at all; there were the nurses too, looking like nurses all the world over, excepting for their caps, which she thought rather sweet, anyway. She turned from contemplating all these things to find a porter with a wheelchair at her elbow and the Baron on the point of lifting his mother into it. Seconds later she was walking sedately beside her patient with Rolf on the other side. She hadn't expected him to go with them and looked back over her shoulder at the Rolls, which he had left standing carelessly in the forecourt with one of its doors still open. Possibly he was something so grand on the hospital staff that he could do such things with impunity. Certainly the people they passed greeted him with respect; she wondered fleetingly if any of them had ever seen him in a sweater and old trousers, walking through Dialach, swinging fish from one hand... She wanted suddenly to be back there, walking beside him through the little town.

They reached the X-ray department presently, and were handed over to the Sister before Rolf bade them a cheerful goodbye and strode away down one of the hospital's interminable corridors. He had said nothing about seeing them again, or where they were to go when they had finished in

X-ray. Sappha, at a smiling nod from Sister, removed the Baroness to a small cubicle to make her ready, and presently wheeled her out once more to meet the radiographer and Mijnheer de Winter, who wrung her hand delightedly and listened with relish while the Baroness recounted the rescue of the puppy. The radiographer enjoyed it too; they discussed the episode at some length, oblivious of Sister's impatient face peering round the door. Sappha felt sorry for her; probably the poor soul had a waiting room full of patients to be got through before lunchtime. It was a relief when the two gentlemen, having squeezed every ounce of amusement out of the Baroness's story, got down to business; straightforward business which took comparatively little time. This dealt with, the Baroness, once more dressed and in her wheelchair, was invited to take coffee with the Directrice, and since Sappha was pushing the chair, she was included in the invitation.

She sat between the two ladies in the Directrice's comfortable office, listening to the Baroness's soft, excited voice and answering the questions put to her so shrewdly by her hostess, whose English was more than adequate to discuss hospital administration with her. The Directrice had an acquaintance with Scotland too, and presently became involved in a discussion with the Baroness, which left Sappha free to wonder what Rolf was doing. A ward round, probably—her imagination, always vivid, pictured a full complement of pretty nurses and a strikingly beautiful Ward Sister who was in love with him. So real was this picture that when the door opened and Mijnheer de Winter entered, with Rolf behind him, she stared at him as though he were a ghost, her eyes wide and her mouth open. He gave her a keen look and his eyebrows soared in enquiry, but he said nothing, merely giving her a brief nod as he took the coffee cup he was offered, leaving her to school her features as best she might; not that they mattered, for all the attention was focused upon the Baroness, who had sat up very straight and asked quickly: 'Well, I hope you have good news for me?'

Sappha looked at Mijnheer de Winter's face and decided that the news wasn't going to be quite as good as the Baroness expected. She got up casually and went and sat by her patient, who, while unlikely to burst into tears or throw a fit of hysterics, would probably be glad of a little moral support. It was a pity that Mr MacCombie hadn't been more vague when the Baroness had questioned him. He had said 'several more weeks', and they had been in Dokkum just over two weeks, and despite Sappha's gentle discouragement, the Baroness had made up her mind that today was D-Day. She watched the Baroness's face now, for Mijnheer de Winter was speaking in Dutch and she couldn't hope to understand a word. But she understood the expression upon her patient's face—disappointment. When he had finished speaking, Sappha looked anxiously at the Baron, who was standing with his back to the window, watching his mother as well. He crossed the room at once, asking as he came:

'May I translate, de Winter? I daresay Sappha may have some helpful ideas.' He smiled briefly at his mother. 'Mother is naturally disappointed; Mijnheer de Winter wants her to keep the weight off her leg for another three weeks. He suggests a caliper to be worn for a short period each day while Mother takes the gentlest possible walking exercise.'

'I'm not sure what a caliper is,' his mother burst out. 'It sounds horrible, and anyway, what is the use of walking up and down my bedroom for a few minutes at a time—I might just as well be in bed.' She blinked. 'I'm sorry to be so ill-natured.'

The Baron took her hand. 'It's not quite as bad as that, Mother...'

Sappha interrupted him. She said energetically: 'It's not bad at all. Why should you stay upstairs all day? Why shouldn't you be carried down—Rolf can do it'—she was unaware of using his name—'before he goes in the morning—it doesn't matter how early. I can dress you later, downstairs. You can have your friends to luncheon and tea, and can walk for five minutes in the drawing room just as well as in your bedroom.'

She paused and the Baron interposed. 'Good girl, Sappha, but it will make a great deal more work for you.'

She turned on him. 'Oh, rubbish—don't you start…' and came to an abrupt halt. Rolf's eyes were fastened on hers, the gleam in their depths could have been laughter, though his face was blank. She glanced quickly round the room. The Directrice was looking thunderstruck, Mijnheer de Winter amused, and the Baroness had such a look of deep satisfaction on her face that Sappha came to the erroneous conclusion that she hadn't heard what she had said. She meet the Baron's gaze, ignored the gleam and said woodenly: 'I'm sorry, Baron, I quite forgot we weren't alone,' and stopped for a second time, aware that she hadn't improved matters. Rolf allowed her a brief glimpse of his satyr's smile. He said with a graciousness to make her grit her teeth: 'Think nothing of it, Miss Devenish. Your idea is a good one—perhaps you have some further suggestions?'

She lifted her chin. 'As a matter of fact, I have. You suggested that I might drive a car while I was here; I could take the Baroness for drives—she could visit her friends…'

'Splendid—how do you propose to get my mother in and out of the car?'

'I shall think of something.'

'Of that I am sure.' He really was laughing at her now. 'Mother, what do you say? Shall we take advantage of Sappha's idea?' He squeezed the hand he was holding. 'Confess now, it won't be so bad after all. Another few weeks and you'll be quite well.'

His mother studied his face. 'Yes, dear. But I should like to know the reason for these extra weeks—and I am to be cured completely, or are you trying to make things easy for me?'

He laughed. 'No, dearest, you will be as good as new. The reason you must go slowly for another week or so is because the nature of your illness has made it more difficult for your bones to heal and unite.'

He looked across the room to Mijnheer de Winter, who nodded.

'Indeed, yes,' he said. 'If you will have just a little more patience, Baroness, and that shouldn't be too difficult now that your excellent nurse has made her suggestions,' he smiled kindly at Sappha, 'I think that we might have a glass of sherry to celebrate the happy ending, don't you?'

Rolf had moved nearer Sappha. 'Excuse us, will you?' he asked casually. 'I want Sappha to see something of the hospital. Come along, Sappha.'

She went with him, smiling a little uncertainly at the others as she went through the door. Outside in the corridor, Rolf took her arm.

'I've a ward round to do,' he said blandly, 'but I've asked Theatre Sister to take you to some of the wards—we'll go and collect her.'

Sappha walked beside him because there wasn't much else she could do. A dozen remarks, all unsuitable, trembled on her lips. She reminded herself just in time that there was no reason at all why he should go to the trouble of escorting her and composed her features into a pleasant smile in time to greet Theatre Sister, who was waiting for them at the end of the corridor and was, to Sappha's disgust, a raving beauty. What was more, she seemed to be on terms of the greatest possible friendliness with the Baron, who addressed her as Jan with the easy air of a very old friend. He said goodbye vaguely and disappeared up a staircase without looking back.

The hospital was large and well-equipped; despite her unhappy feelings, Sappha couldn't help but be interested in it; besides, Jan turned out to be great fun and when she mentioned, in her excellent English, that she was leaving to get married in a week's time, Sappha felt quite a glow of friendship towards her. The morning hadn't been too successful, but at least this news cheered her up a little. They went over the theatre block thoroughly, for it was cleaning day, which meant that they could go anywhere they wished save for the one theatre kept ready for emergencies. They spent a long time in the children's ward too, and still longer in Women's Medical, and if it hadn't been for the fact that everyone was speaking a language different from her own, Sappha could have imagined herself at Greggs'.

As they went through the ward doors, Jan looked at her watch, murmured. 'It is just time, I think,' and started up the stone staircase to the floor above. Here there was another ward, its swing doors were opened wide as they approached, and Rolf, followed by his registrar, housemen, the Ward Sister and a nurse burdened with all the paraphernalia judged necessary for a consultant's round, stalked through. He stopped at the door, bade farewell to his companions with no apparent haste, and joined Sappha and her companion, who said: 'There, did I not get the time exactly right?' She smiled at them both, bade Sappha goodbye in her turn, and flew down the stairs, leaving them standing together while Rolf's recent entourage, still hanging around the ward doors, tried not to look curious. He glanced at them over his shoulder. 'Downstairs,' he said firmly, propelling her with a compelling hand down to the floor below. They passed a number of people on the way, all of whom stood back to let them pass, rather as though they had been royalty. When they reached the ground floor and were walking side by side along one of its corridors, Sappha observed nastily: 'You must be frightfully important.'

He flung open a door and she found herself in a dark brown room which could have been comfortable but wasn't. He shut the door carefully and leaned against it, facing her.

He said in a silky voice: 'Of course I'm important—just as I'm bold and bad—and what else was it?—a brigand.

What did you expect? Oh, yes, Sappha, I take every possible advantage of my birth and position—a man with my deplorable character could do no less, could he? I like to be. I'm even an elder at St Martin's Church—that should make you laugh.'

She had taken the precaution of putting the width of the room between them, but now she turned away from the window and stormed across the wooden floor. She said furiously:

'I'm not amused, it's nothing to laugh about. How dare you talk like that? Of course you're an elder in the church, how could you be anything else when half the people buried there are your ancestors? You should be proud...'

She got no further, for he plucked her from the solid little table she was leaning against and caught her round the waist. 'Oh, Sappha,' he sighed, and kissed her.

'I don't think the elders would approve,' she said shakily when she had her breath back.

'In that case...' There was a knock at the door and he let her go as a young man came in—she recognised the Registrar, who smiled at her awkwardly and broke into earnest speech. Rolf listened, asked one or two questions and started for the door, taking her with him.

'Something's cropped up,' he gave her a little push in the opposite direction to the one he was taking himself. 'Fourth door on your right,' he said shortly. 'I'll see you later.'

She knocked and went inside, and was relieved to see the Baroness, still with her two companions. They all looked at her as she went in and the Baroness said: 'Back already, dear? We have had such a nice talk.' Her eyes searched Sappha's face. 'You enjoyed yourself, I hope?'

Sappha sat down on the nearest chair. 'Yes,' she replied, surprised to find herself still breathless. 'Very much, Baroness.'

She had plenty of opportunity to recover from her enjoyment during the following days. It was true that she saw

Rolf each morning, for he carried his mother downstairs before he left the house. He carried her back in the evenings too, but these operations were hardly conducive to more than an exchange of commonplace remarks and he made no attempt to be alone with her. Not that she would have had much opportunity anyway, for now that the Baroness spent her days downstairs, Sappha had a great deal more to do besides the walking exercises several times a day and the massage. She rather welcomed the extra work, it kept her fully occupied and the improvement in her patient's condition was well worth the effort; besides, she still had an hour or two free in the afternoons.

On one of them she had begged the loan of the Mini and explored the flat, tranquil land around Dokkum. It had been a cold day and windy with a pale blue sky of which there seemed a great deal by reason of the horizon being so wide. She had gone to Bolwerd and watched the ferry leaving for Ameland, a few miles off the coast. It was bare and bleak on the dyke and the sea looked unfriendly. She preferred the little town, where she bought some cakes because standing on the windblown shore had made her hungry; she bought postcards to send home and went back to the car and wrote them before driving back again.

It wasn't until the following Sunday that Rolf appeared at breakfast. To Sappha's surprise the Baroness had expressed a wish to stay in bed for the day. She had, she declared happily, made a great deal of progress in the last few days, so she was going to write letters and read. Sappha went down to her breakfast wondering if she might suggest to her patient that she might have at least part of the day off. The morning routine wouldn't take long; Antonia and Rolf were both home and Victoria and her husband were coming to lunch. She took her place at the table, returned her companions' good mornings, and commenced her breakfast. She was buttering a roll when Rolf said formally:
'Antonia and I would be delighted if you would accompany us to church.'

Sappha stared at her knife, poised above the roll, vividly remembering her awful remarks about him being an elder. She said, with a politeness equal to his own: 'How kind—but I don't see how I can. There are things to do for the Baroness...'

Rolf said patiently: 'I am aware of that. Annie and Mrs Burns will be delighted to do them for you. Church is at ten o'clock, we will meet in the hall at ten minutes to the hour.' He got up. 'If you will excuse me?'

When he had gone Antonia observed sympathetically: 'When he comes the baron over you there's nothing much you can do about it, is there? I stop him, of course, but I don't suppose you feel you should. Still, I'm glad you're coming to church.'

Sappha helped herself to some rye bread and reached for the cheese.

'I'm coming,' she declared clearly, 'because I am interested in attending one of your church services. Not that I shall understand a word.'

The Baroness proved unexpectedly brisk. Sappha, convinced that she had done all she could for her patient's comfort, went to her own room to dress. It was a gloomy day and cold, so there was nothing for it but to wear the tweed coat again, only this time she wore a wool dress of a pleasing shade of brown beneath it. She went down the stairs at exactly ten minutes to ten and found Antonia in the hall, sitting on the arm of one of the great carved chairs, reading a letter which she stuffed hastily into her handbag when she saw Sappha coming towards her. She broke into speech at once. 'How nice you look. Here's Rolf...it's only a short walk.' She prattled on with an artlessness and speed that made Sappha wonder thoughtfully about the hastily concealed letter. There was no chance to find out, for Rolf, calmly unhurried beside her, was listening to his sister with a half smile, obviously diverted. Sappha stole a look at him as they went; he appeared immaculate and aloof in his well-cut clothes, as unlike the unshaven man she had met on her journey to Dialach as it was possible to find. He looked down suddenly and caught her staring, then smiled, and she saw how completely wrong she was. He was indeed the same man.

The church was full, which was something she had expected. She had read a great deal about Dokkum and asked questions besides; she knew all about its religious history. Religion, she thought, was important to people of the little town, probably to the whole province. Perhaps that was why they seemed so content with their lives, and why they were friendly and good-natured, although she had the idea that any of the large, calm men around her could show a magnificent rage in a good cause.

It was a pleasant surprise to find that she knew most of the hymn tunes although she was the only person there not singing. She listened to the volume of sound rising to the roof, almost drowning the organ, and she listened to Antonia's clear treble too, and Rolf's deep, well-controlled roar.

The service wasn't so hard to follow with Tonia and Rolf to look after her. When Rolf got up to join the other elders and take the collection she didn't look up from her hymn book; not until he was standing beside their pew, holding the little black velvet bag on its long cane handle—which she might have found amusing if it hadn't been Rolf holding it—did she look up to find him gazing at her, his face grave but with a look in his eye to send the delicate pink sweeping over her face. She bent her head and kept it bent when he returned to sit beside her for the sermon, which was long, so that her thoughts began to wander. Presently, when she thought it was safe to do so, she peeped at him. In profile he looked haughty, due, no doubt, to the arrogant thrust of his domineering nose, but when he turned his head and smiled at her, he looked kind and gentle...he would smile like that at his children...

She became lost in a daydream, in which the pew was peopled with several delightful children, with Rolf at one

end and herself at the other—or perhaps she would be at
home with the baby—no, there would probably be a nanny.
He laid a gentle hand on hers and she jumped so hard that
she dropped her book. The sermon was ended, they sang
another hymn and then the congregation surged out into the
grey day, breaking up into groups which disintegrated into
little streams of people making their way across the square
to the various streets leading them home.

Victoria had arrived when they returned and coffee was
being served in the Baroness's bedroom; Sappha, on some
pretext or another, slipped away—the family would want
to talk, to say things that were no concern of hers. She
went to her room and tossed off her hat, and was unbut-
toning her coat when there was a knock on the door and
Rolf came in.

'Put your hat on again,' he said affably. 'You've got the
rest of the day off—we're going out.' He crossed the room
to where she was standing and rebuttoned her coat and she
said, puzzled: 'I don't understand.'

His voice was bland. 'It's quite simple and very harm-
less. We are going to Menkemaborg—remember? Where
the pancakes are. If we go now we shall have time to eat
some before we look round the castle.'

'Your sister—and her husband, they've come to
lunch…and your mother—you see so little of them all.'

'I see so little of you, Sappha.'

She started to unbutton her coat again, unaware of what
she was doing.

'Yes, but you don't need to see me.'

He sighed. 'Sappha, allow me to know what I need—
and now I have to do up your coat once more. Have you
heard from Glover lately?'

It was the last thing she had expected him to say. She
shook her head.

He said, frowning: 'He's not for you, Sappha—not a girl
like you. If you were my sister I should take good care that
he didn't get you.'

Sappha's heart, which had been thumping excitedly against her ribs did a double knock of disappointment and then began a renewed hammering when he went on: 'Not that I regard you in the light of a sister, my dear Sappha.'

She looked at him and found him smiling. 'Put on your hat,' he wheedled. 'I want you to myself.' He went to the door and opened it. 'I'll be in the hall in five minutes.'

Five minutes wasn't long; she achieved the repair of her make-up, the exact and most becoming angle of her hat, a discreet spray of *Ma Griffe* and a short visit to the Baroness's room. Her patient knew all about it, apparently, for she said: 'There you are, dear. I'm so glad you're going to Menkemaborg, I know you will love it and Rolf can answer your questions so much better than I.'

'It's very kind...' began Sappha, to be cut short by the Baroness's quick 'Nonsense—you've had no fun at all. I'm perfectly comfortable and Victoria will be here until after tea. Tonia is meeting some school friends, but Annie is in, and so is Mrs Burns, so you see, I shall be well looked after,' She gave Sappha a bright glance. 'That's a dear little hat,' she commented. 'Now run along.'

Thus dismissed, Sappha went down to the hall, to find Rolf waiting with Charlie beside him. He smiled at her.

'Hush wanted to come too, but I think he's better in the kitchen with Moggy, don't you? She thinks he's a kitten and the mothering is doing him good. When he's a little older we'll try him on short runs.'

He opened the car door and she got in and sat silent while he fastened her seat belt and then turned away to let Charlie into the back of the car before getting in beside her. As the big car purred into life, he said: 'We'll go through Kollom and take the byroads to Munnekezijl and Ulrum, that'll cut off a corner and bring us to Warffum. We can turn off there for Uithuizen.'

Sappha nodded happily; if he had said that they would be going by way of the North Pole or the South Sea Islands, it would have made no difference to her feelings. She leaned back against the soft leather and allowed herself to forget all but the delights of the moment. Rolf looked at his watch. 'A quarter to twelve,' he remarked, 'we should take about an hour—just nice time to work up an appetite for the *spek pannekoeken*.'

'Pancakes,' and Sappha, anxious to air her Dutch, 'but haven't I seen *spek* in the butcher's?'

'Yes, it's fat pork, fried very crisp and eaten with syrup.'

She asked faintly: 'Oh, shall I like it? It sounds rather—rather...'

'Wait and see. If it revolts you you shall have something else, but I think you'll like it. What are your plans for the future—have you any?'

He had snapped his questions out so fast that she was still thinking about the pancakes; now she paused before she answered. She would have dearly loved to tell him then and there that she had no future, not with Andrew at any rate, but it seemed unfair to take advantage of his recent efforts to get on a more friendly footing with her, for she had endangered it on several occasions in the past. She had been, she realised now, far too quick to squabble, and she should have told him about Andrew. It was too late now, he so obviously thought that she and Andrew...she said now with an assumption of ease: 'No—at least, no cut and dried ones. I shall wait until I get back to London.'

'Andrew,' said Rolf pleasantly, and she echoed like a fool, 'Andrew,' letting him believe what he liked. It was strange, though, that the mention of Andrew's name seemed to clear the air before they forgot him completely. There was so much to talk about; so many questions Sappha wanted to ask, and such an exchange of views and opinions about everything under the sun, the journey passed in a flash and she noticed nothing of the country through which they passed.

Menkemaborg was a lovely surprise. She hadn't quite known what to expect—Dutch castles were a little deceptive, judging from those that had already been pointed out to her, for they resembled English country houses, but this really was a castle, not large as castles go, but old, its three wings grey-stoned and moated. Sappha wandered to the edge of the paved courtyard and studied the gardens; they were beautiful too, even in the sombre light of the chilly day. She turned round to meet Rolf, who had been dealing with Charlie's wants, and caught the sleeve of his coat to draw his attention to the swans on the moat. She said happily, forgetful of everything but the delight of his company: 'It's lovely here—the Baroness said that someone in her family lived here, a long time ago, I suppose.'

Rolf possessed himself of her hand and tucked it under his arm.

'The Albarda family—extinct, at least this branch is— that was at the turn of the century. I can't remember who inherited it, but it was given to the Province of Groningen—rather like the National Trust.'

'So no one lives here now. That's sad.'

He smiled a little. 'Yes, it is—but on the other hand it would cost a fortune to keep the place warm in winter. Come and eat that pancake.'

The restaurant was in the old barn-like building in the courtyard, there were quite a few people in it and it was gloriously warm and smelled of something freshly baked. They sat down at a red-checked covered table and drank coffee while they waited for their pancakes and when they came, Sappha exclaimed: 'But I couldn't possibly eat all that!' for they were enormous, the size of the large plates upon which they were served, and thick too. Rolf passed her the stone jar of syrup.

'At least see how far you can get.' He gave her a tolerant look that put her in mind of a good-natured, coaxing father, and when he saw the expression on her face, he asked: 'Why do you look at me like that?'

She was disconcerted that her thoughts had shown in her face and for want of anything better she said lamely: 'Nothing.'

He put his handsome head on one side. 'You are the most unconvincing liar I have ever had to do with.' His voice was light and robbed his words of any seriousness and he said nothing more, but turned away to speak to a passing waitress who presently returned with two tall glasses.

'To wash down the pancakes,' he explained, 'Pilsener beer.'

She took a sip and found it to her liking. 'Nice,' she said approvingly. 'Do you often do this?'

He was intent on adding a little more syrup to his pancake. 'Not often, it's hardly a place one would come to on one's own.'

She opened her lovely eyes wide. 'But I don't suppose you go anywhere on your own, at least, you don't need to.'

'You allude to girl-friends, am I right? Of course you have made up your mind that I have a large number—they fit nicely into my degenerate life, do they not? For your information, I have one girl-friend...' he stopped because Sappha had dropped her fork, he passed her a fresh one and went on smoothly: 'Unfortunately she happens to be someone else's girl-friend as well.'

Sappha sat looking at the food of her plate—it would be impossible to swallow any more of it because her heart was in her throat which was making breathing difficult, let alone swallowing.

'I'm sure you'd like to know her name,' Rolf went on, still smooth and she said urgently. 'No—oh, no,' in a small choking voice which he paid no attention to at all. 'Her name's Sappha,' he smiled at her as he said her name and waited, still without breath, for what he would say next. 'I thought you might like to know,' he said softly, his satyr's grin came and went. 'You see, my hands are tied until she decides who she will have. Though perhaps I should warn her that that would make no difference to me—I shall wait for her, if I have to, all my life. I have one virtue which even she must allow me—patience.'

He looked at his watch and when he spoke again it was in quite a different voice. 'If you've gone as far as you can with your pancake, shall we go—the door opens at one o'clock.'

Sappha went around the castle without seeing a thing. She gazed, when told to do so, at furniture, wallpapers, tiled floors, state beds and the like, without seeing any of them. They were in the kitchen, a large semi-basement room with tiled walls and floor, and their small sightseeing party had fanned out, the better to examine its accoutrements. Sappha studied a nappy dryer, circa seventeenth century, until she could have drawn it blindfold, and then realised that the others had gone into one of the little side rooms and she and Rolf were alone. She caught his amused eye and plunged at once into conversation which became more and more involved as she persevered with it. She had commented at least twice upon a goffering iron on the table before them, and was enlarging upon the beauties of the copper warming pans hanging on the walls when Rolf said gently, cutting her off in mid-sentence:

'Dear girl, you're not afraid of me?'

His calm calmed her too so that she said at once in a serious little voice: 'No, Rolf.'

'Then you can't make up your mind to tell me something.'

She said, still serious: 'Yes,' thinking how easy it would be to tell him that she loved him now, but she had to tell him about Andrew first and it was really rather difficult in the middle of a mediaeval kitchen with a number of people likely to rejoin them at any moment. She looked at him helplessly.

'All right, Sappha, I can wait—I'll not ask you to pluck up courage today, tell me in your own time. And now if you've finished examining this dull object, whatever it is, I see the guide is looking at us with every sign of impatience.'

For the rest of the afternoon, Rolf was nothing but a

charming, agreeable companion, who talked amusingly and knowledgeably upon a dozen topics. By the time they were home again she was completely at her ease once more; the evening passed pleasantly and the only references made to their afternoon's outing had been of a most impersonal nature. She got ready for bed in a dreamy state which allowed of no other thoughts than those of Rolf. He had said very little to her the whole evening, but she hadn't minded; she wanted time to savour the happiness she had almost given up. She walked about the pretty room, brushing her hair and finally sat down before the delicate Louis Seize dressing table. She was staring at her face in its mirror when there was a light tap on the door and Antonia came in.

'I hoped you would be awake, Sappha. I want to tell you something. It's exciting.' She smiled seraphically and flung herself down on the bed. 'You'll never guess...'

'No, I shan't,' said Sappha with a touch of asperity, because she wanted to be alone with her thoughts, 'unless you choose to tell me.'

'Andrew's here—in Dokkum—I went out with him this afternoon!'

Sappha said nothing for several seconds; her forebodings had been right, she felt them crowding back, shutting out her happiness. At last she said quietly: 'Why is he here, and does your mother or—or Rolf know?'

'He's here because I wrote and asked him to come, and no one knows, only you, and you aren't a bit thrilled, are you, Sappha? I don't believe you love him after all. I thought perhaps you didn't, but I didn't tell him that because I had to use you as an excuse to get him to come,' she paused and smiled naughtily. 'We had a lovely afternoon together; I think he likes me very much and he thinks I'm the prettiest girl he's ever met, and I told him I should have a lot of money when I'm eighteen...'

Sappha looked at her in horror. 'Tonia, you didn't!'

Antonia nodded happily. 'Yes, I did. I think he's marvellous—he said he could fall for a girl like me, and I expect I could twist him round my little finger if I wanted to.'

Sappha said gently, trying to be calm and say the right thing: 'Look, Tonia dear, you're sixteen, you'll meet lots of boys—men—in the next few years. Andrew is much older than you—of course he thinks you're pretty, you are, very, but that doesn't mean he's serious about you.'

Antonia rolled over on her back. 'If you weren't such a nice girl, Sappha, I might think you were jealous.'

Sappha let this pass, she said earnestly: 'Tonia, you must tell your mother or Rolf—promise me, you must!'

Antonia got off the bed and came across the room to fling an arm around Sappha's dressing-gowned shoulders. 'Darling Sappha, of course I'll tell.' She danced to the door where she paused. 'You won't sneak on me, Sappha—you won't tell Rolf?'

Sappha said soberly: 'No, I won't tell,' and Antonia blew her a kiss and slipped out of the room. Sappha sat for a long time, her thoughts busy as well as unhappy. Rolf was going to be furious, for he adored his young sister; on the other hand Antonia, despite her flippancy, stood a little in awe of her brother. Sappha longed to rush down to the study and tell Rolf all about it, but of course she couldn't— she had promised. Besides, she could imagine the incredulity on his face when she told him—he might even think that she was using Antonia as an excuse for Andrew's sudden visit. After all, she hadn't told Rolf that she loved him and she had told him that very afternoon that there was something she had to tell him. He would draw his own conclusions and hate her coldly for being a fickle hussy.

She got into bed at last, her thoughts chasing each other round and round inside her tired head until, from sheer weariness, she fell asleep.

CHAPTER NINE

THERE was no one at breakfast when Sappha went downstairs the next morning, and when Mrs Burns, who had popped her head round the door to enquire if she had all she wanted, volunteered the information that Antonia had had breakfast with her brother and gone off early because she was going to school in a friend's car, Sappha's doubts and fears came rushing back tenfold, especially when Mrs Burns went on to say that the master and his sister hadn't been so gay for a long time. 'Laughing and joking, they were,' she chuckled, 'all about a fur hat Miss Antonia's set her heart on.' There was a great deal more in the same vein, but Sappha, while contriving to look interested, wasn't really listening. It would seem that Antonia hadn't told Rolf about Andrew. She finished her breakfast without appetite and set about the rather slow business of getting the Baroness dressed, thinking what a pity it was that she had missed Rolf when he had gone to carry his mother downstairs, even though she would have been able to say nothing to him, but it would have been nice, she thought wistfully, just to have seen him. Perhaps Antonia intended to tell him when she got back from school. She stifled a sigh and started to strap on the Baroness's caliper, preparatory to the morning exercises.

Sia arrived unexpectedly just before lunch, declared her intention of staying for the meal and spending an hour or so with her mother afterwards, and suggested that Sappha might like to go out directly the meal was over, an offer which Sappha was only too glad to accept—a long walk might help her think, besides there was something she had to do. If Andrew was in Dokkum he would be staying in one of the two hotels—probably De Posthoorn; she would go there and see him and make him see that the sensible thing to do would be to go back to London before anyone else knew that he was there. Probably he would be difficult, for Antonia had behaved very badly and he wasn't a man to trifle with when it came to his own dignity. Fired by this decision, Sappha pulled on her raincoat, tied a scarf carelessly under her chin, snatched up her gloves, and made her way to the hotel.

There was no one in the warm welcoming hall, nor was there anyone in the little bar beyond, for it was that quiet hour after luncheon which occurs in most hotels. She opened the door of the coffee room and that was empty too; she was just about to explore more deeply into the passages behind the staircase when a man and a woman came down it, and they were speaking English, or at least, Sappha amended, they were Americans speaking English. The woman was middle-aged, well dressed and still pretty, the man—her husband, almost for certain her husband—was tall, thin and stooping. Sappha advanced upon them and began: 'Excuse me...'

The man paused in front of her and smiled nicely. 'Why, honey,' he observed, 'this little lady speaks English.' They stood together, looking at her as though they had made a delightful discovery.

'Well, I am English,' said Sappha composedly, 'and you must forgive me for butting in like this, but I can't find anyone to ask if Mr Glover is staying here or not,' she added. 'My name's Devenish—Miss Sappha Devenish.'

They shook her by the hand and introduced themselves as Mr and Mrs Winkelman, and Mrs Winkelman added with a touch of pride: 'My husband's got Dutch ancestry—and we just had to come and see where they're from.' She smiled proudly. 'To think they came from a little town like this! You wanted to know about Doctor Glover, my dear—yes, he's staying here—and a very talented young man he is by all accounts—he went away quite early this morning—he had to drive someone to Leeuwarden, wasn't it, John?'

She appealed to her husband, who said that he thought that was the town and would Sappha like them to give him a message when he got back?

Sappha said no, thank you in a polite voice which successfully disguised how appalled she was at their news, for it must surely mean that Andrew had gone with Antonia, and even if she had gone to school, there was still the midday break when they could have met. She said: 'I'll come back later,' and smiled and wished them a pleasant stay and hoped that they would meet again, before she made her escape.

Less than an hour later, as the Winkelmans were on their way upstairs again after a walk through the town, Rolf pushed open the hotel door and strode down the hall to speak to the porter in the bar. Mrs Winkelman paused to look at him, for, as she was at pains to tell her husband later, he was well worth looking at. 'So tall—almost a giant, one might say—and so dark, and did you hear his voice, John? Sort of compelling.' She thought for a moment and then said with satisfaction: 'Arrogant, that's the word I want, but nice with it—I wonder what he wanted?'

Sappha had gone out of the hotel not really caring where she went just so long as she could think. She turned in the direction of the bridge, crossed the Zijl, and walked briskly along its further bank, past the picturesque apothecary's shop and the smaller, just as quaint houses beyond it and presently crossed a narrow bridge which led her back into the town, where she walked up one street and down the next, not noticing where she was at all, her thoughts busy with the fact that Rolf would be home that evening. There was nothing she wanted to do more than throw herself in his arms and pour out the whole story—but that was for Antonia. She shivered, and quickened her steps, for it was cold as well as wet; she could have gone into the hotel and had some tea, but for once the idea didn't appeal to her; instead she made her way to the museum.

If the curator found it strange that this was her third visit within a fortnight, he allowed nothing of the thought to show, but opened the door wide to admit her, commented briefly in his basic English upon the weather and asked her if she wanted to see anything in particular.

She said at once: 'Oh, yes please. The first floor—those cases of ornaments and jewellery.' She added hesitantly: 'Do you have to be with me? I mean, I only want to look around for half an hour—it's so quiet here.'

He caught the gist of her remarks and smiled. 'You know your way, miss,' he smiled again, and watched while she mounted the plank staircase.

It was blissfully peaceful, with the deep quiet of aged things and she pottered slowly round, half of her mind trying to decipher the cards on the exhibits while the other half thought about Rolf. She was standing in front of a case containing the gold and silver ornaments worn by Friesian women of earlier times, when there was a murmur of voices below and a step on the stair. Sappha frowned, because it looked as though her peace was about to be disturbed, and kept her back to the staircase to discourage even the 'Good day', which was the custom even with strangers.

But this was no stranger. Rolf said from the head of the stairs:

'Hello—I should have come here first, instead of peering into every shop in town. I thought you might have been in De Posthoorn, drinking your English tea, but they said they hadn't seen you.'

She went a little pale at that—he couldn't know about Andrew then, and of course the only people to have seen her there were that nice American couple. She said faintly: 'Hello, I thought you would be working.' The white of her cheeks pinkened a little. 'That is, you usually do…'

'I took the afternoon off. What's the use of having an excellent Registrar if he can't do my work for me occasionally? Besides, I owe him one for bursting in on us the other day in the hospital.'

He crossed the creaking wood floor and stood before her eyeing her narrowly. 'What are you looking at?' he wanted to know.

She spoke in a nervous rush. 'I like these ornaments, only I don't know what they are—I can guess some of them, but this?'

She pointed to a small silver box, embellished with scrollwork; it was oblong and only a few inches in length; it was nicely lined with velvet. When Rolf saw at what she was pointing he laughed with such genuine amusement that she asked a little sharply: 'What's so funny about it?'

'It's not funny, Sappha, only appropriate. You see, it's an engagement box—once upon a time young Friesians took such a box with them when they went courting, and when they proposed they handed it to the girl of their choice—it held the ring.'

'That's charming,' and then, although she hadn't meant to say it, 'Why is it appropriate?'

He caught her suddenly round the waist. 'Because if I had such a box, I should give it to you, dear girl.'

And when she looked up into his face he smiled at her with a tenderness to touch her heart and said: 'This will have to do instead,' and bent and kissed her with slow deliberation, then kissed her for the second time with no deliberation at all so that she was left breathless.

Neither of them had heard the footsteps on the stairs until the American exclaimed jovially: 'Why, hullo there!' Rolf loosed her slowly, tucking her arm under his as he did so. He said politely, 'Good afternoon,' and Sappha saw the American's wife pluck at his sleeve and frown, so that instead of advancing towards them as he had obviously intended to do, he said feebly: 'Well, nice to see you,' and allowed himself to be led away to the other end of the long room, where he was presently joined by the curator. Rolf murmured—and she could hear the laugh in his voice as he spoke: 'The study, I think—with the door locked!' He gave her a wicked look as they went downstairs and out through the side door which gave on to the paved path at the side of the museum. The Rolls was on the other side of the road, parked by the water, and it was only when they were both in it and Rolf had switched on the engine that he spoke again.

'We'll go through the town, Sappha, as I have to call at the surgery.' He gave her a singularly sweet smile as he put the car into gear.

They would have to turn up into the town past De Posthoorn to reach the surgery. In the midst of her happiness Sappha knew with devastating certainty that Andrew's car would be parked in front of the hotel.

It was. And what was far worse, Andrew was just getting out of it. She made a small sound, half sigh, half sob when she saw him, but it wasn't until they had almost reached the centre of the town that Rolf spoke. 'Did you know Andrew Glover was here?' His voice was silkily polite.

Sappha said miserably: 'Yes.'

'You called at the hotel this afternoon? Before I met you?'

'Yes—I...'

He interrupted her smoothly. 'Shall we talk about it later?' He had pulled up in front of the surgery. 'I shan't be many minutes.'

She sat, utterly miserable, rehearsing what she would say to him presently. Perhaps she should wait until they got home, because Antonia would be there and if she explained he would know that she herself had had no part in meeting Andrew—indeed, she thought crossly, she hadn't met him, and didn't intend to except on Antonia's behalf. Rolf got back into the car again, and began almost immediately to discuss the practice in a perfectly natural voice which nonetheless made it impossible for her to say anything about Andrew. The short ride became a nightmare which she couldn't wish over fast enough, but the nightmare didn't

end when they reached the house, for they were met by
Mrs Burns with the news that Antonia thought she had a
wee cold and had thought it prudent to go to bed. She had
taken some Disprin and hot lemon and begged that no one
should disturb her.

Sappha went upstairs to change into uniform, for naturally there was no question of going to Rolf's study. He
had opened its door and gone inside himself with not so
much as a look in her direction. She supposed that a girl
with more spirit might have said something or done something, but she felt strangely empty inside and quite dim in
her wits. Probably a good thing, she thought wryly, if she
was to get through the evening without making a fool of
herself.

Sia was still with her mother, and as Sappha went into
the room, both ladies looked at her closely, so that she felt
constrained to start an animated description of Mr and Mrs
Winkelman. When she had finally finished and was busying
herself with her patient's medicine, the Baroness asked casually: 'Did Rolf find you, dear? I told him of all the places
you usually visit.'

Sappha came across the room with a medicine glass. She
said colourlessly: 'Yes, thank you—in the Museum.' Her
voice faltered a little as she said it, because she remembered
what had happened there. 'Shall I let the doctor know
you're ready to go down, Baroness?'

'Am I, dear?' asked her patient absent-mindedly. 'Well,
Sia's going now, she will no doubt want a word with Rolf
as she leaves—she'll tell him.'

Sia got up without demur, kissed her mother, collected
her handbag, slung her expensive fur coat over one shoulder, and with a friendly wave to Sappha went out of the
door, closing it gently behind her. Scarcely had she done
so when the Baroness said:

'Sappha, there's something the matter—tell me quickly.'
She added wistfully: 'You were so happy...'

Sappha summoned a smile and said with forced cheerfulness:

'It's nothing, Baroness—not worth talking about.' She went on, in the same determinedly cheerful voice. 'I've been thinking, how about a drive tomorrow? You could visit some friends perhaps—I'll wrap you up warm and I promise you I'll drive carefully...' She broke off as Rolf came in and to avoid his look she turned away and made a pretence of picking up Leo, who wouldn't allow her to touch him anyway.

Listening to Rolf talking at dinner later on, Sappha began to wonder if she had dreamed that awful bit about Andrew, for she could detect no crack in the Baron's facade of cheerful friendliness, only towards the end of the meal she looked up unexpectedly and found his eyes upon her. They looked black and held no expression whatsoever.

When, finally, she had put the Baroness to bed, she went to Antonia's room, because she knew that unless she talked to Antonia she wouldn't sleep at all that night. She knocked gently, and when there was no answer, she went in.

Antonia wasn't there. If she had gone to bed as she had said, then she had got up again, and most unlikely of all, she had made her bed with Joke's incredible neatness. Sappha looked round the room. The clothes Antonia usually wore to school were cast down upon a chair—the closet door was open and it didn't take much intelligence on Sappha's part to see that the new outfit she had badgered Rolf to buy for her and which had arrived only the day before wasn't among the dresses and coats hanging there. Sappha switched out the light and went back to her room, and then, because she didn't lack courage, went downstairs to the drawing room, so that if Rolf wanted to talk to her she would be there, although she had no idea of what she was going to say to him.

At eleven o'clock Mrs Burns, coming in to put the fireguard before the fire, looked at her in surprise. 'What,' she said, 'sitting here all alone, and the house so quiet? Miss

Tonia in bed, puir wee lass, and the master gone to Leeuwarden to some big reception at the Burgemeester's house. He won't be back until the small hours—there'll be those to amuse him, I've no doubt.' She took a good look at Sappha's face and said comfortably: 'Och, lassie, go to ye bed, ye're tired to death.'

Sappha obediently got to her feet, for there was no point in waiting any longer now—Rolf didn't want to talk about Andrew. Probably he would be coldly polite until she left his house, and that, she thought shrewdly, wouldn't be long if he had the arranging of it. Obviously he thought that she had been fooling him—all the same, he could have given her the chance to explain. She went tiredly upstairs under Mrs Burns' motherly eye and once in her room, went and sat by the window, her thoughts still busy. Of course Antonia would have known about Rolf going out—probably she had taken a key with her. All the same, Sappha decided to wait up and see her—she wasn't likely to be very late.

She stayed by the window, and after careful thought turned out the light. She could just see the street and there was enough light from the distant street lamps to identify any car which might stop at the gates. She dozed a little as the night wore on, and presently, fearful of falling sound asleep, she got to her feet, doing odds and ends of jobs to pass the time. It was almost three o'clock when she heard a car coming down the street. She had been busy for the last half hour or so altering one of her dresses—one she had never worn in Dokkum—a green silk jersey, a little too elaborate for the quiet life she led in Dokkum. She had been trying it on before the long mirror on the closet door and now she hastily switched off the wall light she had been using and ran to the window, pulling back the heavy curtain the better to peer through the streaming rain as Andrew's car came through the gates and pulled up before the door.

She ran from the room, flew soundlessly down the stairs and crossed the hall to the front door. There was a solitary wall light casting a soft glow over the shot bolts and heavy key in the great door's lock. It was a matter of moments to draw the bolts, for they were well oiled, as was the key, and pausing only to snatch up her umbrella from the inner porch, she slipped outside and down the steps to the car. Antonia was getting out and although it was dark for Sappha to see either of its occupants, she was aware of tension in the air, although there was no time to investigate its cause. She caught Antonia by the hand, bustled her under the shelter of the umbrella and into the house, and only then, as they reached the door, did she realise that no one had spoken a word.

She pushed the girl gently inside, shook the umbrella free of raindrops and put it back in its place before turning to close the door. She did this carefully and without haste, for although her instinct was to question Antonia immediately, she realised there would be time enough to do so when they were in one or other of the bedrooms, the thing was to get her upstairs and into bed… She was easing the final bolt gently home when she heard a gasp from her companion and turned round. The study door was open, and Rolf, leaning relaxed against it, was watching her. She stood speechless, aware that there was truth after all in that old saying about being rooted to the spot. She stood like stone, while her eyes registered the fact that Rolf, in a white tie and tails, was quite magnificent. Of course, he had been to the Burgemeester's reception, and he must have returned while she dozed; the possibility of that happening hadn't occurred to her.

He said pleasantly: 'Have I disturbed you? Naturally you would have expected me to be in bed.' He put out a deliberate hand and switched on the light, flooding them all in the brilliance of the great crystal chandelier above their heads, and looked at his watch, and then at Sappha. She caught her breath at the anger in his eyes and made a small nervous gesture with a hand to smooth her hair—to find it soaking wet, as was her dress. She had forgotten the rain, but when she darted a look at Antonia she saw that she was miraculously, and because of the umbrella, bone dry. She licked her dry lips, trying to think of something to say before Antonia gave herself away by blurting out the whole sorry business. She stalled for time. 'It's my fault—Andrew...' she began, to be interrupted by Rolf's strangely harsh voice.

'Don't bother with excuses, Sappha. I am, I believe, a tolerant man, you may do as you please with your own life, but surely you realise that to drag Antonia into your—nocturnal junketings is rather more than I can tolerate?'

He walked over to his sister and put a large comforting arm around her shoulders. His voice held icy contempt. 'Could you not have borrowed the back door key from one of the servants?'

Sappha, her mouth slightly open, listened to him. He believed that she had been the one to go out, and, meanly enough, had prevailed upon Tonia to let her in—logical enough on the face of things, for she was not drenched with circumstantial evidence, even to the kind of dress a girl might wear for an evening out with a boy-friend—and she was wet, while Antonia was most innocently dry and on top of that he had, in his arrogance, taken it for granted that she had gone to see Andrew that afternoon; if he chose to think she was capable of such behaviour after what had occurred in the museum that afternoon, then she had no intention of telling him the truth; besides, she couldn't, even if she wanted to, because of Antonia, standing there like a frightened child, terrified of being found out. Sappha, with tremendous effort, managed to smile.

'I'm sorry, Tonia, I should have known better—I hope it is quite understood that I am to blame.'

She was rewarded by such a look of gratitude from Antonia that for the time being at any rate the lie had been worthwhile. She watched while Antonia, with a murmured good night, started up the staircase, and after a moment's hesitation, essayed to follow her, to be stopped by Rolf's cold voice.

'Perhaps you will spare a few minutes? I daresay a brief talk will make little difference to you at this hour of night—or should I say morning?' He held the door behind him wide and stood aside as she passed him and went into his study. It was lighted only by a powerful reading lamp on his desk, which was a jumble of papers and medical journals and opened letters. He shut the door quietly and walked across to his desk and sat down behind it, leaving her to stand. She lifted her chin at the slight as she waited for him to speak. Which presently he did, in a chill, remote voice which made him seem like a stranger.

'You will agree with me, will you not, that it is best that you leave my house as soon as possible?'

And Sappha, who was a reasonable girl and knew how to make allowances for people's bad temper even when her heart was breaking, agreed with him, her voice wooden with the emotion she was determined to suppress. She wasn't looking at him as she spoke and so failed to see the gleam of surprise in his eyes. Her own were fixed firmly upon an ancestral family group upon the wall before her, her whole body stiff with a strong resolve not to apologise or make excuses for her conduct in case he started asking awkward questions.

Rolf stirred in his chair, and said, still with icy politeness: 'It should be possible for you to travel tomorrow—there will be no difficulties, I imagine. Andrew should be delighted to drive you. I shall be away for the day, but I will arrange for you to be paid whatever is owing to you before you go.'

He got up slowly, and walked, just as slowly, towards her and stood staring down at the top of her head. He said in a quiet voice:

'I am indebted to you for the care you have given my mother—you are a good nurse and she has become fond of you. I should be grateful if you will say nothing of this to her. I will arrange for you to receive a telegram within the next hour or so, recalling you to England—family illness, shall we say? I'm sure you will know how to act.' His voice had an edge to it, and she thought miserably that he took it for granted that she was an expert in deceit. He paused, and the pause was so long that she felt compelled to look at him, though it was against her will. His face held no expression save a faint mockery. The desire to tell him everything was so great that she was forced to clench her teeth to prevent the words from pouring out. He spoke with a sudden fierceness to surprise her.

'This afternoon, in the Museum, I could have sworn…it meant nothing to you, did it? Probably you were amused.' His voice was bitter.

Sappha looked away. Her heart, leaping in her throat in such a ridiculous fashion, made it difficult for her to answer him, and he gave her no opportunity to do so; he was at the door, holding it open with an exaggerated politeness which was as insulting as leaving her to stand. She said: 'Goodnight, Doctor van Duyren,' in a quiet little voice as she passed him.

'Not goodnight,' he answered, still pleasant. 'goodbye.'

In her room she undressed very carefully, as though it mattered how each garment was folded. Only when she was ready for bed did she take the green dress and bundle it up as though it were so much waste paper, and push it into the wastepaper basket, then she packed with methodical neatness, walked aimlessly around the room doing nothing at all, and finally lay down on the bed and closed her eyes. Incredibly, she slept.

She was awakened by Joke with her morning tea, and on the tray, true to his word, was Rolf's telegram. It helped enormously that Joke should linger at the door, because Sappha was able to convey to her that it contained bad news—Joke would spread the tidings, which would enable her to lie more convincingly. She was almost dressed when Antonia came in. She was in her dressing gown and her blotched, puffy face gave ample evidence of her lack of sleep. Her eyes lighted upon Sappha's packed case as she paused just inside the door and she ran across the room to cast herself in Sappha's arms and wail: 'Sappha, you're leaving. Oh, what did Rolf say to you—did he think…?'

Sappha disengaged herself gently, took the hairpins out of her mouth long enough to say: 'Now, now,' in a heartening manner, then pushed them in rather haphazardly and went on: 'Tonia, haven't you slept at all? Sit down, I'll tell you what happened.'

She did so, beginning with the telegram and working backwards, so that by the time she got to the humiliating talk with Rolf she was able to present it in a far different light to her listener. When she had finished, she sat back, quietly pleased at the good job she had made of it. She almost believed it herself. All the same, she whisked the telegram form the tray and put it safely in her pocket, so that Antonia, who had sharp eyes, wouldn't notice that its postmark was no further afield than Dokkum.

'I'll have to tell,' said Antonia. 'Rolf has a way of finding things out. Oh, Sappha, I have been a fool, haven't I?'

Sappha ignored this last obvious remark and answered the first one.

'No, you won't tell,' she said positively. 'It won't help a bit if you do. You see, dear, Rolf isn't just going to be angry if you do, he's going to be dreadfully hurt as well. He—he loves you very much, you know, he might even think he's failed you in some way, because when your father died, Rolf tried to take his place, didn't he?' She sat up straight, pierced by a sudden dreadful thought. 'Tonia, where did you go? What did you do? Andrew didn't try any…?'

Antonia interrupted her with a light-hearted giggle. 'Sappha, you sound just like Mother! No, of course not—he didn't get a chance. I may be only sixteen, but Mother and Rolf have primed me thoroughly, you know. We quarrelled, Andrew and I, and he called me a little prude. I'm not sure

I know what it means, but I didn't like him any more then.'
She broke off. 'Did you really love him, Sappha?' she
asked. 'I can't think why.'

'Nor can I,' said Sappha simply, much struck by the fact
that she had no feelings, good bad or indifferent, for Andrew any more, and at the same time sighing with relief
that Antonia had fallen out of love almost as quickly as she
had fallen in.

'Was Rolf cross with you?' asked Antonia. 'If he was, I
shall tell him I let you take the blame last night—I was so
frightened I couldn't think. Have you ever felt like that?'

Sappha smiled wryly. 'Frequently, and of course Rolf
wasn't annoyed—why should he be? He knows about Andrew.'

'Yes, but he was furious when we came in—his voice
was all cold like it goes when he's angry.'

Sappha got up; she didn't think she could bear to talk
about Rolf any more. 'Yes, well, he wasn't,' she said positively. 'Look, I'm going to see your mother now to tell
her I must go back to England. Why don't you go back to
bed and I'll get someone to bring you up some breakfast—
no one need know—they'll think you've got a cold.'

It was a happy thought. Within five minutes Antonia was
tucked up in bed again, and she herself was free to break
the news to the Baroness, not such a hard task as she had
anticipated, for Joke had indeed spread the news and the
Baroness was prepared for ill tidings. Sappha showed her
patient the telegram, with her thumb placed strategically
over the date stamp, and that, coupled with her white face,
was evidence enough.

'Oh dear, and Rolf went away very early,' said the Baroness unhappily. 'Examinations or something for the first-
year students—he did tell me—you must make your own
arrangements, my dear. Have you enough money? And take
the car if you need it. Ask for anything you want. Shall I
telephone Rolf, or would you prefer to do it yourself? He'll
be so upset.'

Sappha went even paler, for this was something she had forgotten. She said quickly: 'May I telephone him, Baroness? I can find out about the trains and flights and let him know and—and say goodbye at the same time.'

The Baroness turned a mournful face to her. 'Yes, dear. I can't imagine what it will be like without you—just as I'm almost well, too. You've been like another daughter. Do you suppose you will be needed at home for very long—is there a possibility that you might come back before very long?'

She looked so wistful that Sappha gave her a heartening little hug.

'I don't see why not,' she lied cheerfully. 'I must go home and see what it's all about first, though. I'll write to you as soon as I know how things are.'

'Yes, of course, I know you will. How selfish of me to talk like that when you look worried to death. Go and get your journey arranged, dear, Annie can help me.' She smiled and wiped away a tear. 'I shall have to get used to doing without you, shan't I?'

Sappha, feeling mean, could have cried herself as she put on her outdoor clothes. She went to the kitchen and saw Annie and Mrs Burns and then left the house, glad to get away for a little while; everyone had been so kind and she felt such a fraud. She hadn't given any serious thought as to how she was going to get back to England and she had quite forgotten about Andrew; even if she had remembered, to accept a lift with him was the last thing she would have done. Now she went to the station and not without difficulty, discovered that there was a train in the late afternoon which would connect up with the boat train from Leeuwarden. She had allowed the Baroness to think that she would fly home, but there was no hurry, she might just as well go by boat. For the first time, it struck her that she had no plans and no job, she would have to go home and start looking for work, she didn't much care where, but she

had to earn her living, and if she had work to do, it would
fill the intolerable emptiness she saw looming ahead.

She walked back from the station, thinking she would
leave Rolf's house just as soon as she could. If she left
immediately after lunch, the car could take her to the station—she could leave her case there and go to De Posthoorn until it was time for her train, then if Rolf came
home before his usual hour, he would suppose that she had
left either with Andrew or to catch the plane. She stopped
suddenly. Andrew—she had forgotten Andrew. If he hadn't
already gone, it might be a good idea to go and see him
and hurry him on his way, then if Rolf did find out about
Antonia, it might not be quite so bad. She looked at her
watch; she had time enough; she started to walk down the
main street in the direction of the hotel.

There was no sign of Andrew in the coffee room—probably he was still in his rom. When the waiter brought her
coffee she asked him, to learn that he had left quite early
that morning. She stirred her coffee, thinking how like Andrew it was to avoid an awkward situation, but at least she
could leave knowing that he wasn't likely to bother Antonia
again—in a couple of weeks he would be forgotten. She
drank her coffee, and got up to go, trying not to think that
she would be forgotten too.

Back in the house, sitting with the Baroness in the lovely
drawing room, she enlarged a little upon her journey back,
telling her that she had booked on a flight which would
mean her leaving immediately after lunch, and when the
Baroness cried, something she hadn't done for quite some
time, Sappha very nearly blurted out the whole tale from
very shame.

It was after lunch, which she had eaten in the company
of a silent Antonia, that Joke came in with a letter. Sappha
took it from the salver, her heart leaping foolishly at the
sight of Rolf's handwriting. She opened it, conscious of
Antonia's look, to find nothing but a cheque inside. It was
while she was folding it neatly back into the envelope that

Antonia enquired of Joke: 'Is my brother home? I didn't hear him come in.'

Joke was on her way to the door; she paused and said:

'No, *Juffrouw*. He gave me this letter before he left this morning and told me to give it to Miss Devenish before she left.' Having dropped this bombshell, she left the room and before Sappha could ask what she had said, Antonia burst out: 'But that's impossible! Rolf went before you had the telegram—Mother said so, so how could he know?' She stopped and stared across the table at Sappha, who for want of anything better to do was writing aimlessly in the little notebook she had drawn from her handbag. She went on writing even though she knew that Antonia was still staring at her.

'Sappha, did Rolf tell you to go? He was angry, wasn't he?'

Sappha had no answer ready, which as it turned out, didn't matter, because Antonia didn't wait for one, but went on: 'He was—he did—I know it. It's all a botched-up story so that Mama won't know. I shall telephone him now and tell him…'

'Don't you dare!' snapped Sappha. She felt sick with unhappiness and after the things Rolf had said she told herself she didn't care any more—all she wanted to do was to get away. She said in a more reasonable voice:

'Look, Tonia, there's very little harm done—I would have been leaving in another week or two, and it's not likely that any of us will ever meet again. It's best that we should forget the whole thing, no one's come to any harm.' She got up, because if she went on talking like that she would burst into tears and spoil the whole thing. 'I'm going to say goodbye to everyone, because it's almost time to go.'

She was actually on the steps, her goodbyes said, and Jan waiting by the car, when Antonia said suddenly: 'I'm even more of a fool than I thought. You love Rolf, don't you, Sappha?'

She turned her lovely blue eyes on to Sappha's rigidly composed face; they were solemn and unhappy and ashamed.

Sappha looked away from her, across the garden to where she could see the dull gleam of water. It was a pity, she thought savagely, that she hadn't drowned when she had gone after Hush. He was cuddled in Antonia's arms now, his ugly little head, not quite as ugly as it had been, stretched to its utmost so that he should miss nothing of what was going on around him. Sappha pulled his ears gently and smiled quite naturally at Antonia. She said: 'Yes, dear. But don't let that worry you—life's not always what we want it to be, you know—things happen...'

She kissed the pretty, unhappy face. 'Goodbye, Tonia. I shan't write to you and you mustn't write to me because I don't think Rolf would like that.'

She got into the car, and as it went down the short drive, waved and smiled at the Baroness, sitting at the drawing room window. She waved to Antonia too, but Antonia had gone inside, straight to her brother's study and picked up the receiver and dialled Rolf's consulting rooms. She wasn't sure where he was, but his secretary would know.

There was no one in the coffee room when Sappha arrived at De Posthoorn. She ordered a pot of coffee, since she would have to sit there for an hour at least, and sat drinking it, her mind a merciful blank. She had begun on her second cup when Mr and Mrs Winkelman came in, ordered coffee in their turn and asked, in the nicest possible way, what she was doing there. Sappha said simply: 'I'm going home,' and when Mrs Winkelman said kindly: 'Not bad news, I hope my dear,' replied, because she was sick of lying: 'No—no, thank you. I'm going on the night boat, and I've a little time to spare before my train goes, so I thought I'd come here.'

Mr Winkelman frowned. 'The people you worked for—surely they should have sent you into Leeuwarden by car—or at least seen you to the station.'

He sounded so indignant that she hastened to explain. 'Well, they couldn't very well, you see, my patient is still very much an invalid, and Baron van Duyren is a doctor and—isn't always home.'

Mrs Winkelman leaned a little forward in her chair. 'A baron!' she breathed. 'Was he here yesterday? Tall and large and very dark?'

Sappha put down her cup. 'Yes, it sounds like him,' she admitted and tried to smile without much success. She busied herself pouring another cup of coffee so that they wouldn't be able to see her face, and Mrs Winkelman said forthrightly: 'Well, it all seems a bit sudden to me, if there's anything we can do...' She got no further. A kind of fury shook the front door of the hotel, it shook the door of the coffee room too, which flew open to admit Rolf. Sappha looked at him through her puffy, red-rimmed eyes and prepared for battle, for it was obvious that he was controlling vast feelings of some sort or another. He was also, she noticed with a sinking heart, very much a baron; it was as though he had wrapped the invisible cloak of his ancient title around himself so that he had become wholly inaccessible. Sappha sniffed back threatening tears, telling herself it didn't matter any more, she hadn't anything else to say and she wasn't going to make excuses or plead forgiveness.

He stood just inside the open door, letting all the cold air in and taking his time. His eyes lighted upon Mr and Mrs Winkelman and he wished them a good day with an icy civility which failed to dislodge them from their table in the corner. As Mrs Winkelman pointed out to her husband much later, they had every right to stay—were they not guests at the hotel, and moreover, was he not of Dutch blood with a real ancestor whose gravestone was to be seen in St Martin's church? Surely that fact alone was enough to allow them to sit tight.

As far as Sappha and Rolf were concerned, however, there was no one else in the room, or, for that matter, the world. From the still open doorway he demanded thunderously:

'Where are you going, and why are you here and where is Glover?' He had made no effort to lower his voice: it beat around Sappha's head to increase its ache, so that she said peevishly: 'Don't shout.'

He answered her with a deliberate clarity which was far worse than any roar would have been. 'I am not shouting. And I want an answer to my questions.'

'You won't get them,' said Sappha rudely, 'coming in here like a—a hurricane and shouting at me.' She didn't answer his questions either, so that when next he spoke it was in a subdued roar which had made her jump.

'Sappha, I'm waiting!'

She was plaiting the silky fringe of the Smyrna table rug, with which the Dutch, as a nation, adorn their coffee tables. She already had five little pigtails; she embarked on the sixth and said without looking at him:

'I'm going home—you told me to go, remember? Andrew went this morning, I don't know when because I haven't seen him, not at all. I'm sitting here waiting until it's time for me to catch my train to Leeuwarden, because I don't care to stay in your house a moment longer than I must.'

She had spoken in a calm, colourless voice and then spoilt the whole thing by bursting into tears, whereupon, to Mrs Winkelman's delight, Rolf crossed the room in a couple of strides to offer a very large, freshly laundered handkerchief, which Sappha snatched from him and defiantly blew her nose. She said furiously: 'I never want to see you again—never!' she repeated, as if by saying it twice she could convince herself as well as her audience. 'One minute you were...' she paused, left her sentence unfinished and tried again, 'and the next you...' She sniffed. 'You don't trust me.'

Rolf was standing very close. He said in a surprisingly mild voice:

'Did I ever say that—that I didn't trust you?'

She sniffed again, it was quite true, he hadn't. 'Well, you thought that I was meeting Andrew, and,' she declared with rising indignation, 'you told me to go back to England with him.'

'And what else was I supposed to say?' His voice was rough and had a bitter ring, 'and what the hell was I supposed to think—I'm only human, you know; bad-tempered and arrogant and God help me, jealous—one moment you were melting in my arms and five minutes later you were telling me that you'd just been to see Glover, damn him.'

Sappha stood up, pushing her chair back as she did so because he was so near. 'I'm going,' she said in a soggy voice. She would have liked to say something clever and cutting about melting in his arms, but she could think of nothing nasty enough. She went past him and he made no move to stop her, but as she reached the door he said, almost as thought it didn't matter any more: 'Antonia telephoned me—I can deal with her later, but I had to see you because I don't understand why you couldn't have told me, instead of having me to imagine that you and Glover...'

Sappha stared at the fine specimen of a Friesian clock hanging on the wall before her. 'I did—at least I tried, and you said we'd talk about it later, but you went out and then in the hall you didn't give me the chance to say anything even if I could have done, and you know I couldn't because I'd promised Tonia.' During this muddled observation her voice had risen considerably, she paused for breath and continued rather loudly. 'Why should I tell you anything, you're—you're...' What with tears and temper she was bereft of words. She went through the door and closed it quietly behind her and went out into the cold blustery late afternoon.

She wanted to hide and the only place she could think of was the Museum; at least it would be warm and dry there and it didn't close until five. She rang the bell and when the curator opened the door and saw her tear-streaked face he opened it still wider and said kindly, 'Another visit, miss?' He smiled at her kindly, pretending not to see how awful she looked. 'There's plenty of time before we close.'

She managed a tired little smile. 'Please may I go upstairs, just for a little while—it's peaceful.'

Sappha made straight for the case where the little silver box was displayed and stared at it with sad eyes. It was only a little more than twenty-four hours since she had last seen it, and then she had been so happy. She turned away at last and got out her lipstick and compact and with the aid of its little mirror did things to her miserable little face. It didn't look much better when she had finished, but at least it was the first step taken towards the new life she would have to build. She closed her bag, put her hand into her pocket and drew out Rolf's handkerchief—it was very fine linen, she saw idly, with his initials beautifully embroidered in one corner, but the sight of it was bad for her so she pushed it back again and walked over to the display case once more.

The door bell rang as she did so and she frowned because she wanted the place to herself. Sappha gave a last defiant sniff, thinking sadly that in a novel it would have been the hero ringing the bell, intent on catching up with the heroine before the last page—only there was not going to be a last page to this particular story. She put her hand in her pocket again and clutched the handkerchief because it was all she had left, and at the same time became aware that someone was coming up the stairs. She knew it was Rolf and turned round to face him as he came across the room to her. He said in a gentle voice:

'I knew you would be here, my dear—my darling Sappha,' and when she opened her mouth to speak he went on: 'No, we're not going to talk any more, my dearest love, not at present, for nothing we can say to each other can alter the fact that I love you with all my heart, and I believe that you love me.'

He caught her close and smiled down at her and kissed her mouth and then her pale face until it pinkened and glowed with her happiness. Only then did he loosen his hold, and that just long enough to fish something out of a pocket. It was a little silver box with a beautifully engraved lid. He put it into Sappha's hand. 'Open it, my love.'

There was a ring inside, a diamond and ruby ring in an old-fashioned gold setting. Sappha looked at it and because she appeared to be about to burst into tears again, Rolf kissed her again before he spoke.

'The ring has been in my pocket for several weeks, Sappha, but the box I found this morning because I couldn't think of a better way of telling you how ashamed I was for making you unhappy.'

Sappha stared up at him, her eyes like stars. She said obscurely: 'But I wouldn't have been here.'

'I should have come after you.'

'Even if I'd been with Andrew?'

'Even if you had been with Andrew, my darling.'

'What would you have done?'

'Put the ring on your finger, of course.'

Sappha smiled. 'Please put it on now, dear Rolf,' and when he had done so she reached up and kissed him, standing within the circle of his arms. His face, she thought, studying it, was neither bold nor bad—just loving.

It was the curator who disturbed them, and that in the kindest possible fashion. He had been prowling round them for some time without either of them noticing; now he said almost apologetically: 'It's well past closing time,' and smiled at them; he was a happily married man himself and he liked to see young people happy, as these two were. He went downstairs behind them and waited patiently by the door while Sappha paused to admire her ring. He asked diffidently:

'I suppose you won't be coming any more now, miss?'

It was Rolf who answered him in Dutch. 'Oh, yes she will—when we're married and she wants a bolthole from

me and our children,' and the man chuckled as he shut the
door behind them.

They stopped to kiss on the steps outside; the rain had
turned to snow, but neither of them noticed as they strolled
down the little path.

'We'll be married in Dialach—as soon as possible, my
lovely one,' said Rolf, 'because that's where we met.'

Sappha smiled at him and said meekly: 'Yes, dear.' Dialach was perhaps not an ideal place in which to have a
wedding in midwinter. She said, thinking out loud: 'I shall
have to be wrapped from top to toes in white fur.' She
laughed at the idea and Rolf plucked her to him and kissed
her with pleasure.

'And so you shall,' he promised. 'You shall have anything in the world you want, Sappha.'

She stopped and looked up at him. The snow had pow-
dered his dark hair, making it darker than ever by contrast—his eyes looked black in the feeble light of the street
lamps ahead of them. She put up a gentle finger and traced
the outline of his awe inspiring nose. He looked very handsome, but it wasn't good looks she was looking for. Apparently she found what she was seeking in his face, for
she smiled at him and put up her face to be kissed, knowing
that she loved him dearly, just as he loved her. 'I only want
you,' she said.

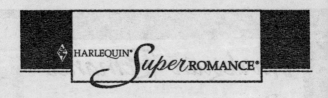

HARLEQUIN *Presents*

The world's bestselling romance series...
The series that brings you your favorite authors,
month after month:

Helen Bianchin...Emma Darcy
Lynne Graham...Penny Jordan
Miranda Lee...Sandra Marton
Anne Mather...Carole Mortimer
Susan Napier...Michelle Reid

and many more uniquely talented authors!

Wealthy, powerful, gorgeous men...
Women who have feelings just like your own...
The stories you love, set in exotic, glamorous locations...

HARLEQUIN *Presents*

Seduction and passion guaranteed!

From rugged lawmen and valiant knights to defiant heiresses and spirited frontierswomen, Harlequin Historicals will capture your imagination with their dramatic scope, passion and adventure.

Harlequin Historicals... they're too good to miss!

HHDIR1